KU-379-242

THE CODE OF THE WOOSTERS

The Code of the Woosters decrees that one must never let a pal down. So Bertie must hop off to Totleigh Towers in order to mend a lovers' rift between the daffy Madeline Bassett and newt-fancier Gussie Fink-Nottle. As if patching up things between those two drips wasn't sufficient, Bertie also finds himself required to secure the nuptials of Stiffy Byng and Stinker Pinker — not to mention becoming embroiled in a plot to swipe an antique silver cow-creamer. As misunderstandings mount and conspiracies collide, there's only one man who can sort out the whole mess — Jeeves, naturally.

Books by P. G. Wodehouse
Published in Ulverscroft Collections:

JEEVES & WOOSTER:
CARRY ON, JEEVES
THE INIMITABLE JEEVES
VERY GOOD, JEEVES
THANK YOU, JEEVES
RIGHT HO, JEEVES

BLANDINGS:
SOMETHING FRESH
SUMMER LIGHTNING

3800 18 0007674 1

||||||||||||||||||||||||||||||||||

HIGH LIFE HIGHLAND

SPECIAL ERS

THE ULVERSCROFT FOUNDATION
(registered UK charity number 264873)
was established in 1972 to provide funds for research, diagnosis and treatment of eye diseases. Examples of major projects funded by the Ulverscroft Foundation are:-

- The Children's Eye Unit at Moorfields Eye Hospital, London
- The Ulverscroft Children's Eye Unit at Great Ormond Street Hospital for Sick Children
- Funding research into eye diseases and treatment at the Department of Ophthalmology, University of Leicester
- The Ulverscroft Vision Research Group, Institute of Child Health
- Twin operating theatres at the Western Ophthalmic Hospital, London
- The Chair of Ophthalmology at the Royal Australian College of Ophthalmologists

You can help further the work of the Foundation by making a donation or leaving a legacy. Every contribution is gratefully received. If you would like to help support the Foundation or require further information, please contact:

HIGHLAND LIBRARIES

WITHDRAWN

THE ULVERSCROFT FOUNDATION
The Green, Bradgate Road, Anstey
Leicester LE7 7FU, England
Tel: (0116) 236 4325

website: www.foundation.ulverscroft.com

SPECIAL MESSAGE TO READERS

THE ULVERSCROFT FOUNDATION
(registered UK charity number 264873)

was established in 1972 to provide funds for
research, diagnosis and treatment of eye diseases.
Examples of major projects funded by
the Ulverscroft Foundation are:-

• The Children's Eye Unit at Moorfields Eye
Hospital, London

• The Ulverscroft Children's Eye Unit at Great
Ormond Street Hospital for Sick Children

• Funding research into eye diseases and
treatment at the Department of Ophthalmology,
University of Leicester

• The Ulverscroft Vision Research Group,
Institute of Child Health

• Twin operating theatres at the Western
Ophthalmic Hospital, London

• The Chair of Ophthalmology at the Royal
Australian College of Ophthalmologists

You can help further the work of the Foundation
by making a donation or leaving a legacy.
Every contribution is gratefully received. If you
would like to help support the Foundation or
require further information, please contact:

THE ULVERSCROFT FOUNDATION
The Green, Bradgate Road, Anstey
Leicester LE7 7FU, England
Tel: (0116) 236 4325

website: www.foundation.ulverscroft.com

P. G. WODEHOUSE

---◆---

THE CODE
OF THE
WOOSTERS

Complete and Unabridged

HIGHLAND
LIBRARIES

1 8 0 0 0 7 6 7 4 1

ULVERSCROFT
Leicester

First published in Great Britain in 1938 by
Herbert Jenkins
London

This Ulverscroft Edition
published 2018
by arrangement with
Rogers, Coleridge & White Literary Agency
London

Copyright © 1938 by P. G. Wodehouse
All rights reserved

The moral right of the author has been asserted

A catalogue record for this book is available
from the British Library.

ISBN 978–1–4448–3819–0

Published by
F. A. Thorpe (Publishing)
Anstey, Leicestershire

Set by Words & Graphics Ltd.
Anstey, Leicestershire
Printed and bound in Great Britain by
T. J. International Ltd., Padstow, Cornwall

This book is printed on acid-free paper

1

I reached out a hand from under the blankets, and rang the bell for Jeeves.

'Good evening, Jeeves.'

'Good morning, sir.'

This surprised me.

'Is it morning?'

'Yes, sir.'

'Are you sure? It seems very dark outside.'

'There is a fog, sir. If you will recollect, we are now in autumn — season of mists and mellow fruitfulness.'

'Season of what?'

'Mists, sir, and mellow fruitfulness.'

'Oh? Yes. Yes, I see. Well, be that as it may, get me one of those bracers of yours, will you?'

'I have one in readiness, sir, in the ice box.'

He shimmered out, and I sat up in bed with that rather unpleasant feeling you get sometimes that you're going to die in about five minutes. On the previous night, I had given a little dinner at the Drones to Gussie Fink-Nottle as a friendly send-off before his approaching nuptials with Madeline, only daughter of Sir Watkyn Bassett, CBE, and these things take their toll. Indeed, just before Jeeves came in, I had been dreaming that some bounder was driving spikes through my head — not just ordinary spikes, as used by Jael the wife of Heber, but red-hot ones.

He returned with the tissue-restorer. I loosed

it down the hatch, and after undergoing the passing discomfort, unavoidable when you drink Jeeves's patent morning revivers, of having the top of the skull fly up to the ceiling and the eyes shoot out of their sockets and rebound from the opposite wall like racquet balls, felt better. It would have been overstating it to say that even now Bertram was back again in mid-season form, but I had at least slid into the convalescent class and was equal to a spot of conversation.

'Ha!' I said, retrieving the eyeballs and replacing them in position. 'Well, Jeeves, what goes on in the great world? Is that the paper you have there?'

'No, sir. It is some literature from the Travel Bureau. I thought that you might care to glance at it.'

'Oh?' I said. 'You did, did you?'

And there was a brief and — if that's the word I want — pregnant silence.

I suppose that when two men of iron will live in close association with one another, there are bound to be occasional clashes, and one of these had recently popped up in the Wooster home. Jeeves was trying to get me to go on a Round-The-World cruise, and I would have none of it. But in spite of my firm statements to this effect, scarcely a day passed without him bringing me a sheaf or nosegay of those illustrated folders which the Ho-for-the-open-spaces birds send out in the hope of drumming up custom. His whole attitude recalled irresistibly to the mind that of some assiduous hound who will persist in laying a dead rat on the drawing-room carpet, though repeatedly apprised by word and gesture that the market for same is sluggish or even non-existent.

'Jeeves,' I said, 'this nuisance must now cease.'

'Travel is highly educational, sir.'

'I can't do with any more education. I was full up years ago. No, Jeeves, I know what's the matter with you. That old Viking strain of yours has come out again. You yearn for the tang of the salt breezes. You see yourself walking the deck in a yachting cap. Possibly someone has been telling you about the Dancing Girls of Bali. I understand, and I sympathize. But not for me. I refuse to be decanted into any blasted ocean-going liner and lugged off round the world.'

'Very good, sir.'

He spoke with a certain what-is-it in his voice, and I could see that, if not actually disgruntled, he was far from being gruntled, so I tactfully changed the subject.

'Well, Jeeves, it was quite a satisfactory binge last night.'

'Indeed, sir?'

'Oh, most. An excellent time was had by all. Gussie sent his regards.'

'I appreciate the kind thought, sir. I trust Mr Fink-Nottle was in good spirits?'

'Extraordinarily good, considering that the sands are running out and that he will shortly have Sir Watkyn Bassett for a father-in-law. Sooner him than me, Jeeves, sooner him than me.'

I spoke with strong feeling, and I'll tell you why. A few months before, while celebrating Boat Race night, I had fallen into the clutches of the Law for trying to separate a policeman from his helmet, and after sleeping fitfully on a plank bed had been hauled up at Bosher Street next morning and fined five of the best. The magistrate who had inflicted this monstrous sentence — to the accompaniment, I may add, of some very offensive remarks from the bench — was none other than old Pop Bassett, father of Gussie's bride-to-be.

As it turned out, I was one of his last customers, for a couple of weeks later he inherited a pot of money from a distant relative and retired to the country. That, at least, was the story that had been put about. My own view was that he had got the stuff by sticking like glue to the fines. Five quid here, five quid there — you can see how it would mount up over a period of years.

'You have not forgotten that man of wrath, Jeeves? A hard case, eh?'

'Possibly Sir Watkyn is less formidable in private life, sir.'

'I doubt it. Slice him where you like, a hellhound is always a hellhound. But enough of this Bassett. Any letters today?'

'No, sir.'

'Telephone communications?'

'One, sir. From Mrs Travers.'

'Aunt Dahlia? She's back in town, then?'

'Yes, sir. She expressed a desire that you would ring her up at your earliest convenience.'

'I will do even better,' I said cordially. 'I will call in person.'

And half an hour later I was toddling up the

4

steps of her residence and being admitted by old Seppings, her butler. Little knowing, as I crossed that threshold, that in about two shakes of a duck's tail I was to become involved in an imbroglio that would test the Wooster soul as it had seldom been tested before. I allude to the sinister affair of Gussie Fink-Nottle, Madeline Bassett, old Pop Bassett, Stiffy Byng, the Rev. H. P. ('Stinker') Pinker, the eighteenth-century cow-creamer and the small, brown, leather-covered notebook.

★   ★   ★

No premonition of an impending doom, however, cast a cloud on my serenity as I buzzed in. I was looking forward with bright anticipation to the coming reunion with this Dahlia — she, as I may have mentioned before, being my good and deserving aunt, not to be confused with Aunt Agatha, who eats broken bottles and wears barbed wire next the skin. Apart from the mere intellectual pleasure of chewing the fat with her, there was the glittering prospect that I might be able to cadge an invitation to lunch. And owing to the outstanding virtuosity of Anatole, her French cook, the browsing at her trough is always of a nature to lure the gourmet.

The door of the morning-room was open as I went through the hall, and I caught a glimpse of Uncle Tom messing about with his collection of old silver. For a moment I toyed with the idea of pausing to pip-pip and inquire after his indigestion, a malady to which he is extremely subject, but wiser counsels prevailed. This uncle is a bird who, sighting a nephew, is apt to buttonhole him and become a bit informative on the subject of sconces and foliation, not to mention scrolls, ribbon wreaths in high relief and gadroon borders, and it seemed to me that silence was best. I whizzed by, accordingly, with sealed lips, and headed for the library, where I had been informed that Aunt Dahlia was at the moment rooting.

I found the old flesh-and-blood up to her Marcelwave in proof sheets. As all the world knows, she is the courteous and popular proprietress of a weekly sheet for the delicately nurtured entitled *Milady's Boudoir*. I once contributed an article to it on 'What the Well-Dressed Man is Wearing'.

My entry caused her to come to the surface, and she greeted me with one of those cheery view-halloos which, in the days when she went in for hunting, used to make her so noticeable a figure of the Quorn, the Pytchley and other organizations for doing the British fox a bit of no good.

'Hullo, ugly,' she said. 'What brings you here?'

'I understood, aged relative, that you wished to confer with me.'

'I didn't want you to come barging in, interrupting my work. A few words on the telephone would have met the case. But I suppose some instinct told you that this was my busy day.'

'If you were wondering if I could come to lunch, have no anxiety. I shall be delighted, as always. What will Anatole be giving us?'

'He won't be giving you anything, my gay young tapeworm. I am entertaining Pomona Grindle, the novelist, to the midday meal.'

'I should be charmed to meet her.'

'Well, you're not going to. It is to be a strictly tête-à-tête affair. I'm trying to get a serial out of her for the *Boudoir*. No, all I wanted was to tell you to go to an antique shop in the Brompton Road — it's just past the Oratory — you can't miss it — and sneer at a cow-creamer.'

I did not get her drift. The impression I received was that of an aunt talking through the back of her neck.

'Do what to a what?'

'They've got an eighteenth-century cow-creamer there that Tom's going to buy this afternoon.'

The scales fell from my eyes.

'Oh, it's a silver whatnot, is it?'

'Yes. A sort of cream jug. Go there and ask them to show it to you, and when they do, register scorn.'

'The idea being what?'

'To sap their confidence, of course, chump. To sow doubts and misgivings in their mind and make them clip the price a bit. The cheaper he gets the thing, the better he will be pleased. And I want him to be in cheery mood, because if I succeed in signing the Grindle up for this serial, I shall be compelled to get into his ribs for a biggish sum of money. It's sinful what these best-selling women novelists want for their stuff. So pop off there without delay and shake your head at the thing.'

7

I am always anxious to oblige the right sort of aunt, but I was compelled to put in what Jeeves would have called a *nolle prosequi*. Those morning mixtures of his are practically magical in their effect, but even after partaking of them one does not oscillate the bean.

'I can't shake my head. Not today.'

She gazed at me with a censorious waggle of the right eyebrow.

'Oh, so that's how it is? Well, if your loathsome excesses have left you incapable of headshaking, you can at least curl your lip.'

'Oh, rather.'

'Then carry on. And draw your breath in sharply. Also try clicking the tongue. Oh, yes, and tell them you think it's modern Dutch.'

'Why?'

'I don't know. Apparently it's something a cow-creamer ought not to be.'

She paused, and allowed her eye to roam thoughtfully over my perhaps somewhat corpse-like face.

'So you were out on the tiles last night, were you, my little chickadee? It's an extraordinary thing — every time I see you, you appear to be recovering from some debauch. Don't you ever stop drinking? How about when you're asleep?'

I rebutted the slur.

'You wrong me, relative. Except at times of special revelry, I am exceedingly moderate in my potations. A brace of cocktails, a glass of wine at dinner and possibly a liqueur with the coffee — that is Bertram Wooster. But last night I gave a small bachelor binge for Gussie Fink-Nottle.'

8

'You did, did you?' She laughed — a bit louder than I could have wished in my frail state of health, but then she is always a woman who tends to bring plaster falling from the ceiling when amused. 'Spink-Bottle, eh? Bless his heart! How was the old newt-fancier?'

'Pretty roguish.'

'Did he make a speech at this orgy of yours?'

'Yes. I was astounded. I was all prepared for a blushing refusal. But no. We drank his health, and he rose to his feet as cool as some cucumbers, as Anatole would say, and held us spellbound.'

'Tight as an owl, I suppose?'

'On the contrary. Offensively sober.'

'Well, that's a nice change.'

We fell into a thoughtful silence. We were musing on the summer afternoon down at her place in Worcestershire when Gussie, circumstances having so ordered themselves as to render him full to the back teeth with the right stuff, had addressed the young scholars of Market Snodsbury Grammar School on the occasion of their annual prize giving.

A thing I never know, when I'm starting out to tell a story about a chap I've told a story about before, is how much explanation to bung in at the outset. It's a problem you've got to look at from every angle. I mean to say, in the present case, if I take it for granted that my public knows all about Gussie Fink-Nottle and just breeze ahead, those publicans who weren't hanging on my lips the first time are apt to be fogged. Whereas, if before kicking off I give about eight

9

volumes of the man's life and history, other bimbos, who were so hanging, will stifle yawns and murmur 'Old stuff. Get on with it.'

I suppose the only thing to do is to put the salient facts as briefly as possible in the possession of the first gang, waving an apologetic hand at the second gang the while, to indicate that they had better let their attention wander for a minute or two and that I will be with them shortly.

This Gussie, then, was a fish-faced pal of mine who, on reaching man's estate, had buried himself in the country and devoted himself entirely to the study of newts, keeping the little chaps in a glass tank and observing their habits with a sedulous eye. A confirmed recluse you would have called him, if you had happened to know the word, and you would have been right. By all the rulings of the form book, a less promising prospect for the whispering of tender words into shell-like ears and the subsequent purchase of platinum ring and licence for wedding it would have seemed impossible to discover in a month of Sundays.

But Love will find a way. Meeting Madeline Bassett one day and falling for her like a ton of bricks, he had emerged from his retirement and started to woo, and after numerous vicissitudes had clicked and was slated at no distant date to don the spongebag trousers and gardenia for buttonhole and walk up the aisle with the ghastly girl.

I call her a ghastly girl because she was a ghastly girl. The Woosters are chivalrous, but they can speak their minds. A droopy, soupy, sentimental exhibit, with melting eyes and a cooing voice and the most extraordinary views on such things as stars and rabbits. I remember her telling me once that rabbits were gnomes in attendance on the Fairy Queen and that the stars were God's daisy chain. Perfect rot, of course. They're nothing of the sort.

Aunt Dahlia emitted a low, rumbling chuckle, for that speech of Gussie's down at Market Snodsbury has always been one of her happiest memories.

'Good old Spink-Bottle! Where is he now?'

'Staying at the Bassett's father's place — Totleigh Towers, Totleigh-in-the-Wold, Glos. He went back there this morning. They're having the wedding at the local church.'

'Are you going to it?'

'Definitely no.'

'No, I suppose it would be too painful for you. You being in love with the girl.'

I stared.

'In love? With a female who thinks that every time a fairy blows its wee nose a baby is born?'

'Well, you were certainly engaged to her once.'

'For about five minutes, yes, and through no fault of my own. My dear old relative,' I said, nettled, 'you are perfectly well aware of the inside facts of that frightful affair.'

I winced. It was an incident in my career on which I did not care to dwell. Briefly, what had occurred was this. His nerve sapped by long association with newts, Gussie had shrunk from pleading his cause with Madeline Bassett, and

11

had asked me to plead it for him. And when I did so, the fat-headed girl thought I was pleading mine. With the result that when, after that exhibition of his at the prize giving, she handed Gussie the temporary mitten, she had attached herself to me, and I had had no option but to take the rap. I mean to say, if a girl has got it into her nut that a fellow loves her, and comes and tells him that she is returning her *fiancé* to store and is now prepared to sign up with him, what can a chap do?

Mercifully, things had been straightened out at the eleventh hour by a reconciliation between the two pills, but the thought of my peril was one at which I still shuddered. I wasn't going to feel really easy in my mind till the parson had said: 'Wilt thou, Augustus?' and Gussie had whispered a shy 'Yes.'

'Well, if it is of any interest to you,' said Aunt Dahlia, 'I am not proposing to attend that wedding myself. I disapprove of Sir Watkyn Bassett, and don't think he ought to be encouraged. There's one of the boys, if you want one!'

'You know the old crumb, then?' I said, rather surprised, though of course it bore out what I often say — viz that it's a small world.

'Yes, I know him. He's a friend of Tom's. They both collect old silver and snarl at one another like wolves about it all the time. We had him staying at Brinkley last month. And would you care to hear how he repaid me for all the loving care I lavished on him while he was my guest? Sneaked round behind my back and tried to steal Anatole!'

'No!'

'That's what he did. Fortunately, Anatole proved staunch — after I had doubled his wages.'

'Double them again,' I said earnestly. 'Keep on doubling them. Pour out money like water rather than lose that superb master of the roasts and hashes.'

I was visibly affected. The thought of Anatole, that peerless disher-up, coming within an ace of ceasing to operate at Brinkley Court, where I could always enjoy his output by inviting myself for a visit, and going off to serve under old Bassett, the last person in the world likely to set out a knife and fork for Bertram, had stirred me profoundly.

'Yes,' said Aunt Dahlia, her eye smouldering as she brooded on the frightful thing, 'that's the sort of hornswoggling high-binder Sir Watkyn Bassett is. You had better warn Spink-Bottle to watch out on the wedding day. The slightest relaxation of vigilance, and the old thug will probably get away with his tie-pin in the vestry. And now,' she said, reaching out for what had the appearance of being a thoughtful essay on the care of the baby in sickness and in health, 'push off. I've got about six tons of proofs to correct. Oh, and give this to Jeeves, when you see him. It's the 'Husbands' Corner' article. It's full of deep stuff about braid on the side of men's dress trousers, and I'd like him to vet it. For all I know, it may be Red propaganda. And I can rely on you not to bungle that job? Tell me in your own words what it is you're supposed to do.'

'Go to antique shop — '

' — in the Brompton Road — '

' — in, as you say, the Brompton Road. Ask to see cow-creamer — '

' — and sneer. Right. Buzz along. The door is behind you.'

★ ★ ★

It was with a light heart that I went out into the street and hailed a passing barouche. Many men, no doubt, might have been a bit sick at having their morning cut into in this fashion, but I was conscious only of pleasure at the thought that I had it in my power to perform this little act of kindness. Scratch Bertram Wooster, I often say, and you find a Boy Scout.

The antique shop in the Brompton Road proved, as foreshadowed, to be an antique shop in the Brompton Road and, like all antique shops except the swanky ones in the Bond Street neighbourhood, dingy outside and dark and smelly within. I don't know why it is, but the proprietors of these establishments always seem to be cooking some sort of stew in the back room.

'I say,' I began, entering; then paused as I perceived that the bloke in charge was attending to two other customers.

'Oh, sorry,' I was about to add, to convey the idea that I had horned in inadvertently, when the words froze on my lips.

Quite a slab of misty fruitfulness had drifted into the emporium, obscuring the view, but in spite of the poor light I was able to note that the

14

smaller and elder of these two customers was no stranger to me.

It was old Pop Bassett in person. Himself. Not a picture.

★ ★ ★

There is a tough, bulldog strain in the Woosters which has often caused comment. It came out in me now. A weaker man, no doubt, would have tiptoed from the scene and headed for the horizon, but I stood firm. After all, I felt, the dead past was the dead past. By forking out that fiver, I had paid my debt to Society and had nothing to fear from this shrimp-faced little son of a whatnot. So I remained where I was, giving him the surreptitious once-over.

My entry had caused him to turn and shoot a quick look at me, and at intervals since then he had been peering at me sideways. It was only a question of time, I felt, before the hidden chord in his memory would be touched and he would realize that the slight distinguished-looking figure leaning on its umbrella in the background was an old acquaintance. And now it was plain that he was hep. The bird in charge of the shop had pottered off into an inner room, and he came across to where I stood, giving me the up-and-down through his wind-shields.

'Hallo, hallo,' he said. 'I know you, young man. I never forget a face. You came up before me once.'

I bowed slightly.

'But not twice. Good! Learned your lesson,

15

eh? Going straight now? Capital. Now, let me see, what was it? Don't tell me. It's coming back. Of course, yes. Bag-snatching.'

'No, no. It was — '

'Bag-snatching,' he repeated firmly. 'I remember it distinctly. Still, it's all past and done with now, eh? We have turned over a new leaf, have we not? Splendid. Roderick, come over here. This is most interesting.'

His buddy, who had been examining a salver, put it down and joined the party.

He was, as I had already been able to perceive, a breath-taking cove. About seven feet in height, and swathed in a plaid ulster which made him look about six feet across, he caught the eye and arrested it. It was as if Nature had intended to make a gorilla, and had changed its mind at the last moment.

But it wasn't merely the sheer expanse of the bird that impressed. Close to, what you noticed more was his face, which was square and powerful and slightly moustached towards the centre. His gaze was keen and piercing. I don't know if you have ever seen those pictures in the papers of Dictators with tilted chins and blazing eyes, inflaming the populace with fiery words on the occasion of the opening of a new skittle alley, but that was what he reminded me of.

'Roderick,' said old Bassett, 'I want you to meet this fellow. Here is a case which illustrates exactly what I have so often maintained — that prison life does not degrade, that it does not warp the character and prevent a man rising on stepping-stones of his dead self to higher things.'

16

I recognized the gag — one of Jeeves's — and wondered where he could have heard it.

'Look at this chap. I gave him three months not long ago for snatching bags at railway stations, and it is quite evident that his term in jail has had the most excellent effect on him. He has reformed.'

'Oh, yes?' said the Dictator.

Granted that it wasn't quite 'Oh, yeah?' I still didn't like the way he spoke. He was looking at me with a nasty sort of supercilious expression. I remember thinking that he would have been the ideal man to sneer at a cow-creamer.

'What makes you think he has reformed?'

'Of course he has reformed. Look at him. Well groomed, well dressed, a decent member of Society. What his present walk in life is, I do not know, but it is perfectly obvious that he is no longer stealing bags. What are you doing now, young man?'

'Stealing umbrellas, apparently,' said the Dictator. 'I notice he's got yours.'

And I was on the point of denying the accusation hotly — I had indeed, already opened my lips to do so — when there suddenly struck me like a blow on the upper maxillary from a sock stuffed with wet sand the realization that there was a lot in it.

I mean to say, I remembered now that I had come out without my umbrella, and yet here I was, beyond any question of doubt, umbrellaed to the gills. What had caused me to take up the one that had been leaning against a seventeenth-century chair, I cannot say, unless it was the

17

primeval instinct which makes a man without an umbrella reach out for the nearest one in sight, like a flower groping towards the sun.

A manly apology seemed in order. I made it as the blunt instrument changed hands.

'I say, I'm most frightfully sorry.'

Old Bassett said he was, too — sorry and disappointed. He said it was this sort of thing that made a man sick at heart.

The Dictator had to shove his oar in. He asked if he should call a policeman, and old Bassett's eyes gleamed for a moment. Being a magistrate makes you love the idea of calling policemen. It's like a tiger tasting blood. But he shook his head.

'No, Roderick. I couldn't. Not today — the happiest day of my life.'

The Dictator pursed his lips, as if feeling that the better the day, the better the deed.

'But listen,' I bleated, 'it was a mistake.'

'Ha!' said the Dictator.

'I thought that umbrella was mine.'

'That,' said old Bassett, 'is the fundamental trouble with you, my man. You are totally unable to distinguish between *meum* and *tuum*. Well, I am not going to have you arrested this time, but I advise you to be very careful. Come, Roderick.'

They biffed off, the Dictator pausing at the door to give me another look and say 'Ha!' again.

A most unnerving experience all this had been for a man of sensibility, as you may well imagine, and my immediate reaction was a disposition to give Aunt Dahlia's commission the miss-in-balk and return to the flat and get outside another of Jeeves's pick-me-ups. You know how harts pant

18

for cooling streams when heated in the chase. Very much that sort of thing. I realized now what madness it had been to go out into the streets of London with only one of them under my belt, and I was on the point of melting away and going back to the fountain head, when the proprietor of the shop emerged from the inner room, accompanied by a rich smell of stew and a sandy cat, and inquired what he could do for me. And so, the subject having come up, I said that I understood that he had an eighteenth-century cow-creamer for sale.

He shook his head. He was a rather mildewed bird of gloomy aspect, almost entirely concealed behind a cascade of white whiskers.

'You're too late. It's promised to a customer.'

'Name of Travers?'

'Ah.'

'Then that's all right. Learn, O thou of unshuffled features and agreeable disposition,' I said, for one likes to be civil, 'that the above Travers is my uncle. He sent me here to have a look at the thing. So dig it out, will you? I expect it's rotten.'

'It's a beautiful cow-creamer.'

'Ha!' I said, borrowing a bit of the Dictator's stuff. 'That's what you think. We shall see.'

I don't mind confessing that I'm not much of a lad for old silver, and though I have never pained him by actually telling him so, I have always felt that Uncle Tom's fondness for it is evidence of a goofiness which he would do well to watch and check before it spreads. So I wasn't expecting the heart to leap up to any great extent at the sight of this exhibit. But when the whiskered ancient pottered off into the shadows and came back with the thing, I scarcely knew whether to laugh or weep. The thought of an uncle paying hard cash for such an object got right in amongst me.

It was a silver cow. But when I say 'cow', don't go running away with the idea of some decent, self-respecting cudster such as you may observe loading grass into itself in the nearest meadow. This was a sinister, leering, Underworld sort of animal, the kind that would spit out of the side of its mouth for twopence. It was about four inches high and six long. Its back opened on a hinge. Its tail was arched, so that the tip touched the spine — thus, I suppose, affording a handle for the cream-lover to grasp. The sight of it seemed to take me into a different and dreadful world.

It was, consequently, an easy task for me to carry out the programme indicated by Aunt Dahlia. I curled the lip and clicked the tongue, all in one movement. I also drew in the breath sharply. The whole effect was that of a man absolutely out of sympathy with this cow-creamer, and I saw the mildewed cove start, as if he had been wounded in a tender spot.

'Oh, tut, tut, tut!' I said, 'Oh, dear, dear, dear! Oh, no, no, no, no, no! I don't think much of this,' I said, curling and clicking freely. 'All wrong.'

'All wrong?'

'All wrong. Modern Dutch.'

'Modern Dutch?' He may have frothed at the

mouth, or he may not. I couldn't be sure. But the agony of spirit was obviously intense. 'What do you mean, Modern Dutch? It's eighteenth-century English. Look at the hallmark.'

'I can't see any hallmark.'

'Are you blind? Here, take it outside in the street. It's lighter there.'

'Right ho,' I said, and started for the door, sauntering at first in a languid sort of way, like a connoisseur a bit bored at having his time wasted.

I say 'at first,' because I had only taken a couple of steps when I tripped over the cat, and you can't combine tripping over cats with languid sauntering. Shifting abruptly into high, I shot out of the door like someone wanted by the police making for the car after a smash-and-grab raid. The cow-creamer flew from my hands, and it was a lucky thing that I happened to barge into a fellow citizen outside, or I should have taken a toss in the gutter.

Well, not absolutely lucky, as a matter of fact, for it turned out to be Sir Watkyn Bassett. He stood there goggling at me with horror and indignation behind the pince-nez, and you could almost see him totting up the score on his fingers. First, bag-snatching, I mean to say; then umbrella-pinching; and now this. His whole demeanour was that of a man confronted with the last straw.

'Call a policeman, Roderick!' he cried, skipping like the high hills.

The Dictator sprang to the task.

'Police!' he bawled.

21

'Police!' yipped old Bassett, up in the tenor clef.

'Police!' roared the Dictator, taking the bass.

And a moment later something large loomed up in the fog and said: 'What's all this?'

Well, I dare say I could have explained everything, if I had stuck around and gone into it, but I didn't want to stick around and go into it. Sidestepping nimbly, I picked up the feet and was gone like the wind. A voice shouted 'Stop!' but of course I didn't. Stop, I mean to say! Of all the damn silly ideas. I legged it down byways and along side streets, and eventually fetched up somewhere in the neighbourhood of Sloane Square. There I got aboard a cab and started back to civilization.

My original intention was to drive to the Drones and get a bite of lunch there, but I hadn't gone far when I realized that I wasn't equal to it. I yield to no man in my appreciation of the Drones Club . . . its sparkling conversation, its camaraderie, its atmosphere redolent of all that is best and brightest in the metropolis . . . but there would, I knew, be a goodish bit of bread thrown hither and thither at its luncheon table, and I was in no vein to cope with flying bread. Changing my strategy in a flash, I told the man to take me to the nearest Turkish bath.

It is always my practice to linger over a Turkish b., and it was consequently getting late by the time I returned to the flat. I had managed to put in two or three hours' sleep in my cubicle, and that, taken in conjunction with the healing flow of persp in the hot room and the plunge into the icy tank, had brought the roses back to my cheeks to no little extent. It was, indeed, practically with a merry tra-la-la on my lips that I latchkeyed my way in and made for the sitting-room.

And the next moment my fizziness was turned off at the main by the sight of a pile of telegrams on the table.

2

I don't know if you were among the gang that followed the narrative of my earlier adventures with Gussie Fink-Nottle — you may have been one of those who didn't happen to get around to it — but if you were you will recall that the dirty work on that occasion started with a tidal wave of telegrams, and you will not be surprised to learn that I found myself eyeing this mound of envelopes askance. Ever since then, telegrams in any quantity have always seemed to me to spell trouble.

I had had the idea at first glance that there were about twenty of the beastly things, but a closer scrutiny revealed only three. They had all been dispatched from Totleigh-in-the-Wold, and they all bore the same signature.

They ran as follows:

The first:

Wooster,
    Berkeley Mansions,
        Berkeley Square,
            London.
Come immediately. Serious rift Madeline and self. Reply.

GUSSIE.

The second:

Surprised receive no answer my telegram saying Come immediately serious rift Madeline and self. Reply.

GUSSIE.

And the third:

I say, Bertie, why don't you answer my telegrams? Sent you two today saying Come immediately serious rift Madeline and self. Unless you come earliest possible moment prepared lend every effort effect reconciliation, wedding will be broken off. Reply.

GUSSIE.

I have said that that sojourn of mine in the T. bath had done much to re-establish the *mens sana in corpore* whatnot. Perusal of these frightful communications brought about an instant relapse. My misgivings, I saw, had been well founded. Something had whispered to me on seeing those bally envelopes that here we were again, and here we were.

The sound of the familiar footstep had brought Jeeves floating out from the back premises. A glance was enough to tell him that all was not well with ye employer.

'Are you ill, sir?' he inquired solicitously.

I sank into a c. and passed an agitated h. over the b.

'Not ill, Jeeves, but all of a twitter. Read these.'

He ran his eye over the dossier, then transferred it to mine, and I could read in it the respectful anxiety he was feeling for the well-being of the young seigneur.

'Most disturbing, sir.'

His voice was grave. I could see that he hadn't missed the gist. The sinister import of those telegrams was as clear to him as it was to me.

We do not, of course, discuss the matter, for to do so would rather come under the head of speaking lightly of a woman's name, but Jeeves is in full possession of the facts relating to the Bassett-Wooster mix-up and thoroughly cognizant of the peril which threatens me from that quarter. There was no need to explain to him why I now lighted a feverish cigarette and hitched the lower jaw up with a visible effort.

'What do you suppose has happened, Jeeves?'

'It is difficult to hazard a conjecture, sir.'

'The wedding may be scratched, he says. Why? That is what I ask myself.'

'Yes, sir.'

'And I have no doubt that that is what you ask yourself?'

'Yes, sir.'

'Deep waters, Jeeves.'

'Extremely deep, sir.'

'The only thing we can say with any certainty is that in some way — how, we shall presumably learn later — Gussie has made an ass of himself again.'

I mused on Augustus Fink-Nottle for a moment, recalling how he had always stood by himself in the chump class. The best judges had been saying it for years. Why, at our private school, where I had first met him, he had been known as 'Fathead', and that was in competition with fellows like Bingo Little, Freddie Widgeon and myself.

'What shall I do, Jeeves?'

'I think it would be best to proceed to Totleigh Towers, sir.'

'But how can I? Old Bassett would sling me out the moment I arrived.'

'Possibly if you were to telegraph to Mr Fink-Nottle, sir, explaining your difficulty, he might have some solution to suggest.'

This seemed sound. I hastened out to the post office, and wired as follows:

Fink-Nottle,
 Totleigh Towers,
  Totleigh-in-the-Wold.
Yes, that's all very well. You say come here immediately, but how dickens can I? You don't understand relations between Pop Bassett and self. These not such as to make him welcome visit Bertram. Would inevitably hurl out on ear and set dogs on. Useless suggest putting on false whiskers and pretending be fellow come inspect drains, as old blighter familiar with features and would instantly detect imposture. What is to be done? What has happened? Why serious rift?

What serious rift? How do you mean wedding broken off? Why dickens? What have you been doing to the girl? Reply.

BERTIE.

The answer to this came during dinner:

27

Wooster,
   Berkeley Mansions,
    Berkeley Square,
     London.
See difficulty, but think can work it. In spite strained relations, still speaking terms Madeline. Am telling her have received urgent letter from you pleading be allowed come here. Expect invitation shortly.

                    GUSSIE.

And on the morrow, after a tossing-on-pillow night, I received a bag of three.

The first ran:

Have worked it. Invitation dispatched. When you come, will you bring book entitled My Friends the Newts by Loretta Peabody published Popgood and Grooly get any bookshop.

                    GUSSIE.

The second:

Bertie, you old ass, I hear you are coming here. Delighted, as something very important want you do for me.

                    STIFFY.

The third:

Please come here if you wish, but, oh Bertie, is this wise? Will not it cause you needless pain *seeing me? Surely merely twisting knife wound.*

MADELINE.

Jeeves was bringing me the morning cup of tea when I read these missives, and I handed them to him in silence. He read them in same. I was able to imbibe about a fluid ounce of the hot and strengthening before he spoke.

'I think that we should start at once, sir.'

'I suppose so.'

'I will pack immediately. Would you wish me to call Mrs Travers on the telephone?'

'Why?'

'She has rung up several times this morning.'

'Oh? Then perhaps you had better give her a buzz.'

'I think it will not be necessary, sir. I fancy that this would be the lady now.'

A long and sustained peal had sounded from the front door, as if an aunt had put her thumb on the button and kept it there. Jeeves left the presence, and a moment later it was plain that his intuition had not deceived him. A booming voice rolled through the flat, the voice which once, when announcing the advent of a fox in their vicinity, had been wont to cause members of the Quorn and Pytchley to clutch their hats and bound in their saddles.

'Isn't that young hound awake yet, Jeeves? . . . Oh, there you are.'

Aunt Dahlia charged across the threshold.

★   ★   ★

At all times and on all occasions, owing to years of fox-chivvying in every kind of weather, this relative has a fairly purple face, but one noted now an even deeper mauve than usual. The breath came jerkily, and the eyes gleamed with a goofy light. A man with far less penetration than Bertram Wooster would have been able to divine that there before him stood an aunt who had got the pip about something.

It was evident that information which she yearned to uncork was bubbling within her, but she postponed letting it go for a moment in order to reproach me for being in bed at such an hour. Sunk, as she termed it in her forthright way, in hoggish slumber.

'Not sunk in hoggish slumber,' I corrected. 'I've been awake some little time. As a matter of fact, I was just about to partake of the morning meal. You will join me, I hope? Bacon and eggs may be taken as read, but say the word and we can do you a couple of kippers.'

She snorted with a sudden violence which twenty-four hours earlier would have unmanned me completely. Even in my present tolerably robust condition, it affected me rather like one of those gas explosions which slay six.

'Eggs! Kippers! What I want is a brandy and soda. Tell Jeeves to mix me one. And if he forgets to put in the soda, it will be all right with me. Bertie, a frightful thing has happened.'

'Push along into the dining-saloon, my fluttering old aspen,' I said. 'We shall not be interrupted there. Jeeves will want to come in here to pack.'

'Are you off somewhere?'

'Totleigh Towers. I have had a most disturb-ing — '

'Totleigh Towers? Well, I'm dashed! That's just where I came to tell you you had jolly well got to go immediately.'

'Eh?'

'Matter of life and death.'

'How do you mean?'

'You'll soon see, when I've explained.'

'Then come along to the dining-room and explain at your earliest convenience.'

'Now then, my dear old mysterious hinter,' I said, when Jeeves had brought the foodstuffs and withdrawn, 'tell me all.'

For an instant, there was silence, broken only by the musical sound of an aunt drinking brandy and soda and self lowering a cup of coffee. Then she put down her beaker, and drew a deep breath.

'Bertie,' she said, 'I wish to begin by saying a few words about Sir Watkyn Bassett, CBE. May greenfly attack his roses. May his cook get tight on the night of the big dinner-party. May all his hens get the staggers.'

'Does he keep hens?' I said, putting a point.

'May his cistern start leaking, and may white ants, if there are any in England, gnaw away the foundations of Totleigh Towers. And when he walks up the aisle with his daughter Madeline, to give her away to that ass Spink-Bottle, may he get a sneezing fit and find that he has come out without a pocket handkerchief.'

She paused, and it seemed to me that all this,

31

while spirited stuff, was not germane to the issue.

'Quite,' I said. 'I agree with you *in toto*. But what has he done?'

'I will tell you. You remember that cowcreamer?'

I dug into a fried egg, quivering a little.

'Remember it? I shall never forget it. You will scarcely believe this, Aunt Dahlia, but when I got to the shop, who should be there by the most amazing coincidence but this same Bassett — '

'It wasn't a coincidence. He had gone there to have a look at the thing, to see if it was all Tom had said it was. For — can you imagine such lunacy, Bertie? — that chump of an uncle of yours had told the man about it. He might have known that the fiend would hatch some devilish plot for his undoing. And he did. Tom lunched with Sir Watkyn Bassett at the latter's club yesterday. On the bill of fare was a cold lobster, and this Machiavelli sicked him on to it.'

I looked at her incredulously.

'You aren't going to tell me,' I said, astounded, for I was familiar with the intensely delicate and finely poised mechanism of his tummy, 'that Uncle Tom ate lobster? After what happened last Christmas?'

'At this man's instigation, he appears to have eaten not only pounds of lobster, but forests of sliced cucumber as well. According to his story, which he was able to tell me this morning — he could only groan when he came home yesterday — he resisted at first. He was strong and resolute. But then circumstances were too much for him. Bassett's club, apparently, is one of those clubs where they have the cold dishes on a table in the middle of the room, so placed that wherever you sit you can't help seeing them.'

I nodded.

'They do at the Drones, too. Catsmeat Potter-Pirbright once hit the game pie from the far window six times with six consecutive rolls.'

'That was what caused poor old Tom's downfall. Bassett's lobster sales-talk he might have been strong enough to ignore, but the sight of the thing was too much for him. He yielded, tucked in like a starving Esquimau, and at six o'clock I got a call from the hall porter, asking me if I would send the car round to fetch away the remains, which had been discovered by a page boy writhing in a corner of the library. He arrived half an hour later, calling weakly for bicarbonate of soda. Bicarbonate of soda, my foot!' said Aunt Dahlia, with a bitter, mirthless laugh. 'He had to have two doctors and a stomach-pump.'

'And in the meantime — ?' I said, for I could see whither the tale was tending.

'And in the meantime, of course, the fiend Bassett had nipped down and bought the cow-creamer. The man had promised to hold it for Tom till three o'clock, but naturally when three o'clock came and he didn't turn up and there was another customer clamouring for the thing, he let it go. So there you are. Bassett has the cow-creamer, and took it down to Totleigh last night.'

It was a sad story, of course, and one that bore

out what I had so often felt about Pop Bassett — to wit, that a magistrate who could nick a fellow for five pounds, when a mere reprimand would more than have met the case, was capable of anything, but I couldn't see what she thought there was to be done about it. The whole situation seemed to me essentially one of those where you just clench the hands and roll the eyes mutely up to Heaven and then start a new life and try to forget. I said as much, while marmalading a slice of toast.

She gazed at me in silence for a moment.

'Oh? So that's how you feel, is it?'

'I do, yes.'

'You admit, I hope, that by every moral law that cow-creamer belongs to Tom?'

'Oh, emphatically.'

'But you would take this foul outrage lying down? You would allow this stick-up man to get away with the swag? Confronted with the spectacle of as raw a bit of underhanded skulduggery as has ever been perpetrated in a civilized country, you would just sit tight and say 'Well, well!' and do nothing?'

I weighed this.

'Possibly not 'Well, well!' I concede that the situation is one that calls for the strongest comment. But I wouldn't do anything.'

'Well, I'm going to do something. I'm going to pinch the damn thing.'

I stared at her, astounded. I uttered no verbal rebuke, but there was a distinct 'Tut, tut!' in my gaze. Even though the provocation was, I admitted, severe, I could not approve of these strong-arm methods. And I was about to try to awaken her dormant conscience by asking her gently what the Quorn would think of these goings-on — or, for the matter of that, the Pytchley — when she added:

'Or, rather, you are!'

I had just lighted a cigarette as she spoke these words, and so, according to what they say in the advertisements, ought to have been nonchalant. But it must have been the wrong sort of cigarette, for I shot out of my chair as if somebody had shoved a bradawl through the seat.

'Who, me?'

'That's right. See how it all fits in. You're going to stay at Totleigh. You will have a hundred excellent opportunities of getting your hooks on the thing — '

'But, dash it!'

' — and I must have it, because otherwise I shall never be able to dig a cheque out of Tom for that Pomona Grindle serial. He simply won't be in the mood. And I signed the old girl up yesterday at a fabulous price, half the sum agreed upon to be paid in advance a week from current date. So snap into it, my lad. I can't see what you're making all this heavy weather about. It doesn't seem to me much to do for a loved aunt.'

'It seems to me a dashed lot to do for a loved aunt, and I'm jolly well not going to dream — '

'Oh, yes you are, because you know what will happen, if you don't.' She paused significantly. 'You follow me, Watson?'

I was silent. She had no need to tell me what she meant. This was not the first time she had displayed the velvet hand beneath the iron glove — or, rather, the other way about — in this manner.

For this ruthless relative has one all-powerful weapon which she holds constantly over my head like the sword of — who was the chap? — Jeeves would know — and by means of which she can always bend me to her will — viz the threat that if I don't kick in she will bar me from her board and wipe Anatole's cooking from my lips. I shall not lightly forget the time when she placed sanctions on me for a whole month — right in the middle of the pheasant season, when this superman is at his incomparable best.

I made one last attempt to reason with her.

'But why does Uncle Tom want this frightful cow-creamer? It's a ghastly object. He would be far better without it.'

'He doesn't think so. Well, there it is. Perform this simple, easy task for me, or guests at my dinner table will soon be saying: 'Why is it that we never seem to see Bertie Wooster here any more?' Bless my soul, what an amazing lunch that was that Anatole gave us yesterday! 'Superb' is the only word. I don't wonder you're fond of his cooking. As you sometimes say, it melts in the mouth.'

I eyed her sternly.

'Aunt Dahlia, this is blackmail!'

'Yes, isn't it?' she said, and beetled off.

I resumed my seat, and ate a moody slice of cold bacon.

Jeeves entered.

'The bags are packed, sir.'

'Very good, Jeeves,' I said. 'Then let us be starting.'

★ ★ ★

'Man and boy, Jeeves,' I said, breaking a thoughtful silence which had lasted for about eighty-seven miles, 'I have been in some tough spots in my time, but this one wins the mottled oyster.'

We were bowling along in the old two-seater on our way to Totleigh Towers, self at the wheel, Jeeves at my side, the personal effects in the dickey. We had got off round about eleven-thirty, and the genial afternoon was now at its juiciest. It was one of those crisp, sunny, bracing days with a pleasant tang in the air, and had circumstances been different from what they were, I should no doubt have been feeling at the peak of my form, chatting gaily, waving to passing rustics, possibly even singing some light snatch.

Unfortunately, however, if there was one thing circumstances weren't, it was different from what they were, and there was no suspicion of a song on the lips. The more I thought of what lay before me at these bally Towers, the boweddowner did the heart become.

'The mottled oyster,' I repeated.

'Sir?'

I frowned. The man was being discreet, and this was no time for discretion.

'Don't pretend you don't know all about it, Jeeves,' I said coldly. 'You were in the next room throughout my interview with Aunt Dahlia, and her remarks must have been audible in Piccadilly.'

He dropped the mask.

'Well, yes, sir, I must confess that I did gather the substance of the conversation.'

'Very well, then. You agree with me that the situation is a lulu?'

'Certainly a somewhat sharp crisis in your affairs would appear to have been precipitated, sir.'

I drove on, brooding.

'If I had my life to live again, Jeeves, I would start it as an orphan without any aunts. Don't they put aunts in Turkey in sacks and drop them in the Bosphorus?'

'Odalisques, sir, I understand. Not aunts.'

'Well, why not aunts? Look at the trouble they cause in the world. I tell you, Jeeves, and you may quote me as saying this — behind every poor, innocent, harmless blighter who is going down for the first time in the soup, you will find, if you look carefully enough, the aunt who shoved him into it.'

'There is much in what you say, sir.'

'It is no use telling me that there are bad aunts and good aunts. At the core, they are all alike. Sooner or later, out pops the cloven hoof. Consider this Dahlia, Jeeves, As sound an egg as ever cursed a foxhound for chasing a rabbit, I have always considered her. And she goes and hands me an assignment like this. Wooster, the pincher of policemen's helmets, we know. We are familiar with Wooster, the supposed bag-snatcher. But it was left for this aunt to present to the world a Wooster who goes to the houses of retired magistrates and, while eating their bread and salt, swipes their cow-creamers. Faugh!' I said, for I was a good deal overwrought.

'Most disturbing, sir.'

'I wonder how old Bassett will receive me, Jeeves.'

'It will be interesting to observe his reactions, sir.'

'He can't very well throw me out, I suppose, Miss Bassett having invited me?'

'No, sir.'

'On the other hand, he can — and I think he will — look at me over the top of his pince-nez and make rummy sniffing noises. The prospect is not an agreeable one.'

'No, sir.'

'I mean to say, even if this cow-creamer thing had not come up, conditions would be sticky.'

'Yes, sir. Might I venture to inquire if it is your intention to endeavour to carry out Mrs Travers's wishes?'

You can't fling the hands up in a passionate gesture when you are driving a car at fifty miles an hour. Otherwise, I should have done so.

'That is the problem which is torturing me, Jeeves. I can't make up my mind. You remember that fellow you've mentioned to me once or twice, who let something wait upon something? You know who I mean — the cat chap.'

'Macbeth, sir, a character in a play of that

name by the late William Shakespeare. He was described as letting 'I dare not' wait upon 'I would', like the poor cat i' th' adage.'

'Well, that's how it is with me. I wobble, and I vacillate — if that's the word?'

'Perfectly correct, sir.'

'I think of being barred from those menus of Anatole's, and I say to myself that I will take a pop. Then I reflect that my name at Totleigh Towers is already mud and that old Bassett is firmly convinced that I am a combination of Raffles and a pea-and-thimble man and steal everything I come upon that isn't nailed down — '

'Sir?'

'Didn't I tell you about that? I had another encounter with him yesterday, the worst to date. He now looks upon me as the dregs of the criminal world — if not Public Enemy Number One, certainly Number Two or Three.'

I informed him briefly of what had occurred, and conceive my emotion when I saw that he appeared to be finding something humorous in the recital. Jeeves does not often smile, but now a distinct simper had begun to wreathe his lips.

'A laughable misunderstanding, sir.'

'Laughable, Jeeves?'

He saw that his mirth had been ill-timed. He reassembled the features, ironing out the smile.

'I beg your pardon, sir. I should have said 'disturbing'.'

'Quite.'

'It must have been exceedingly trying, meeting Sir Watkyn in such circumstances.'

'Yes, and it's going to be a dashed sight more trying if he catches me pinching his cow-creamer. I keep seeing a vision of him doing it.'

'I quite understand, sir. And thus the native hue of resolution is sicklied o'er with the pale cast of thought, and enterprises of great pitch and moment in this regard their currents turn awry and lose the name of action.'

'Exactly. You take the words out of my mouth.'

I drove on, brooding more than ever.

'And here's another point that presents itself, Jeeves. Even if I want to steal cow-creamers, how am I going to find the time? It isn't a thing you can just take in your stride. You have to plan and plot and lay schemes. And I shall need every ounce of concentration for this business of Gussie's.'

'Exactly, sir. One appreciates the difficulty.'

'And, as if that wasn't enough to have on my mind, there is that telegram of Stiffy's. You remember the third telegram that came this morning. It was from Miss Stephanie Byng, Miss Bassett's cousin, who resides at Totleigh Towers. You've met her. She came to lunch at the flat a week or two ago. Smallish girl of about the tonnage of Jessie Matthews.'

'Oh, yes, sir. I remember Miss Byng. A charming young lady.'

'Quite. But what does she want me to do for her? That's the question. Probably something completely unfit for human consumption. So I've got that to worry about, too. What a life!'

'Yes, sir.'

'Still, stiff upper lip, I suppose, Jeeves, what?'

41

'Precisely, sir.'

During these exchanges, we had been breezing along at a fairish pace, and I had not failed to note that on a signpost which we had passed some little while back there had been inscribed the words 'Totleigh-in-the-Wold, 8 miles'. There now appeared before us through the trees a stately home of E.

I braked the car.

'Journey's End, Jeeves?'

'So I should be disposed to imagine, sir.'

And so it proved. Having turned in at the gateway and fetched up at the front door, we were informed by the butler that this was indeed the lair of Sir Watkyn Bassett.

'Childe Roland to the dark tower came, sir,' said Jeeves, as we alighted, though what he meant I hadn't an earthly. Responding with a brief 'Oh, ah,' I gave my attention to the butler, who was endeavouring to communicate something to me.

What he was saying, I now gathered, was that if desirous of mixing immediately with the inmates I had chosen a bad moment for hitting the place. Sir Watkyn, he explained, had popped out for a breather.

'I fancy he is somewhere in the grounds with Mr Roderick Spode.'

I started. After that affair at the antique shop, the name Roderick was, as you may imagine, rather deeply graven on my heart.

'Roderick Spode? Big chap with a small moustache and the sort of eye that can open an oyster at sixty paces?'

42

'Yes, sir. He arrived yesterday with Sir Watkyn from London. They went out shortly after lunch. Miss Madeline, I believe, is at home, but it may take some little time to locate her.'

'How about Mr Fink-Nottle?'

'I think he has gone for a walk, sir.'

'Oh? Well, right ho. Then I'll just potter about a bit.'

I was glad of the chance of being alone for a while, for I wished to brood. I strolled off along the terrace, doing so.

The news that Roderick Spode was on the premises had shaken me a good deal. I had supposed him to be some mere club acquaintance of old Bassett's, who confined his activities exclusively to the metropolis, and his presence at the Towers rendered the prospect of trying to unnerve the stoutest, twice as intimidating as it had been before, when I had supposed that I should be under the personal eye of Sir Watkyn alone.

Well, you can see that for yourself, I mean to say. I mean, imagine how some unfortunate Master Criminal would feel, on coming down to do a murder at the old Grange, if he found that not only was Sherlock Holmes putting in the weekend there, but Hercule Poirot, as well.

The more I faced up to the idea of pinching that cow-creamer, the less I liked it. It seemed to me that there ought to be a middle course, and that what I had to do was explore avenues in the hope of finding some formula. To this end, I paced the terrace with bent bean, pondering.

Old Bassett, I noted, had laid out his money to

43

excellent advantage. I am a bit of a connoisseur of country houses, and I found this one well up to sample. Nice façade, spreading grounds, smoothly shaven lawns, and a general atmosphere of what is known as old-world peace. Cows were mooing in the distance, sheep and birds respectively bleating and tootling, and from somewhere near at hand there came the report of a gun, indicating that someone was having a whirl at the local rabbits. Totleigh Towers might be a place where Man was vile, but undoubtedly every prospect pleased.

And I was strolling up and down, trying to calculate how long it would have taken the old bounder, fining, say, twenty people a day five quid apiece, to collect enough to pay for all this, when my attention was arrested by the interior of a room on the ground floor, visible through an open french window.

It was a sort of minor drawing-room, if you know what I mean, and it gave the impression of being overfurnished. This was due to the fact that it was stuffed to bursting point with glass cases, these in their turn stuffed to bursting point with silver. It was evident that I was looking at the Bassett collection.

I paused. Something seemed to draw me through the french window. And the next moment, there I was, *vis-à-vis*, as the expression is, with my old pal the silver cow. It was standing in a smallish case over by the door, and I peered in at it, breathing heavily on the glass.

It was with considerable emotion that I perceived that the case was not locked.

I turned the handle. I dipped in, and fished it out.

Now, whether it was my intention merely to inspect and examine, or whether I was proposing to shoot the works, I do not know. The nearest I can remember is that I had no really settled plans. My frame of mind was more or less that of a cat in an adage.

However, I was not accorded leisure to review my emotions in what Jeeves would call the final analysis, for at this point a voice behind me said 'Hands up!' and, turning, I observed Roderick Spode in the window. He had a shotgun in his hand, and this he was pointing in a negligent sort of way at my third waistcoat button. I gathered from his manner that he was one of those fellows who like firing from the hip.

3

I had described Roderick Spode to the butler as a man with an eye that could open an oyster at sixty paces, and it was an eye of this nature that he was directing at me now. He looked like a Dictator on the point of starting a purge, and I saw that I had been mistaken in supposing him to be seven feet in height. Eight, at least. Also the slowly working jaw muscles.

I hoped he was not going to say 'Ha!' but he did. And as I had not yet mastered the vocal cords sufficiently to be able to reply, that concluded the dialogue sequence for the moment. Then, still keeping his eyes glued on me, he shouted:

'Sir Watkyn!'

There was a distant sound of Eh-yes-here-I-am-what-is-it-ing.

'Come here, please, I have something to show you.'

Old Bassett appeared in the window, adjusting his pince-nez.

I had seen this man before only in the decent habiliments suitable to the metropolis, and I confess that even in the predicament in which I found myself I was able to shudder at the spectacle he presented in the country. It is, of course, an axiom, as I have heard Jeeves call it, that the smaller the man, the louder the check suit, and old Bassett's apparel was in keeping with his lack of inches. Prismatic is the only word for those frightful tweeds and, oddly enough, the spectacle of them had the effect of steadying my nerves. They gave me the feeling that nothing mattered.

'Look!' said Spode. 'Would you have thought such a thing possible?'

Old Bassett was goggling at me with a sort of stunned amazement.

'Good God! It's the bag-snatcher!'

'Yes. Isn't it incredible?'

'It's unbelievable. Why, damn it, it's persecution. Fellow follows me everywhere, like Mary's lamb. Never a free moment. How did you catch him?'

'I happened to be coming along the drive, and I saw a furtive figure slink in at the window. I hurried up, and covered him with my gun. Just in time. He had already begun to loot the place.'

'Well, I'm most obliged to you, Roderick. But what I can't get over is the chap's pertinacity. You would have thought that when we foiled that attempt of his in the Brompton Road, he would have given up the thing as a bad job. But no. Down he comes here next day. Well, he will be sorry he did.'

'I suppose this is too serious a case for you to deal with summarily?'

'I can issue a warrant for his arrest. Bring him along to the library, and I'll do it now. The case will have to go to the Assizes or the Sessions.'

'What will he get, do you think?'

'Not easy to say. But certainly not less than — '

'Hoy!' I said.

I had intended to speak in a quiet, reasonable

voice — going on, after I had secured their attention, to explain that I was on these premises as an invited guest, but for some reason the word came out like something Aunt Dahlia might have said to a fellow member of the Pytchley half a mile away across a ploughed field, and old Bassett shot back as if he had been jabbed in the eye with a burned stick.

Spode commented on my methods of voice production.

'Don't shout like that!'

'Nearly broke my eardrum,' grumbled old Bassett.

'But listen!' I yelled. 'Will you listen!'

A certain amount of confused argument then ensued, self trying to put the case for the defence and the opposition rather harping a bit on the row I was making. And in the middle of it all, just as I was showing myself in particularly good voice, the door opened and somebody said 'Goodness gracious!'

I looked round. Those parted lips . . . those saucerlike eyes . . . that slender figure, drooping slightly at the hinges . . .

Madeline Bassett was in our midst.

'Goodness gracious!' she repeated.

I can well imagine that a casual observer, if I had confided to him my qualms at the idea of being married to this girl, would have raised his eyebrows and been at a loss to understand. 'Bertie,' he would probably have said, 'you don't know what's good for you,' adding, possibly, that he wished he had half my complaint. For Madeline Bassett was undeniably of attractive

48

exterior — slim, *svelte*, if that's the word, and bountifully equipped with golden hair and all the fixings.

But where the casual observer would have been making his bloomer was in overlooking that squashy soupiness of hers, that subtle air she had of being on the point of talking baby-talk. It was that that froze the blood. She was definitely the sort of girl who puts her hands over a husband's eyes, as he is crawling in to breakfast with a morning head, and says: 'Guess who!'

I once stayed at the residence of a newly married pal of mine, and his bride had had carved in large letters over the fire-place in the drawing-room, where it was impossible to miss it, the legend: 'Two Lovers Built This Nest,' and I can still recall the look of dumb anguish in the other half of the sketch's eyes every time he came in and saw it. Whether Madeline Bassett, on entering the marital state, would go to such an awful extreme, I could not say, but it seemed most probable.

She was looking at us with a sort of pretty, wide-eyed wonder.

'Whatever is all the noise about?' she said. 'Why, Bertie! When did you get here?'

'Oh, hallo. I've just arrived.'

'Did you have a nice journey down?'

'Oh, rather, thanks. I came in the two-seater.'

'You must be quite exhausted.'

'Oh, no, thanks, rather not.'

'Well, tea will be ready soon. I see you've met Daddy.'

'And Mr Spode.'

'And Mr Spode.'

'I don't know where Augustus is, but he's sure to be in for tea.'

'I'll count the moments.'

Old Bassett had been listening to these courtesies with a dazed expression on the map — gulping a bit from time to time, like a fish that has been hauled out of a pond on a bent pin and isn't at all sure it is equal to the pressure of events. One followed the mental processes, of course. To him, Bertram was a creature of the underworld who stole bags and umbrellas and, what made it worse, didn't even steal them well. No father likes to see his ewe lamb on chummy terms with such a one.

'You don't mean you know this man?' he said.

Madeline Bassett laughed the tinkling, silvery laugh which was one of the things that had got her so disliked by the better element.

'Why, Daddy, you're too absurd. Of course I know him. Bertie Wooster is an old, old, a very dear old friend of mine. I told you he was coming here today.'

Old Bassett seemed not abreast. Spode didn't seem any too abreast, either.

'This isn't your friend Mr Wooster?'

'Of course.'

'But he snatches bags.'

'Umbrellas,' prompted Spode, as if he had been the King's Remembrancer or something.

'And umbrellas,' assented old Bassett. 'And makes daylight raids on antique shops.'

Madeline was not abreast — making three in all.

'Daddy!'

Old Bassett stuck to it stoutly.

'He does, I tell you. I've caught him at it.'

'*I've* caught him at it,' said Spode.

'We've both caught him at it,' said old Bassett. 'All over London. Wherever you go in London, there you will find this fellow stealing bags and umbrellas. And now in the heart of Gloucestershire.'

'Nonsense!' said Madeline.

I saw that it was time to put an end to all this rot. I was about fed up with that bag-snatching stuff. Naturally, one does not expect a magistrate to have all the details about the customers at his fingers' ends — pretty good, of course, remembering his *clientèle* at all — but one can't just keep passing a thing like that off tactfully.

'Of course it's nonsense,' I thundered. 'The whole thing is one of those laughable misunderstandings.'

I must say I was expecting that my explanation would have gone better than it did. What I had anticipated was that after a few words from myself, outlining the situation, there would have been roars of jolly mirth, followed by apologies and backslappings. But old Bassett, like so many of these police court magistrates, was a difficult man to convince. Magistrates' natures soon get warped. He kept interrupting and asking questions, and cocking an eye at me as he asked them. You know what I mean — questions beginning with 'Just a moment — ' and 'You say — ' and 'Then you are asking us to believe — ' Offensive, very.

51

However, after a good deal of tedious spadework, I managed to get him straight on the umbrella, and he conceded that he might have judged me unjustly about that.

'But how about the bags?'

'There weren't any bags.'

'I certainly sentenced you for something at Bosher Street. I remember it vividly.'

'I pinched a policeman's helmet.'

'That's just as bad as snatching bags.'

Roderick Spode intervened unexpectedly. Throughout this — well, dash it, this absolute Trial of Mary Dugan — he had been standing by, thoughtfully sucking the muzzle of his gun and listening to my statement as if he thought it all pretty thin; but now a flicker of human feeling came into his granite face.

'No,' he said, 'I don't think you can go so far as that. When I was at Oxford, I once stole a policeman's helmet myself.'

I was astounded. Nothing in my relations with this man had given me the idea that he, too, had, so to speak, once lived in Arcady. It just showed, as I often say, that there is good in the worst of us.

Old Bassett was plainly taken aback. Then he perked up.

'Well, how about that affair at the antique shop? Hey? Didn't we catch him in the act of running off with my cow-creamer? What has he got to say to that?'

Spode seemed to see the force of this. He removed the gun, which he had replaced between his lips, and nodded.

'The bloke at the shop had given it to me to look at,' I said shortly. 'He advised me to take it outside, where the light was better.'

'You were rushing out.'

'Staggering out. I trod on the cat.'

'What cat?'

'It appeared to be an animal attached to the personnel of the emporium.'

'H'm! I saw no cat. Did you see a cat, Roderick?'

'No, no cat.'

'Ha! Well, we will pass over the cat — '

'But I didn't,' I said, with one of my lightning flashes.

'We will pass over the cat,' repeated old Bassett, ignoring the gag and leaving it lying there, 'and come to another point. What were you doing with that cow-creamer? You say you were looking at it. You are asking us to believe that you were merely subjecting it to a perfectly innocent scrutiny. Why? What was your motive? What possible interest could it have for a man like you?'

'Exactly,' said Spode. 'The very question I was going to ask myself.'

This bit of backing-up from a pal had the worst effect on old Bassett. It encouraged him to so great an extent that he now yielded completely to the illusion that he was back in his bally police court.

'You say the proprietor of the shop handed it to you. I put it to you that you snatched it up and were making off with it. And now Mr Spode catches you here, with the thing in your hands.

53

How do you explain that? What's your answer to that? Hey?'

'Why, Daddy!' said Madeline.

I dare say you have been wondering at this pancake's silence during all the cut-and-thrust stuff which had been going on. It is readily explained. What had occurred was that shortly after saying 'Nonsense!' in the earlier portion of the proceedings, she had happened to inhale some form of insect life, and since then had been choking quietly in the background. And as the situation was far too tense for us to pay any attention to choking girls, she had been left to carry on under her own steam while the men threshed out the subject on the agenda paper.

She now came forward, her eyes still watering a bit.

'Why, Daddy,' she said, 'naturally your silver would be the first thing Bertie would want to look at. Of course, he is interested in it. Bertie is Mr Travers's nephew.'

'What!'

'Didn't you know that? Your uncle has a wonderful collection hasn't he, Bertie? I suppose he has often spoken to you of Daddy's.'

There was a pause. Old Bassett was breathing heavily. I didn't like the look of him at all. He glanced from me to the cow-creamer, and from the cow-creamer to me, then back from me to the cow-creamer again, and it would have taken a far less astute observer than Bertram to fail to read what was passing in his mind. If ever I saw a bimbo engaged in putting two and two together, that bimbo was Sir Watkyn Bassett.

'Oh!' he said.

Just that. Nothing more. But it was enough.

'I say,' I said, 'could I send a telegram?'

'You can telephone it from the library,' said Madeline. 'I'll take you there.'

She conducted me to the instrument and left me, saying that she would be waiting in the hall when I had finished. I leaped at it, established connection with the post office, and after a brief conversation with what appeared to be the village idiot, telephoned as follows:

Mrs Travers,
    47, Charles Street,
      Berkeley Square,
        London.

I paused for a moment, assembling the ideas, then proceeded thus:

Deeply regret quite impossible carry out assignment re you know what. Atmosphere one of keenest suspicion and any sort of action instantly fatal. You ought to have seen old Bassett's eye just now on learning of blood relationship of self and Uncle Tom. Like ambassador finding veiled woman snooping round safe containing secret treaty. Sorry and all that, but nothing doing. Love.

BERTIE.

I then went down to the hall to join Madeline Bassett.

She was standing by the barometer, which, if it had had an ounce of sense in its head, would have been pointing to 'Stormy' instead of 'Set Fair': and as I hove alongside she turned and gazed at me with a tender goggle which sent a thrill of dread creeping down the Wooster spine. The thought that there stood one who was on distant terms with Gussie and might 'ere long return the ring and presents afflicted me with a nameless horror.

I resolved that if a few quiet words from a man of the world could heal the breach, they should be spoken.

'Oh, Bertie,' she said, in a low voice like beer trickling out of a jug, 'you ought not to be here!'

My recent interview with old Bassett and Roderick Spode had rather set me thinking along those lines myself. But I hadn't time to explain that this was no idle social visit, and that if Gussie hadn't been sending out SOSs I wouldn't have dreamed of coming within a hundred miles of the frightful place. She went on, looking at me as if I were a rabbit which she was expecting shortly to turn into a gnome.

'Why did you come? Oh, I know what you are going to say. You felt that, cost what it might, you had to see me again, just once. You could not resist the urge to take away with you one last memory, which you could cherish down the lonely years. Oh, Bertie, you remind me of Rudel.'

The name was new to me.

'Rudel?'

'The Seigneur Geoffrey Rudel, Prince of Blay-en-Saintonge.'

I shook my head.

'Never met him, I'm afraid. Pal of yours?'

'He lived in the Middle Ages. He was a great poet. And he fell in love with the wife of the Lord of Tripoli.'

I stirred uneasily. I hoped she was going to keep it clean.

'For years he loved her, and at last he could resist no longer. He took ship to Tripoli, and his servants carried him ashore.'

'Not feeling so good?' I said, groping. 'Rough crossing?'

'He was dying. Of love.'

'Oh, ah.'

'They bore him into the Lady Melisande's presence on a litter, and he had just strength enough to reach out and touch her hand. Then he died.'

She paused, and heaved a sigh that seemed to come straight up from the cami-knickers. A silence ensued.

'Terrific,' I said, feeling I had to say something, though personally I didn't think the story a patch on the one about the travelling salesman and the farmer's daughter. Different, of course, if one had known the chap.

She sighed again.

'You see now why I said you reminded me of Rudel. Like him, you came to take one glimpse of the woman you loved. It was dear of you, Bertie, and I shall never forget it. It will always remain with me as a fragrant memory, like a flower pressed between the leaves of an old album.

But was it wise? Should you not have been strong? Would it not have been better to have ended it all cleanly, that day when we said goodbye at Brinkley Court, and not to have reopened the wound? We had met, and you had loved me, and I had had to tell you that my heart was another's. That should have been our farewell.'

'Absolutely,' I said. I mean to say, all that was perfectly sound, as far as it went. If her heart really was another's, fine. Nobody more pleased than Bertram. The whole nub of the thing was — was it? 'But I had a communication from Gussie, more or less indicating that you and he were *p'fft*.'

She looked at me like someone who has just solved the crossword puzzle with a shrewd 'Emu' in the top right-hand corner.

'So that was why you came! You thought that there might still be hope? Oh, Bertie, I'm sorry . . . sorry . . . so sorry.' Her eyes were misty with the unshed, and about the size of soup plates. 'No, Bertie, really there is no hope, none. You must not build dream castles. It can only cause you pain. I love Augustus. He is my man.'

'And you haven't parted brass rags?'

'Of course not.'

'Then what did he mean by saying 'Serious rift Madeline and self'?'

'Oh, that?' She laughed another tinkling, silvery one. 'That was nothing. It was all too perfectly silly and ridiculous. Just the teeniest, weeniest little misunderstanding. I thought I had found him flirting with my cousin Stephanie, and I was silly and jealous. But he explained

58

everything this morning. He was only taking a fly out of her eye.'

I suppose I might legitimately have been a bit shirty on learning that I had been hauled all the way down here for nothing, but I wasn't. I was amazingly braced. As I have indicated, that telegram of Gussie's had shaken me to my foundations, causing me to fear the worst. And now the All Clear had been blown, and I had received absolute inside information straight from the horse's mouth that all was hotsy-totsy between this blister and himself.

'So everything's all right, is it?'

'Everything. I have never loved Augustus more than I do now.'

'Haven't you, by Jove?'

'Each moment I am with him, his wonderful nature seems to open before me like some lovely flower.'

'Does it, egad?'

'Every day I find myself discovering some new facet of his extraordinary character. For instance . . . you have seen him quite lately, have you not?'

'Oh, rather. I gave him a dinner at the Drones only the night before last.'

'I wonder if you noticed any difference in him?'

I threw my mind back to the binge in question. As far as I could recollect, Gussie had been the same fish-face freak I had always known.

'Difference? No, I don't think so. Of course, at that dinner I hadn't the chance to observe him very closely — subject his character to the final analysis, if you know what I mean. He sat next to

59

me, and we talked of this and that, but you know how it is when you're a host — you have all sorts of thing to divert your attention . . . keeping an eye on the waiters, trying to make the conversation general, heading Catsmeat Potter-Pirbright off from giving his imitation of Beatrice Lillie . . . a hundred little duties. But he seemed to me much the same. What sort of difference?'

'An improvement, if such a thing were possible. Have you not sometimes felt in the past, Bertie, that, if Augustus had a fault, it was a tendency to be a little timid?'

I saw what she meant.

'Oh, ah, yes, of course, definitely.' I remembered something Jeeves had once called Gussie. 'A sensitive plant, what?'

'Exactly. You know your Shelley, Bertie.'

'Oh, do I?'

'That is what I have always thought him — a sensitive plant, hardly fit for the rough and tumble of life. But recently — in this last week, in fact — he has shown, together with that wonderful dreamy sweetness of his, a force of character which I had not suspected that he possessed. He seems completely to have lost his diffidence.'

'By Jove, yes,' I said, remembering. 'That's right. Do you know, he actually made a speech at that dinner of mine, and a most admirable one. And, what is more — '

I paused. I had been on the point of saying that, what was more, he had made it from start to finish on orange juice, and not — as had been the case at the Market Snodsbury prize giving — with about three quarts of mixed alcoholic stimulants lapping about inside him: and I saw that the statement might be injudicious. That Market Snodsbury exhibition on the part of the adored object was, no doubt, something which she was trying to forget.

'Why, only this morning,' she said, 'he spoke to Roderick Spode quite sharply.'

'He did?'

'Yes. They were arguing about something, and Augustus told him to go and boil his head.'

'Well, well!' I said.

Naturally, I didn't believe it for a moment. Well, I mean to say! Roderick Spode, I mean — a chap who even in repose would have made an all-in wrestler pause and pick his words. The thing wasn't possible.

I saw what had happened, of course. She was trying to give the boyfriend a build-up and, like all girls, was overdoing it. I've noticed the same thing in young wives, when they're trying to kid you that Herbert or George or whatever the name may be has hidden depths which the vapid and irreflective observer might overlook. Women never know when to stop on these occasions.

I remember Mrs Bingo Little once telling me, shortly after their marriage, that Bingo said poetic things to her about sunsets — his best friends being perfectly well aware, of course, that the odd egg never noticed a sunset in his life and that, if he did by a fluke ever happen to do so, the only thing he would say about it would be that it reminded him of a slice of roast beef, cooked just right.

However, you can't call a girl a liar; so, as I

say, I said: 'Well, well!'

'It was the one thing that was needed to make him perfect. Sometimes, Bertie, I ask myself if I am worthy of so rare a soul.'

'Oh, I wouldn't ask yourself rot like that,' I said heartily. 'Of course you are.'

'It's sweet of you to say so.'

'Not a bit. You two fit like pork and beans. Anyone could see that it was a what-d'you-call-it . . . ideal union. I've known Gussie since we were kids together, and I wish I had a bob for every time I've thought to myself that the girl for him was somebody just like you.'

'Really?'

'Absolutely. And when I met you, I said: 'That's the bird! There she spouts!' When is the wedding to be?'

'On the twenty-third.'

'I'd make it earlier.'

'You think so?'

'Definitely. Get it over and done with, and then you'll have it off your mind. You can't be married too soon to a chap like Gussie. Great chap. Splendid chap. Never met a chap I respected more. They don't often make them like Gussie. One of the fruitiest.'

She reached out and grabbed my hand and pressed it. Unpleasant, of course, but one has to take the rough with the smooth.

'Ah, Bertie! Always the soul of generosity!'

'No, no, rather not. Just saying what I think.'

'It makes me so happy to feel that . . . all this . . . has not interfered with your affection for Augustus.'

62

'I should say not.'

'So many men in your position might have become embittered.'

'Silly asses.'

'But you are too fine for that. You can still say these wonderful things about him.'

'Oh, rather.'

'Dear Bertie!'

And on this cheery note we parted, she to go messing about on some domestic errand, I to head for the drawing-room and get a spot of tea. She, it appeared, did not take tea, being on a diet.

And I had reached the drawing-room, and was about to shove open the door, which was ajar, when from the other side there came a voice. And what it was saying was:

'So kindly do not talk rot, Spode!'

There was no possibility of mistake as to whose voice it was. From his earliest years, there has always been something distinctive and individual about Gussie's *timbre*, reminding the hearer partly of an escape of gas from a gas pipe and partly of a sheep calling to its young in the lambing season.

Nor was there any possibility of mistake about what he had said. The words were precisely as I have stated, and to say that I was surprised would be to put it too weakly. I saw now that it was perfectly possible that there might be something, after all, in that wild story of Madeline Bassett's. I mean to say, an Augustus Fink-Nottle who told Roderick Spode not to talk rot was an Augustus Fink-Nottle who might

quite well have told him to go and boil his head.
I entered the room, marvelling.

* * *

Except for some sort of dim female abaft the
tea-pot, who looked as if she might be a cousin
by marriage or something of that order, only Sir
Watkyn Bassett, Roderick Spode and Gussie were
present. Gussie was straddling the hearthrug with
his legs apart, warming himself at the blaze which
should, one would have said, been reserved for
the trouser seat of the master of the house, and I
saw immediately what Madeline Bassett had meant
when she said that he had lost his diffidence.
Even across the room one could see that, when it
came to self-confidence, Mussolini could have
taken his correspondence course.

He sighted me as I entered, and waved what
seemed to me a dashed patronizing hand. Quite
the ruddy Squire graciously receiving the deputa-
tion of tenantry.

'Ah, Bertie. So here you are.'

'Yes.'

'Come in, come in and have a crumpet.'

'Thanks.'

'Did you bring that book I asked you to?'

'Awfully sorry. I forgot.'

'Well, of all the muddle-headed asses that every
stepped, you certainly are the worst. Others abide
our question, thou art free.'

And dismissing me with a weary gesture, he
called for another potted-meat sandwich.

I have never been able to look back on my first

meal at Totleigh Towers as among my happiest memories. The cup of tea on arrival at a country house is a thing which, as a rule, I particularly enjoy. I like the crackling logs, the shaded lights, the scent of buttered toast, the general atmosphere of leisured cosiness. There is something that seems to speak to the deeps in me in the beaming smile of my hostess and the furtive whisper of my host, as he plucks at my elbow and says 'Let's get out of here and go and have a whisky and soda in the gun-room.' It is on such occasions as this, it has often been said, that you catch Bertram Wooster at his best.

But now all sense of *bien-être* was destroyed by Gussie's peculiar manner — that odd suggestion he conveyed of having bought the place. It was a relief when the gang had finally drifted away, leaving us alone. There were mysteries here which I wanted to probe.

I thought it best, however, to begin by taking a second opinion on the position of affairs between himself and Madeline. She had told me that everything was now hunky-dory once more, but it was one of those points on which you cannot have too much assurance.

'I saw Madeline just now,' I said. 'She tells me that you are sweethearts still. Correct?'

'Quite correct. There was a little temporary coolness about my taking a fly out of Stephanie Byng's eye, and I got a bit panicked and wired you to come down. I thought you might possibly plead. However, no need for that now. I took a strong line, and everything is all right. Still, stay a day or two, of course, as you're here.'

'Thanks.'

'No doubt you will be glad to see your aunt. She arrives tonight, I understand.'

I could make nothing of this. My Aunt Agatha, I knew, was in a nursing home with jaundice. I had taken her flowers only a couple of days before. And naturally it couldn't be Aunt Dahlia, for she had mentioned nothing to me about any plans for infesting Totleigh Towers.

'Some mistake,' I said.

'No mistake at all. Madeline showed me the telegram that came from her this morning, asking if she could be put up for a day or two. It was dispatched from London, I noticed, so I suppose she has left Brinkley.'

I stared.

'You aren't talking about my Aunt Dahlia?'

'Of course I'm talking about your Aunt Dahlia.'

'You mean Aunt Dahlia is coming here tonight?'

'Exactly.'

This was nasty news, and I found myself chewing the lower lip a bit in undisguised concern. This sudden decision to follow me to Totleigh Towers could mean only one thing, that Aunt Dahlia, thinking things over, had become mistrustful of my will to win, and had felt it best to come and stand over me and see that I did not shirk the appointed task. And as I was fully resolved to shirk it, I could envisage some dirty weather ahead. Her attitude towards a recalcitrant nephew would, I feared, closely resemble that which in the old tally-ho days she had been wont to adopt towards a hound which refused to go to cover.

'Tell me,' continued Gussie, 'what sort of voice is she in these days? I ask, because if she is going to make those hunting noises of hers at me during her visit, I shall be compelled to tick her off pretty sharply. I had enough of that sort of thing when I was staying at Brinkley.'

I would have liked to go on musing on the unpleasant situation which had arisen, but it seemed to me that I had been given the cue to begin my probe.

'What's happened to you, Gussie?' I asked.

'Eh?'

'Since when have you been like this?'

'I don't understand you.'

'Well, to take an instance, saying you're going to tick Aunt Dahlia off. At Brinkley, you cowered before her like a wet sock. And, to take another instance, telling Spode not to talk rot. By the way, what was he talking rot about?'

'I forgot. He talks so much rot.'

'I wouldn't have the nerve to tell Spode not to talk rot,' I said frankly. My candour met with an immediate response.

'Well, to tell you the truth, Bertie,' said Gussie, coming clean, 'neither would I, a week ago.'

'What happened a week ago?'

'I had a spiritual rebirth. Thanks to Jeeves. There's a chap, Bertie!'

'Ah!'

'We are as little children, frightened of the dark, and Jeeves is the wise nurse who takes us by the hand and — '

'Switches the light on?'

'Precisely. Would you care to hear about it?'

I assured him that I was all agog. I settled myself in my chair and, putting match to gasper, awaited the inside story.

* * *

Gussie stood silent for a moment. I could see that he was marshalling his facts. He took off his spectacles and polished them.

'A week ago, Bertie,' he began, 'my affairs had reached a crisis. I was faced by an ordeal, the mere prospect of which blackened the horizon. I discovered that I would have to make a speech at the wedding breakfast.'

'Well, naturally.'

'I know, but for some reason I had not foreseen it, and the news came as a stunning blow. And shall I tell you why I was so overcome by stark horror at the idea of making a speech at the wedding breakfast? It was because Roderick Spode and Sir Watkyn Bassett would be in the audience. Do you know Sir Watkyn intimately?'

'Not very. He once fined me five quid at his police court.'

'Well, you can take it from me that he is a hard nut, and he strongly objects to having me as a son-in-law. For one thing, he would have liked Madeline to marry Spode — who, I may mention, has loved her since she was so high.'

'Oh, yes?' I said, courteously concealing my astonishment that anyone except a certified boob like himself could deliberately love this girl.

'Yes. But apart from the fact that she wanted to marry me, he didn't want to marry her. He

68

looks upon himself as a Man of Destiny, you see, and feels that marriage would interfere with his mission. He takes a line through Napoleon.'

I felt that before proceeding further I must get the low-down on this Spode. I didn't follow all this Man of Destiny stuff.

'How do you mean, his mission? Is he someone special?'

'Don't you ever read the papers? Roderick Spode is the founder and head of the Saviours of Britain, a Fascist organization better known as the Black Shorts. His general idea, if he doesn't get knocked on the head with a bottle in one of the frequent brawls in which he and his followers indulge, is to make himself a Dictator.'

'Well, I'm blowed!'

I was astounded at my keenness of perception. The moment I had set eyes on Spode, if you remember, I had said to myself 'What ho! A Dictator!' and a Dictator he had proved to be. I couldn't have made a better shot, if I had been one of those detectives who see a chap walking along the street and deduce that he is a retired manufacturer of poppet valves named Robinson with rheumatism in one arm, living at Clapham.

'Well, I'm dashed! I thought he was something of that sort. That chin . . . Those eyes . . . And, for the matter of that, that moustache. By the way, when you say 'shorts', you mean 'shirts', or course.'

'No. By the time Spode formed his association, there were no shirts left. He and his adherents wear black shorts.'

'Footer bags, you mean?'

69

'Yes.'

'How perfectly foul.'

'Yes.'

'Bare knees?'

'Bare knees.'

'Golly!'

'Yes.'

A thought struck me, so revolting that I nearly dropped my gasper.

'Does old Bassett wear black shorts?'

'No. He isn't a member of the Saviours of Britain.'

'Then how does he come to be mixed up with Spode? I met them going around London like a couple of sailors on shore leave.'

'Sir Watkyn is engaged to be married to his aunt — a Mrs Wintergreen, widow of the late Colonel H. H. Wintergreen, of Pont Street.'

I mused for a moment, reviewing in my mind the scene in the antique-bin.

When you are standing in the dock, with a magistrate looking at you over his pince-nez and talking about you as 'the prisoner Wooster', you have ample opportunity for drinking him in, and what had struck me principally about Sir Watkyn Bassett that day at Bosher Street had been his peevishness. In that shop, on the other hand, he had given the impression of a man who has found the blue bird. He had hopped about like a carefree cat on hot bricks, exhibiting the merchandise to Spode with little chirps of 'I think your aunt would like this?' and 'How about this?' and so forth. And now a clue to that fizziness had been provided.

'Do you know, Gussie,' I said, 'I've an idea he must have clicked yesterday.'

'Quite possibly. However, never mind about that. That is not the point.'

'No, I know. But it's interesting.'

'No, it isn't.'

'Perhaps you're right.'

'Don't let us go wandering off into side issues,' said Gussie, calling the meeting to order. 'Where was I?'

'I don't know.'

'I do. I was telling you that Sir Watkyn disliked the idea of having me for a son-in-law. Spode also was opposed to the match. Nor did he make any attempt to conceal the fact. He used to come popping out at me from round corners and muttering threats.'

'You couldn't have liked that.'

'I didn't.'

'Why did he mutter threats?'

'Because though he would not marry Madeline, even if she would have him, he looks on himself as a sort of knight, watching over her. He keeps telling me that the happiness of that little girl is very dear to him, and that if ever I let her down, he will break my neck. That is the gist of the threats he mutters, and that was one of the reasons why I was a bit agitated when Madeline became distant in her manner, on catching me with Stephanie Byng.'

'Tell me, Gussie, what were you and Stiffy actually doing?'

'I was taking a fly out of her eye.'

I nodded. If that was his story, no doubt he

was wise to stick to it.

'So much for Spode. We now come to Sir Watkyn Bassett. At our very first meeting I could see that I was not his dream man.'

'Me, too.'

'I became engaged to Madeline, as you know, at Brinkley Court. The news of the betrothal was, therefore, conveyed to him by letter, and I imagine that the dear girl must have hauled up her slacks about me in a way that led him to suppose that what he was getting was a sort of cross between Robert Taylor and Einstein. At any rate, when I was introduced to him as the man who was to marry his daughter, he just stared for a moment and said 'What?' Incredulously, you know, as if he were hoping that this was some jolly practical joke and that the real chap would shortly jump out from behind a chair and say 'Boo!' When he at last got on to it that there was no deception, he went off into a corner and sat there for some time, holding his head in his hands. After that I used to catch him looking at me over the top of his pince-nez. It unsettled me.'

I wasn't surprised. I have already alluded to the effect that over-the-top-of-the-pince-nez look of old Bassett's had had on me, and I could see that, if directed at Gussie, it might quite conceivably have stirred the old egg up a good deal.

'He also sniffed. And when he learned from Madeline that I was keeping newts in my bedroom, he said something very derogatory — under his breath, but I heard him.'

'You've got the troupe with you, then?'

'Of course. I am in the middle of a very delicate experiment. An American professor has discovered that the full moon influences the love life of several undersea creatures, including one species of fish, two starfish groups, eight kinds of worms and a ribbon-like seaweed called Dictyota. The moon will be full in two or three days, and I want to find out if it affects the love life of newts, too.'

'But what *is* the love life of newts, if you boil it right down? Didn't you tell me once that they just waggled their tails at one another in the mating season?'

'Quite correct.'

I shrugged my shoulders.

'Well, all right, if they like it. But it's not my idea of molten passion. So old Bassett didn't approve of the dumb chums?'

'No. He didn't approve of anything about me. It made things most difficult and disagreeable. Add Spode, and you will understand why I was beginning to get thoroughly rattled. And then, out of a blue sky, they sprang it on me that I would have to make a speech at the wedding breakfast — to an audience, as I said before, of which Roderick Spode and Sir Watkyn Bassett would form a part.'

He paused, and swallowed convulsively, like a Pekingese taking a pill.

'I am a shy man, Bertie. Diffidence is the price I pay for having a hyper-sensitive nature. And you know how I feel about making speeches under any conditions. The mere idea appals me.

When you lugged me into that prize-giving affair at Market Snodsbury, the thought of standing on a platform, faced by a mob of pimply boys, filled me with a panic terror. It haunted my dreams. You can imagine, then, what it was like for me to have to contemplate that wedding breakfast. To the task of haranguing a flock of aunts and cousins I might have steeled myself. I don't say it would have been easy, but I might have managed it. But to get up with Spode on one side of me and Sir Watkyn Bassett on the other . . . I didn't see how I was going to face it. And then out of the night that covered me, black as the pit from pole to pole, there shone a tiny gleam of hope. I thought of Jeeves.'

His hand moved upwards, and I think his idea was to bare his head reverently. The project was, however, rendered null and void by the fact that he hadn't a hat on.

'I thought of Jeeves,' he repeated, 'and I took the train to London and placed my problem before him. I was fortunate to catch him in time.'

'How do you mean, in time?'

'Before he left England.'

'He isn't leaving England.'

'He told me that you and he were starting off almost immediately on one of those Round-The-World cruises.'

'Oh, no, that's all off. I didn't like the scheme.'

'Does Jeeves say it's all off?'

'No, but I do.'

'Oh?'

He looked at me rather oddly, and I thought he was going to say something more on the subject. But he only gave a rummy sort of short laugh, and resumed his narrative.

'Well, as I say, I went to Jeeves, and put the facts before him. I begged him to try to find some way of getting me out of this frightful situation in which I was enmeshed — assuring him that I would not blame him if he failed to do so, because it seemed to me, after some days of reviewing this matter, that I was beyond human aid. And you will scarcely credit this, Bertie, I hadn't got more than half-way through the glass of orange juice with which he had supplied me, when he solved the whole thing. I wouldn't have believed it possible. I wonder what that brain of his weighs?'

'A good bit, I fancy. He eats a lot of fish. So it was a winner, was it, this idea?'

'It was terrific. He approached the matter from the psychological angle. In the final analysis, he said, disinclination to speak in public is due to fear of one's audience.'

'Well, I could have told you that.'

'Yes, but he indicated how this might be cured. We do not, he said, fear those whom we despise. The thing to do, therefore, is to cultivate a lofty contempt for those who will be listening to one.'

'How?'

'Quite simple. You fill your mind with scornful thoughts about them. You keep saying to yourself: 'Think of that pimple on Smith's nose' . . . 'Consider Jones's flapping ears' . . . 'Remember the time Robinson got hauled up before the beak for travelling first-class with a third-class ticket' . . . 'Don't forget you once saw the child Brown being sick at a children's party' . . . and so on. So that when you are called upon to address Smith, Jones, Robinson and Brown, they have lost their sting. You dominate them.'

I pondered on this.

'I see. Well, yes, it sounds good, Gussie. But would it work in practice?'

'My dear chap, it works like a charm. I've tested it. You recall my speech at that dinner of yours?'

I started.

'You weren't despising us?'

'Certainly I was. Thoroughly.'

'What, me?'

'You, and Freddie Widgeon, and Bingo Little, and Catsmeat Potter-Pirbright, and Barmy Fotheringay-Phipps, and all the rest of those present. 'Worms!' I said to myself. 'What a crew!' I said to myself. 'There's old Bertie,' I said to myself. 'Golly!' I said to myself, 'what I know about *him*!' With the result that I played on you as on a lot of stringed instruments, and achieved an outstanding triumph.'

I must say I was conscious of a certain chagrin. A bit thick, I mean, being scorned by a goof like Gussie — and that at a moment when he had been bursting with one's meat and orange juice.

But soon more generous emotions prevailed. After all, I told myself, the great thing — the fundamental thing to which all other considerations must yield — was to get this Fink-Nottle safely under the wire and off on his honeymoon.

And but for this advice of Jeeves's, the muttered threats of Roderick Spode and the combined sniffing and looking over the top of the pince-nez of Sir Watkyn Bassett might well have been sufficient to destroy his morale entirely and cause him to cancel the wedding arrangements and go off hunting newts in Africa.

'Well, yes,' I said, 'I see what you mean. But dash it, Gussie, conceding the fact that you might scorn Barmy Fotheringay-Phipps and Catsmeat Potter-Birbright and — stretching the possibilities a bit — me, you couldn't despise Spode.'

'Couldn't I?' He laughed a light laugh. 'I did it on my head. And Sir Watkyn Bassett, too. I tell you, Bertie, I approach this wedding breakfast without a tremor. I am gay, confident, debonair. There will be none of that blushing and stammering and twiddling the fingers and plucking at the tablecloth which you see in most bridegrooms on these occasions. I shall look these men in the eye, and make them wilt. As for the aunts and cousins, I shall have them rolling in the aisles. The moment Jeeves spoke those words, I settled down to think of all the things about Roderick Spode and Sir Watkyn Bassett which expose them to the just contempt of their fellow men. I could tell you fifty things about Sir Watkyn alone which would make you wonder how such a moral and physical blot on the English scene could have been tolerated all these years. I wrote them down in a notebook.'

'You wrote them down in a notebook?'

'A small, leather-covered notebook. I bought it in the village.'

I confess that I was a bit agitated. Even though he presumably kept it under lock and key, the mere existence of such a book made one uneasy. One did not care to think what the upshot and outcome would be were it to fall into the wrong hands. A brochure like that would be dynamite.

'Where do you keep it?'

'In my breast pocket. Here it is. Oh, no, it isn't. That's funny,' said Gussie. 'I must have dropped it somewhere.'

4

I don't know if you have had the same experience, but a thing I have found in life is that from time to time, as you jog along, there occur moments which you are able to recognize immediately with the naked eye as high spots. Something tells you that they are going to remain etched, if etched is the word I want, for ever on the memory and will come back to you at intervals down the years, as you are dropping off to sleep, banishing that drowsy feeling and causing you to leap on the pillow like a gaffed salmon.

One of these well-remembered moments in my own case was the time at my first private school when I sneaked down to the headmaster's study at dead of night, my spies having informed me that he kept a tin of biscuits in the cupboard under the bookshelf; to discover, after I was well inside and a modest and unobtrusive withdrawal impossible, that the old bounder was seated at his desk and — by what I have always thought a rather odd coincidence — actually engaged in the composition of my end-of-term report, which subsequently turned out a stinker.

It was a situation in which it would be paltering with the truth to say that Bertram retained unimpaired his customary *sang-froid*. But I'm dashed if I can remember staring at the Rev. Aubrey Upjohn on that occasion with half the pallid horror which had shot into the map at these words of Gussie's.

'Dropped it?' I quavered.

'Yes, but it's all right.'

'All right?'

'I mean, I can remember every word of it.'

'Oh, I see. That's fine.'

'Yes.'

'Was there much of it?'

'Oh, lots.'

'Good stuff?'

'Of the best.'

'Well, that's splendid.'

I looked at him with growing wonder. You would have thought that by this time even this pre-eminent sub-normal would have spotted the frightful peril that lurked. But no. His tortoiseshell-rimmed spectacles shone with a jovial light. He was full of *élan* and *espièglerie*, without a care in the world. All right up to the neck, but from there on pure concrete — that was Augustus Fink-Nottle.

'Oh, yes,' he said, 'I've got it all carefully memorized, and I'm extremely pleased with it. During this past week I have been subjecting the characters of Roderick Spode and Sir Watkyn Bassett to a pitiless examination. I have probed these two gumboils to the very core of their being. It's amazing the amount of material you can assemble, once you begin really analysing people. Have you ever heard Sir Watkyn Bassett dealing with a bowl of soup? It's not unlike the Scottish express going through a tunnel. Have you ever seen Spode eat asparagus?'

'No.'

'Revolting. It alters one's whole conception of Man as Nature's last word.'

'Those were two of the things you wrote in the book?'

'I gave them about half a page. They were just trivial, surface faults. The bulk of my researches went much deeper.'

'I see. You spread yourself?'

'Very much so.'

'And it was all bright, snappy stuff?'

'Every word of it.'

'That's great. I mean to say, no chance of old Bassett being bored when he reads it.'

'Reads it?'

'Well, he's just as likely to find the book as anyone, isn't he?'

I remember Jeeves saying to me once, apropos of how you can never tell what the weather's going to do, that full many a glorious morning had he seen flatter the mountain tops with sovereign eye and then turn into a rather nasty afternoon. It was the same with Gussie now. He had been beaming like a searchlight until I mentioned this aspect of the matter, and the radiance suddenly disappeared as if it had been switched off at the main.

He stood gaping at me very much as I had gaped at the Rev. A. Upjohn on the occasion to which I have alluded above. His expression was almost identical with that which I had once surprised on the face of a fish, whose name I cannot recall, in the royal aquarium at Monaco.

'I never thought of that!'

'Start now.'

'Oh, my gosh!'

'Yes.'

'Oh, my golly!'

'Quite.'

'Oh, my sainted aunt!'

'Absolutely.'

He moved to the tea table like a man in a dream, and started to eat a cold crumpet. His eyes, as they sought mine, were bulging.

'Suppose old Bassett does find that book, what do you think will ensue?'

I could answer that one.

'He would immediately put the bee on the wedding.'

'You don't really think that?'

'I do.'

He choked over his crumpet.

'Of course he would,' I said. 'You say he has never been any too sold on you as a son-in-law. Reading that book isn't going to cause a sudden change for the better. One glimpse of it, and he will be countermanding the cake and telling Madeline that she shall marry you over his dead body. And she isn't the sort of girl to defy a parent.'

'Oh, my gosh!'

'Still, I wouldn't worry about that, old man,' I said, pointing out the bright side, 'because long before it happened, Spode would have broken your neck.'

He plucked feebly at another crumpet.

'This is frightful, Bertie.'

'Not too good, no.'

'I'm in the soup.'

'Up to the thorax.'

'What's to be done?'

'I don't know.'

'Can't you think of anything?'

'Nothing. We must just put our trust in a higher power.'

'Consult Jeeves, you mean?'

I shook the lemon.

'Even Jeeves cannot help us here. It is a straight issue of finding and recovering that notebook before it can get to old Bassett. Why on earth didn't you keep it locked up somewhere?'

'I couldn't. I was always writing fresh stuff in it. I never knew when the inspiration would come, and I had to have it handy.'

'You're sure it was in your breast pocket?'

'Quite sure.'

'It couldn't be in your bedroom, by any chance?'

'No. I always kept in on me — so as to have it safe.'

'Safe. I see.'

'And also, as I said before, because I had constant need of it. I'm trying to think where I saw it last. Wait a minute. It's beginning to come back. Yes, I remember. By the pump.'

'What pump?'

'The one in the stable yard, where they fill the buckets for the horses. Yes, that is where I saw it last, before lunch yesterday. I took it out to jot down a note about the way Sir Watkyn slopped his porridge about at breakfast, and I had just completed my critique when I met Stephanie

Byng and took the fly out of her eye. Bertie!' he cried, breaking off. A strange light had come into his spectacles. He brought his fist down with a bang on the table. Silly ass. Might have known he would upset the milk. 'Bertie, I've just remembered something. It is as if a curtain had been rolled up and all was revealed. The whole scene is rising before my eyes. I took the book out, and entered the porridge item. I then put it back in my breast pocket. Where I keep my handkerchief.'

'Well?'

'Where I keep my handkerchief,' he repeated. 'Don't you understand? Use your intelligence, man. What is the first thing you do, when you find a girl with a fly in her eye?'

I uttered an exclamash.

'Reach for your handkerchief!'

'Exactly. And draw it out and extract the fly with the corner of it. And if there is a small, brown leather-covered notebook alongside the handkerchief — '

'It shoots out — '

'And falls to earth — '

' — you know not where.'

'But I do know where. That's just the point. I could lead you to the exact spot.'

For an instant I felt braced. Then moodiness returned.

'Yesterday before lunch, you say? Then someone must have found it by this time.'

'That's just what I'm coming to. I've remembered something else. Immediately after I had coped with the fly, I recollect hearing

Stephanie saying 'Hallo, what's that?' and seeing her stoop and pick something up. I didn't pay much attention to the episode at the time, for it was just at that moment that I caught sight of Madeline. She was standing in the entrance of the stable yard, with a distant look on her face. I may mention that in order to extract the fly I had been compelled to place a hand under Stephanie's chin, in order to steady the head.'

'Quite.'

'Essential on these occasions.'

'Definitely.'

'Unless the head is kept rigid, you cannot operate. I tried to point this out to Madeline, but she wouldn't listen. She swept away, and I swept after her. It was only this morning that I was able to place the facts before her and make her accept my explanation. Meanwhile, I had completely forgotten the Stephanie-stooping-picking-up incident. I think it is obvious that the book is now in the possession of this Byng.'

'It must be.'

'Then everything's all right. We just seek her out and ask her to hand it back, and she does so. I expect she will have got a good laugh out of it.'

'Where is she?'

'I seem to remember her saying something about walking down to the village. I think she goes and hobnobs with the curate. If you're not doing anything, you might stroll and meet her.'

'I will.'

'Well, keep an eye open for that Scottie of hers. It probably accompanied her.'

'Oh, yes. Thanks.'

I remembered that he had spoken to me of this animal at my dinner. Indeed, at the moment when the *sole meunière* was being served, he had shown me the sore place on his leg, causing me to skip that course.

'It biteth like a serpent.'

'Right ho. I'll be looking out. And I might as well start at once.'

It did not take me long to get to the end of the drive. At the gates, I paused. It seemed to me that my best plan would be to linger here until Stiffy returned. I lighted a cigarette, and gave myself up to meditation.

Although slightly easier in the mind than I had been, I was still much shaken. Until that book was back in safe storage, there could be no real peace for the Wooster soul. Too much depended on its recovery. As I had said to Gussie, if old Bassett started doing the heavy father and forbidding banns, there wasn't a chance of Madeline sticking out her chin and riposting with a modern 'Is zat so?' A glance at her was enough to tell one that she belonged to that small group of girls who still think a parent should have something to say about things: and I was willing to give a hundred to eight that, in the circumstances which I had outlined, she would sigh and drop a silent tear, but that when all the smoke had cleared away Gussie would be at liberty.

I was still musing in sombre and apprehensive vein, when my meditations were interrupted. A human drama was developing in the road in front of me.

★ ★ ★

The shades of evening were beginning to fall pretty freely by now, but the visibility was still good enough to enable me to observe that up the road there was approaching a large, stout, moon-faced policeman on a bicycle. And he was, one could see, at peace with all the world. His daily round of tasks may or may not have been completed, but he was obviously off duty for the moment, and his whole attitude was that of a policeman with nothing on his mind but his helmet.

Well, when I tell you that he was riding without his hands, you will gather to what lengths the careless gaiety of this serene slop had spread.

And where the drama came in was that it was patent that his attention had not yet been drawn to the fact that he was being chivvied — in the strong, silent, earnest manner characteristic of this breed of animal — by a fine Aberdeen terrier. There he was, riding comfortably along, sniffing the fragrant evening breeze and there was the Scottie, all whiskers and eyebrows, haring after him hell-for-leather. As Jeeves said later, when I described the scene to him, the whole situation resembled some great moment in a Greek tragedy, where somebody is stepping high, wide and handsome, quite unconscious that all the while Nemesis is at his heels, and he may be right.

The constable, I say, was riding without his hands: and but for this the disaster, when it occurred, might not have been so complete. I was a bit of a cyclist myself in my youth — I think I have mentioned that I once won a choir boys' handicap at some village sports — and I can testify that when you are riding without your hands, privacy and a complete freedom from interruption are of the essence. The merest suggestion of an unexpected Scottie connecting with the ankle bone at such a time, and you swoop into a sudden swerve. And, as everybody knows, if the hands are not firmly on the handlebars, a sudden swerve spells a smeller.

And so it happened now. A smeller — and among the finest I have ever been privileged to witness — was what this officer of the law came. One moment he was with us, all merry and bright; the next he was in the ditch, a sort of *macédoine* of arms and legs and wheels, with the terrier standing on the edge, looking down at him with that rather offensive expression of virtuous smugness which I have often noticed on the faces of Aberdeen terriers in their clashes with humanity.

And as he threshed about in the ditch, endeavouring to unscramble himself, a girl came round the corner, an attractive young prune upholstered in heather-mixture tweeds, and I recognized the familiar features of S. Byng.

After what Gussie had said, I ought to have been expecting Stiffy, of course. Seeing an Aberdeen terrier, I should have gathered that it belonged to her. I might have said to myself: If Scotties come, can Stiffy be far behind?

Stiffy was plainly vexed with the policeman.

You could see it in her manner. She hooked the crook of her stick over the Scottie's collar and drew him back; then addressed herself to the man, who had now begun to emerge from the ditch like Venus rising from the foam.

'What on earth,' she demanded, 'did you do that for?'

It was no business of mine, of course, but I couldn't help feeling that she might have made a more tactful approach to what threatened to be a difficult and delicate conference. And I could see that the policeman felt the same. There was a good deal of mud on his face, but not enough to hide the wounded expression.

'You might have scared him out of his wits, hurling yourself about like that. Poor old Bartholomew, did the ugly man nearly squash him flat?'

Again I missed the tactful note. In describing this public servant as ugly, she was undoubtedly technically correct. Only if the competition had consisted of Sir Watkyn Bassett, Oofy Prosser of the Drones, and a few more fellows like that, could he have hoped to win to success in a beauty contest. But one doesn't want to rub these things in. Suavity is what you need on these occasions. You can't beat suavity.

The policeman had now lifted himself and bicycle out of the abyss, and was putting the latter through a series of tests, to ascertain the extent of the damage. Satisfied that it was slight, he turned and eyed Stiffy rather as old Bassett had eyed me on the occasion when I had occupied the Bosher Street dock.

'I was proceeding along the public highway,' he began, in a slow, measured tone, as if he were giving evidence in court, 'and the dorg leaped at me in a verlent manner. I was zurled from the bersicle — '

Stiffy seized upon the point like a practised debater.

'Well, you shouldn't ride a bicycle. Bartholomew hates bicycles.'

'I ride a bersicle, miss, because if I didn't I should have to cover my beat on foot.'

'Do you good. Get some of the fat off you.'

'That,' said the policeman, no mean debater himself, producing a notebook from the recesses of his costume and blowing a water-beetle off it, 'is not the point at issue. The point at issue is that this makes twice that the animal has committed an aggravated assault on my person, and I shall have to summons you once more, miss, for being in possession of a savage dorg not under proper control.'

The thrust was a keen one, but Stiffy came back strongly.

'Don't be an ass, Oates. You can't expect a dog to pass up a policeman on a bicycle. It isn't human nature. And I'll bet you started it, anyway. You must have teased him, or something, and I may as well tell you that I intend to fight this case to the House of Lords. I shall call this gentleman as a material witness.' She turned to me, and for the first time became aware that I was no gentleman, but an old friend. 'Oh, hallo, Bertie.'

'Hallo, Stiffy.'

'When did you get here?'

'Oh, recently.'

'Did you see what happened?'

'Oh, rather. Ringside seat throughout.'

'Well, stand by to be subpoenaed.'

'Right ho.'

The policeman had been taking a sort of inventory and writing it down in the book. He was now in a position to call the score.

'Piecer skin scraped off right knee. Bruise or contusion on left elbow. Scratch on nose. Uniform covered with mud and'll have to go and be cleaned. Also shock — severe. You will receive the summons in due course, miss.'

He mounted his bicycle and rode off, causing the dog Bartholomew to make a passionate bound that nearly unshipped him from the restraining stick. Stiffy stood for a moment looking after him a bit yearningly, like a girl who wished that she had half a brick handy. Then she turned away, and I came straight down to brass tacks.

'Stiffy,' I said, 'passing lightly over all the guff about being charmed to see you again and how well you're looking and all that, have you got a small, brown, leather-covered notebook that Gussie Fink-Nottle dropped in the stable yard yesterday?'

She did not reply, seeming to be musing — no doubt on the recent Oates. I repeated the question, and she came out of the trance.

'Notebook?'

'Small, brown, leather-covered one.'

'Full of a lot of breezy personal remarks?'

'That's the one.'

'Yes, I've got it.'

I flung the hands heavenwards and uttered a joyful yowl. The dog Bartholomew gave me an unpleasant look and said something under his breath in Gaelic, but I ignored him. A kennel of Aberdeen terriers could have rolled their eyes and bared the wisdom tooth without impairing this ecstatic moment.

'Gosh, what a relief!'

'Does it belong to Gussie Fink-Nottle?'

'Yes.'

'You mean to say that it was Gussie who wrote those really excellent character studies of Roderick Spode and Uncle Watkyn? I wouldn't have thought he had it in him.'

'Nobody would. It's a most interesting story. It appears — '

'Though why anyone should waste time on Spode and Uncle Watkyn when there was Oates simply crying out to be written about, I can't imagine. I don't think I have ever met a man, Bertie, who gets in the hair so consistently as this Eustace Oates. He makes me tired. He goes swanking about on that bicycle of his, simply asking for it, and then complains when he gets it. And why should he discriminate against poor Bartholomew in this sickening way? Every red-blooded dog in the village has had a go at his trousers and he knows it.'

'Where's that book, Stiffy?' I said, returning to the *res*.

'Never mind about books. Let's stick to Eustace Oates. Do you think he means to summons me?'

I said that, reading between the lines, that was

rather the impression I had gathered, and she made what I believe is known as a *moue* . . . Is it *moue?* . . . Shoving out the lips, I mean, and drawing them quickly back again.

'I'm afraid so, too. There is only one word for Eustace Oates, and that is 'malignant'. He just goes about seeking whom he may devour. Oh, well, more work for Uncle Watkyn.'

'How do you mean?'

'I shall come up before him.'

'Then he does still operate, even though retired?' I said, remembering with some uneasiness the conversation between this ex-beak and Roderick Spode in the collection room.

'He only retired from Bosher Street. You can't choke a man off magistrating, once it's in his blood. He's a Justice of the Peace now. He holds a sort of Star Chamber court in the library. That's where I always come up. I'll be flitting about, doing the flowers, or sitting in my room with a good book, and the butler comes and says I'm wanted in the library. And there's Uncle Watkyn at the desk, looking like Judge Jeffreys, with Oates waiting to give evidence.'

I could picture the scene. Unpleasant, of course. The sort of thing that casts a gloom over a girl's home life.

'And it always ends the same way, with him putting on the black cap and soaking me. He never listens to a word I say. I don't believe the man understands the ABC of justice.'

'That's how he struck me, when I attended his tribunal.'

'And the worst of it is, he knows just what my

allowance is, so can figure out exactly how much the purse will stand. Twice this year he's skinned me to the bone, each time at the instigation of this man Oates — once for exceeding the speed limit in a built-up area, and once because Bartholomew gave him the teeniest little nip on the ankle.'

I tut-tutted sympathetically, but I was wishing that I could edge the conversation back to that notebook. One so frequently finds in girls a disinclination to stick to the important subject.

'The way Oates went on about it, you would have thought Bartholomew had taken his pound of flesh. And I suppose it's all going to happen again now. I'm fed up with this police persecution. One might as well be in Russia. Don't you loathe policemen, Bertie?'

I was not prepared to go quite so far as this in my attitude towards an, on the whole, excellent body of men.

'Well, not en masse, if you understand the expression. I suppose they vary, like other sections of the community, some being full of quiet charm, others not so full. I've met some very decent policemen. With the one on duty outside the Drones I am distinctly chummy. In re this Oates of yours, I haven't seen enough of him, of course, to form an opinion.'

'Well, you can take it from me that he's one of the worst. And a bitter retribution awaits him. Do you remember the time you gave me lunch at your flat? You were telling me about how you tried to pinch that policeman's helmet in Leicester Square.'

'That was when I first met your uncle. It was that that brought us together.'

'Well, I didn't think much of it at the time, but the other day it suddenly came back to me, and I said to myself: 'Out of the mouths of babes and sucklings!' For months I had been trying to think of a way of getting back at this man Oates, and you had showed it to me.'

I started. It seemed to me that her words could bear but one interpretation.

'You aren't going to pinch his helmet?'

'Of course not.'

'I think you're wise.'

'It's man's work. I can see that. So I've told Harold to do it. He has often said he would do anything in the world for me, bless him.'

Stiffy's map, as a rule, tends to be rather grave and dreamy, giving the impression that she is thinking deep, beautiful thoughts. Quite misleading, of course. I don't suppose she would recognize a deep, beautiful thought, if you handed it to her on a skewer with tartare sauce. Like Jeeves, she doesn't often smile, but now her lips had parted — ecstatically, I think — I should have to check up with Jeeves — and her eyes were sparkling.

'What a man!' she said. 'We're engaged, you know.'

'Oh, are you?'

'Yes, but don't tell a soul. It's frightfully secret. Uncle Watkyn mustn't know about it till he has been well sweetened.'

'And who is this Harold?'

'The curate down in the village.' She turned to

95

the dog Bartholomew. 'Is lovely kind curate going to pinch bad, ugly policeman's helmet for his muzzer, zen, and make her very, very happy?' she said.

Or words to that general trend. I can't do the dialect, of course.

I stared at the young pill, appalled at her moral code, if you could call it that. You know, the more I see of women, the more I think that there ought to be a law. Something has got to be done about this sex, or the whole fabric of Society will collapse, and then what silly asses we shall all look.

'Curate?' I said. 'But, Stiffy, you can't ask a curate to go about pinching policemen's helmets.'

'Why not?'

'Well, it's most unusual. You'll get the poor bird unfrocked.'

'Unfrocked?'

'It's something they do to parsons when they catch them bending. And this will inevitably be the outcome of the frightful task you have apportioned to the sainted Harold.'

'I don't see that it's a frightful task.'

'You aren't telling me that it's the sort of thing that comes naturally to curates?'

'Yes, I am. It ought to be right up Harold's street. When he was at Magdalen, before he saw the light, he was the dickens of a chap. Always doing things like that.'

Her mention of Magdalen interested me. It had been my own college.

'Magdalen man, is he? What year? Perhaps I know him.'

96

'Of course you do. He often speaks of you, and was delighted when I told him you were coming here. Harold Pinker.'

I was astounded.

'Harold Pinker? Old Stinker Pinker? Great Scott! One of my dearest pals. I've often wondered where he had got to. And all the while he had sneaked off and become a curate. It just shows you how true it is that one-half of the world doesn't know how the other three-quarters lives. Stinker Pinker, by Jove! You really mean that old Stinker cures souls?'

'Certainly. And jolly well, too. The nibs think very highly of him. Any moment now, he may get a vicarage, and then watch his smoke. He'll be a Bishop some day.'

The excitement of discovering a long-lost buddy waned. I found myself returning to the practical issues. I became grave.

And I'll tell you why I became grave. It was all very well for Stiffy to say that this thing would be right up old Stinker's street. She didn't know him as I did. I had watched Harold Pinker through the formative years of life, and I knew him for what he was — a large, lumbering, Newfoundland puppy of a chap — full of zeal, yes; doing his best, true; but never quite able to make the grade; a man, in short, who if there was a chance of bungling an enterprise and landing himself in the soup, would snatch at it. At the idea of him being turned on to perform the extraordinarily delicate task of swiping Constable Oates's helmet, the blood froze. He hadn't a chance of getting away with it.

I thought of Stinker, the youth. Built rather on the lines of Roderick Spode, he had played Rugby football not only for his University but also for England, and at the art of hurling an opponent into a mud puddle and jumping on his neck with cleated boots had had few, if any, superiors. If I had wanted someone to help me out with a mad bull, he would have been my first choice. If by some mischance I had found myself trapped in the underground den of the Secret Nine, there was nobody I would rather have seen coming down the chimney than the Rev. Harold Pinker.

But mere thews and sinews do not qualify a man to pinch policemen's helmets. You need finesse.

'He will, will he?' I said. 'A fat lot of bishing he's going to do, if he's caught sneaking helmets from members of his flock.'

'He won't be caught.'

'Of course he'll be caught. At the old Alma Mater he was always caught. He seemed to have no notion whatsoever of going about a thing in a subtle, tactful way. Chuck it, Stiffy. Abandon the whole project.'

'No.'

'Stiffy!'

'No. The show must go on.'

I gave it up. I could see plainly that it would be mere waste of time to try to argue her out of her girlish daydreams. She had the same type of mind, I perceived, as Roberta Wickham, who once persuaded me to go by night to the bedroom of a fellow guest at a country house

98

and puncture his hot-water bottle with a darning needle on the end of a stick.

'Well, if it must be, I suppose,' I said resignedly. 'But at least impress upon him that it is essential, when pinching policemen's helmets, to give a forward shove before applying the upwards lift. Otherwise, the subject's chin catches in the strap. It was to overlooking this vital point that my own downfall in Leicester Square was due. The strap caught, the cop was enabled to turn and clutch, and before I knew what had happened I was in the dock, saying 'Yes, your Honour' and 'No, your Honour' to your Uncle Watkyn.'

I fell into a thoughtful silence, as I brooded on the dark future lying in wait for an old friend. I am not a weak man, but I was beginning to wonder if I had been right in squelching so curtly Jeeves's efforts to get me off on a Round-The-World cruise. Whatever you may say against these excursions — the cramped conditions of shipboard, the possibility of getting mixed up with a crowd of bores, the nuisance of having to go and look at the Taj Mahal — at least there is this to be said in their favour, that you escape the mental agony of watching innocent curates dishing their careers and forfeiting all chance of rising to great heights in the Church by getting caught bonneting their parishioners.

I heaved a sigh, and resumed the conversation.

'So you and Stinker are engaged, are you? Why didn't you tell me when you lunched at the flat?'

'It hadn't happened then. Oh, Bertie, I'm so happy I could bite a grape. At least, I shall be, if we can get Uncle Watkyn thinking along 'Bless you, my children' lines.'

'Oh, yes, you were saying, weren't you? About him being sweetened. How do you mean, sweetened?'

'That's what I want to have a talk with you about. You remember what I said in my telegram, about there being something I wanted you to do for me?'

I started. A well-defined uneasiness crept over me. I had forgotten all about that telegram of hers.

'It's something quite simple.'

I doubted it. I mean to say, if her idea of a suitable job for curates was the pinching of policemen's helmets, what sort of an assignment, I could not but ask myself, was she likely to hand to me? It seemed that the moment had come for a bit of in-the-bud-nipping.

'Oh, yes?' I said. 'Well, let me tell you here and now that I'm jolly well not going to do it.'

'Yellow, eh?'

'Bright yellow. Like my Aunt Agatha.'

'What's the matter with her?'

'She's got jaundice.'

'Enough to give her jaundice, having a nephew like you. Why, you don't even know what it is.'

'I would prefer not to know.'

'Well, I'm going to tell you.'

'I do not wish to listen.'

'You would rather I unleashed Bartholomew? I notice he has been looking at you in that odd way of his. I don't believe he likes you. He does take sudden dislikes to people.'

100

The Woosters are brave, but not rash. I allowed her to lead me to the stone wall that bordered the terrace, and we sat down. The evening, I remember, was one of perfect tranquillity, featuring a sort of serene peace. Which just shows you.

'I won't keep you long,' she said. 'It's all quite simple and straightforward. I shall have to begin, though, by telling you why we have had to be so dark and secret about the engagement. That's Gussie's fault.'

'What has he done?'

'Just been Gussie, that's all. Just gone about with no chin, goggling through his spectacles and keeping newts in his bedroom. You can understand Uncle Watkyn's feelings. His daughter tells him she is going to get married. 'Oh, yes?' he says. 'Well, let's have a dekko at the chap.' And along rolls Gussie. A nasty jar for a father.'

'Quite.'

'Well, you can't tell me that a time when he is reeling under the blow of having Gussie for a son-in-law is the moment for breaking it to him that I want to marry the curate.'

I saw her point. I recollected Freddie Threepwood telling me that there had been trouble at Blandings about a cousin of his wanting to marry a curate. In that case, I gathered, the strain had been eased by the discovery that the fellow was the heir of a Liverpool shipping millionaire; but as a broad, general rule, parents do not like their daughters marrying curates, and I take it that the same thing applies to uncles with their nieces.

'You've got to face it. Curates are not so hot. So before anything can be done in the way of removing the veil of secrecy, we have got to sell Harold to Uncle Watkyn. If we play our cards properly, I am hoping that he will give him a vicarage which he has in his gift. Then we shall begin to get somewhere.'

I didn't like her use of the word 'we', but I saw what she was driving at, and I was sorry to have to insert a spanner in her hopes and dreams.

'You wish me to put in a word for Stinker? You would like me to draw your uncle aside and tell him what a splendid fellow Stinker is? There is nothing I would enjoy more, my dear Stiffy, but unfortunately we are not on those terms.'

'No, no, nothing like that.'

'Well, I don't see what more I can do.'

'You will,' she said, and again I was conscious of that subtle feeling of uneasiness. I told myself that I must be firm. But I could not but remember Roberta Wickham and the hot-water bottle. A man thinks he is being chilled steel — or adamant, if you prefer the expression — and suddenly the mists clear away and he finds that he has allowed a girl to talk him into something frightful. Samson had the same experience with Delilah.

'Oh?' I said, guardedly.

She paused in order to tickle the dog Bartholomew under the left ear. Then she resumed.

'Just praising Harold to Uncle Watkyn isn't any use. You need something much cleverer than that. You want to engineer some terrifically brainy scheme that will put him over with a bang. I thought I had got it a few days ago. Do you ever read *Milady's Boudoir?*'

'I once contributed an article to it on 'What the Well-Dressed Man is Wearing', but I am not a regular reader. Why?'

'There was a story in it last week about a Duke who wouldn't let his daughter marry the young secretary, so the secretary got a friend of his to take the Duke out on the lake and upset the boat, and then he dived in and saved the Duke, and the Duke said 'Right ho'.'

I resolved that no time should be lost in quashing this idea.

'Any notion you may have entertained that I am going to take Sir W. Bassett out in a boat and upset him can be dismissed instanter. To start with, he wouldn't come out on a lake with me.'

'No. And we haven't a lake. And Harold said that if I was thinking of the pond in the village, I could forget it, as it was much too cold to dive into ponds at this time of year. Harold is funny in some ways.'

'I applaud his sturdy common sense.'

'Then I got an idea from another story. It was about a young lover who gets a friend of his to dress up as a tramp and attack the girl's father, and then he dashes in and rescues him.'

I patted her hand gently.

'The flaw in all these ideas of yours,' I pointed out, 'is that the hero always seems to have a half-witted friend who is eager to place himself in the foulest positions on his behalf. In Stinker's

103

case, this is not so. I am fond of Stinker — you could even go so far as to say that I love him like a brother — but there are sharply defined limits to what I am prepared to do to further his interests.'

'Well, it doesn't matter, because he put the presidential veto on that one, too. Something about what the vicar would say if it all came out. But he loves my new one.'

'Oh, you've got a new one?'

'Yes, and it's terrific. The beauty of it is Harold's part in it is above reproach. A thousand vicars couldn't get the goods on him. The only snag was that he has to have someone working with him, and until I heard you were coming down here I couldn't think who we were to get. But now you have arrived, all is well.'

'It is, is it? I informed you before, young Byng, and I now inform you again that nothing will induce me to mix myself up with your loathsome schemes.'

'Oh, but, Bertie, you must! We're relying on you. And all you have to do is practically nothing. Just steal Uncle Watkyn's cow-creamer.'

I don't know what you would have done, if a girl in heather-mixture tweeds had sprung this on you, scarcely eight hours after a mauve-faced aunt had sprung the same. It is possible that you would have reeled. Most chaps would, I imagine. Personally, I was more amused than aghast. Indeed, if memory serves me aright, I laughed. If so, it was just as well, for it was about the last chance I had.

'Oh, yes?' I said. 'Tell me more,' I said, feeling

that it would be entertaining to allow the little blighter to run on. 'Steal his cow-creamer, eh?'

'Yes. It's a thing he brought back from London yesterday for his collection. A sort of silver cow with a kind of blotto look on its face. He thinks the world of it. He had it on the table in front of him at dinner last night, and was gassing away about it. And it was then that I got the idea. I thought that if Harold could pinch it, and then bring it back, Uncle Watkyn would be so grateful that he would start spouting vicarages like a geyser. And then I spotted the catch.'

'Oh, there was a catch?'

'Of course. Don't you see? How would Harold be supposed to have got the thing? If a silver cow is in somebody's collection, and it disappears, and next day a curate rolls round with it, that curate has got to do some good, quick explaining. Obviously, it must be made to look like an outside job.'

'I see. You want me to put on a black mask and break in through the window and snitch this *object d'art* and hand it over to Stinker? I see. I see.'

I spoke with satirical bitterness, and I should have thought that anyone could have seen that satirical bitterness was what I was speaking with, but she merely looked at me with admiration and approval.

'You are clever, Bertie. That's exactly it. Of course you needn't wear a mask.'

'You don't think it would help me throw myself into the part?' I said with s. b., as before.

'Well, it might. That's up to you. But the great

105

thing is to get through the window. Wear gloves, of course, because of the fingerprints.'

'Of course.'

'Then Harold will be waiting outside, and he will take the thing from you.'

'And after that I go off and do my stretch at Dartmoor?'

'Oh, no. You escape in the struggle, of course.'

'What struggle?'

'And Harold rushes into the house, all over blood — '

'Whose blood?'

'Well, I said yours, and Harold thought his. There have got to be signs of a struggle to make it more interesting, and my idea was that he should hit you on the nose. But he said the thing would carry greater weight if he was all covered with gore. So how we've left it is that you both hit each other on the nose. And then Harold rouses the house and comes in and shows Uncle Watkyn the cow-creamer and explains what happened, and everything's fine. Because, I mean, Uncle Watkyn couldn't just say 'Oh thanks' and leave it at that, could he? He would be compelled, if he had a spark of decency in him, to cough up that vicarage. Don't you think it's a wonderful scheme, Bertie?'

I rose. My face was cold and hard.

'Most. But I'm sorry — '

'You don't mean you won't do it, now that you see that it will cause you practically no inconvenience at all? It would only take about ten minutes of your time.'

'I do mean I won't do it.'

'Well, I think you're a pig.'

'A pig, maybe, but a shrewd, level-headed pig. I wouldn't touch the project with a bargepole. I tell you I know Stinker. Exactly how he would muck the thing up and get us all landed in the jug, I cannot say, but he would find a way. And now I'll take that book, if you don't mind.'

'What book? Oh, that one of Gussie's.'

'Yes.'

'What do you want it for?'

'I want it,' I said gravely, 'because Gussie is not fit to be in charge of it. He might lose it again, in which event it might fall into the hands of your uncle, in which event he would certainly kick the stuffing out of the Gussie-Madeline wedding arrangements, in which event I would be up against it as few men have ever been up against it before.'

'You?'

'None other.'

'How do you come into it?'

'I will tell you.'

And in a few terse words I outlined for her the events which had taken place at Brinkley Court, the situation which had arisen from those events and the hideous peril which threatened me if Gussie's entry were to be scratched.

'You will understand,' I said, 'that I am implying nothing derogatory to your cousin Madeline, when I say that the idea of being united to her in the bonds of holy wedlock is one that freezes the gizzard. The fact is in no way to her discredit. I should feel just the same about marrying many of the world's noblest women.

There are certain females whom one respects, admires, reveres, but only from a distance. If they show any signs of attempting to come closer, one is prepared to fight them off with a blackjack. It is to this group that your cousin Madeline belongs. A charming girl, and the ideal mate for Augustus Fink-Nottle, but ants in the pants to Bertram.'

She drank this in.

'I see. Yes, I suppose Madeline is a bit of a Gawd-help-us.'

'The expression 'Gawd-help-us' is one which I would not have gone so far as to use myself, for I think a chivalrous man ought to stop somewhere. But since you have brought it up, I admit that it covers the facts.'

'I never realized that that was how things were. No wonder you want that book.'

'Exactly.'

'Well, all this has opened up a new line of thought.'

That grave, dreamy look had come into her face. She massaged the dog Bartholomew's spine with a pensive foot.

'Come on,' I said, chaffing at the delay. 'Slip it across.'

'Just a moment. I'm trying to straighten it all out in my mind. You know, Bertie, I really ought to take that book to Uncle Watkyn.'

'What!'

'That's what my conscience tells me to do. After all, I owe a lot to him. For years he has been a second father to me. And he ought to know how Gussie feels about him, oughtn't he? I mean to say, a bit tough on the old buster, cherishing what he thinks is a harmless newt-fancier in his bosom, when all the time it's a snake that goes about criticizing the way he drinks soup. However, as you're being so sweet and are going to help Harold and me by stealing that cow-creamer, I suppose I shall have to stretch a point.'

We Woosters are pretty quick. I don't suppose it was more than a couple of minutes before I figured out what she meant. I read her purpose, and shuddered.

She was naming the Price of the Papers. In other words, after being blackmailed by an aunt at breakfast, I was now being blackmailed by a female crony before dinner. Pretty good going, even for this lax post-war world.

'Stiffy!' I cried.

'It's no good saying 'Stiffy!' Either you sit in and do your bit, or Uncle Watkyn gets some racy light reading over his morning egg and coffee. Think it over, Bertie.'

She hoisted the dog Bartholomew to his feet, and trickled off towards the house. The last I saw of her was a meaning look, directed at me over her shoulder, and it went through me like a knife.

I had slumped back on to the wall, and I sat there, stunned. Just how long, I don't know, but it was a goodish time. Winged creatures of the night barged into me, but I gave them little attention. It was not till a voice suddenly spoke a couple of feet or so above my bowed head that I came out of the coma.

'Good evening, Wooster,' said the voice.

I looked up. The cliff-like mass looming over me was Roderick Spode.

* * *

I suppose even Dictators have their chummy moments, when they put their feet up and relax with the boys, but it was plain from the outset that if Roderick Spode had a sunnier side, he had not come with any idea of exhibiting it now. His manner was curt. One sensed the absence of the bonhomous note.

'I should like a word with you, Wooster.'

'Oh, yes?'

'I have been talking to Sir Watkyn Bassett, and he has told me the whole story of the cow-creamer.'

'Oh, yes?'

'And we know why you are here.'

'Oh, yes?'

'Stop saying 'Oh, yes?' you miserable worm, and listen to me.'

Many chaps might have resented his tone. I did myself, as a matter of fact. But you know how it is. There are some fellows you are right on your toes to tick off when they call you a miserable worm, others not quite so much.

'Oh, yes,' he said, saying it himself, dash it, 'it is perfectly plain to us why you are here. You have been sent by your uncle to steal this cow-creamer for him. You needn't trouble to deny it. I found you with the thing in your hands this afternoon. And now, we learn, your aunt is arriving. The muster of the vultures, ha!'

He paused a moment, then repeated 'The muster of the vultures,' as if he thought pretty highly of it as a gag. I couldn't see that it was so very hot myself.

'Well, what I came to tell you, Wooster, was that you are being watched — watched closely. And if you are caught stealing that cow-creamer, I can assure you that you will go to prison. You need entertain no hope that Sir Watkyn will shrink from creating a scandal. He will do his duty as a citizen and a Justice of the Peace.'

Here he laid a hand upon my shoulder, and I can't remember when I have experienced anything more unpleasant. Apart from what Jeeves would have called the symbolism of the action, he had a grip like the bite of a horse.

'Did you say 'Oh, yes?'' he asked.

'Oh, no,' I assured him.

'Good. Now, what you are saying to yourself, no doubt, is that you will not be caught. You imagine that you and this precious aunt of yours will be clever enough between you to steal the cow-creamer without being detected. It will do you no good, Wooster. If the thing disappears, however cunningly you and your female accomplice may have covered your traces, I shall know where it has gone, and I shall immediately beat you to a jelly. To a jelly,' he repeated, rolling the words round his tongue as if they were vintage port. 'Have you got that clear?'

'Oh, quite.'

'You are sure you understand?'

'Oh, definitely.'

'Splendid.'

A dim figure was approaching across the terrace, and he changed his tone to one of a rather sickening geniality.

'What a lovely evening, is it not? Extraordinarily mild for the time of year. Well, I mustn't keep you any longer. You will be wanting to go and dress for dinner. Just a black tie. We are quite informal here. Yes?'

The word was addressed to the dim figure. A familiar cough revealed its identity.

'I wished to speak to Mr Wooster, sir. I have a message for him from Mrs Travers. Mrs Travers presents her compliments, sir, and desires me to say that she is in the Blue Room and would be glad if you could make it convenient to call upon her there as soon as possible. She has a matter of importance which she wishes to discuss.'

I heard Spode snort in the darkness.

'So Mrs Travers has arrived?'

'Yes, sir.'

'And has a matter of importance to discuss with Mr Wooster?'

'Yes, sir.'

'Ha!' said Spode, and biffed off with a short, sharp laugh.

I rose from my seat.

'Jeeves,' I said, 'stand by to counsel and advise. The plot has thickened.'

5

I slid into the shirt, and donned the knee-length underwear.

'Well, Jeeves,' I said, 'how about it?'

During the walk to the house I had placed him in possession of the latest developments, and had left him to turn them over in his mind with a view to finding a formula, while I went along the passage and took a hasty bath. I now gazed at him hopefully, like a seal awaiting a bit of fish.

'Thought of anything, Jeeves?'

'Not yet, sir, I regret to say.'

'What, no results whatever?'

'None, sir, I fear.'

I groaned a hollow one, and shoved on the trousers. I had become so accustomed to having this gifted man weigh in with the ripest ideas at the drop of the hat that the possibility of his failing to deliver on this occasion had not occurred to me. The blow was a severe one, and it was with a quivering hand that I now socked the feet. A strange frozen sensation had come over me, rendering the physical and mental processes below par. It was as though both limbs and bean had been placed in a refrigerator and overlooked for several days.

'It may be, Jeeves,' I said, a thought occurring, 'that you haven't got the whole scenario clear in your mind. I was able to give you only the merest outline before going off to scour the torso. I think it would help if we did what they do in the thrillers. Do you ever read thrillers?'

'Not very frequently, sir.'

'Well, there's always a bit where the detective, in order to clarify his thoughts, writes down a list of suspects, motives, times when, alibis, clues and what not. Let us try this plan. Take pencil and paper, Jeeves, and we will assemble the facts. Entitle the thing 'Wooster, B., — position of.' Ready?'

'Yes, sir.'

'Right. Now, then. Item one — Aunt Dahlia says that if I don't pinch that cow-creamer and hand it over to her, she will bar me from her table, and no more of Anatole's cooking.'

'Yes, sir.'

'We now come to Item Two — viz, if I do pinch the cow-creamer and hand it over to her, Spode will beat me to a jelly.'

'Yes, sir.'

'Furthermore — Item Three — if I pinch it and hand it over to her and don't pinch it and hand it over to Harold Pinker, not only shall I undergo the jellying process alluded to above, but Stiffy will take that notebook of Gussie's and hand it over to Sir Watkyn Bassett. And you know and I know what the result of that would be. Well, there you are. That's the set-up. You've got it?'

'Yes, sir. It is certainly a somewhat unfortunate state of affairs.'

I gave him one of my looks.

'Jeeves,' I said, 'don't try me too high. Not at a moment like this. Somewhat unfortunate,

114

forsooth! Who was it you were telling me about the other day, on whose head all the sorrows of the world had come?'

'The Mona Lisa, sir.'

'Well, if I met the Mona Lisa at this moment, I would shake her by the hand and assure her that I knew just how she felt. You see before you, Jeeves, a toad beneath the harrow.'

'Yes, sir. The trousers perhaps a quarter of an inch higher, sir. One aims at the carelessly graceful break over the instep. It is a matter of the nicest adjustment.'

'Like that?'

'Admirable, sir.'

I sighed.

'There are moments, Jeeves, when one asks oneself 'Do trousers matter?''

'The mood will pass, sir.'

'I don't see why it should. If you can't think of a way out of this mess, it seems to me that it is the end. Of course,' I proceeded on a somewhat brighter note, 'you haven't really had time to get your teeth into the problem yet. While I am at dinner, examine it once more from every angle. It is just possible that an inspiration might pop up. Inspirations do, don't they? All in a flash, as it were?'

'Yes, sir. The mathematician Archimedes is related to have discovered the principle of displacement quite suddenly one morning, while in his bath.'

'Well, there you are. And I don't suppose he was such a devil of a chap. Compared with you, I mean.'

'A gifted man, I believe, sir. It has been a matter of general regret that he was subsequently killed by a common soldier.'

'Too bad. Still, all flesh is as grass, what?'

'Very true, sir.'

I lighted a thoughtful cigarette and, dismissing Archimedes for the nonce, allowed my mind to dwell once more on the ghastly jam into which I had been thrust by young Stiffy's ill-advised behaviour.

'You know, Jeeves,' I said, 'when you really start to look into it, it's perfectly amazing how the opposite sex seems to go out of its way to snooter me. You recall Miss Wickham and the hot-water bottle?'

'Yes, sir.'

'And Gwladys what-was-her-name, who put her boyfriend with the broken leg to bed in my flat?'

'Yes, sir.'

'And Pauline Stoker, who invaded my rural cottage at dead of night in a bathing suit?'

'Yes, sir.'

'What a sex! What a sex, Jeeves! But none of that sex, however deadlier than the male, can be ranked in the same class with this Stiffy. Who was the chap lo whose name led all the rest — the bird with the angel?'

'Abou ben Adhem, sir.'

'That's Stiffy. She's the top. Yes, Jeeves?'

'I was merely about to inquire, sir, if Miss Byng, when she uttered her threat of handing over Mr Fink-Nottle's notebook to Sir Watkyn, by any chance spoke with a twinkle in her eye?'

116

'A roguish one, you mean, indicating that she was merely pulling my leg? Not a suspicion of it. No, Jeeves, I have seen untwinkling eyes before, many of them, but never a pair so totally free from twinkle as hers. She wasn't kidding. She meant business. She was fully aware that she was doing something which even by female standards was raw, but she didn't care. The whole fact of the matter is that all this modern emancipation of women has resulted in them getting it up their noses and not giving a damn what they do. It was not like this in Queen Victoria's day. The Prince Consort would have had a word to say about a girl like Stiffy, what?'

'I can conceive that His Royal Highness might quite possibly not have approved of Miss Byng.'

'He would have had her over his knee, laying into her with a slipper, before she knew where she was. And I wouldn't put it past him to have treated Aunt Dahlia in a similar fashion. Talking of which, I suppose I ought to be going and seeing the aged relative.'

'She appeared very desirous of conferring with you, sir.'

'Far from mutual, Jeeves, that desire. I will confess frankly that I am not looking forward to the séance.'

'No, sir?'

'No. You see, I sent her a telegram just before tea, saying that I wasn't going to pinch that cow-creamer, and she must have left London long before it arrived. In other words, she has come expecting to find a nephew straining at the leash to do her bidding, and the news will have to be broken to her that the deal is off. She will not like this, Jeeves, and I don't mind telling you that the more I contemplate the coming chat, the colder the feet become.'

'If I might suggest, sir — it is, of course, merely a palliative — but it has often been found in times of despondency that the assumption of formal evening dress has a stimulating effect on the morale.'

'You think I ought to put on a white tie? Spode told me black.'

'I consider that the emergency justifies the departure, sir.'

'Perhaps you're right.'

And, of course, he was. In these delicate matters of psychology he never errs. I got into the full soup and fish, and was immediately conscious of a marked improvement. The feet became warmer, a sparkle returned to the lack-lustre eyes, and the soul seemed to expand as if someone had got to work on it with a bicycle pump. And I was surveying the effect in the mirror, kneading the tie with gentle fingers and running over in my mind a few things which I proposed to say to Aunt Dahlia if she started getting tough, when the door opened and Gussie came in.

★   ★   ★

At the sight of this bespectacled bird, a pang of compassion shot through me, for a glance was enough to tell me that he was not abreast of stop-press events. There was visible in his

118

demeanour not one of the earmarks of a man to whom Stiffy had been confiding her plans. His bearing was buoyant, and I exchanged a swift, meaning glance with Jeeves. Mine said 'He little knows!' and so did his.

'What ho!' said Gussie. 'What ho! Hallo, Jeeves.'

'Good evening, sir.'

'Well, Bertie, what's the news? Have you seen her?'

The pang of compash became more acute. I heaved a silent sigh. It was to be my mournful task to administer to this old friend a very substantial sock on the jaw, and I shrank from it.

Still, these things have to be faced. The surgeon's knife, I mean to say.

'Yes,' I said. 'Yes, I've seen her. Jeeves, have we any brandy?'

'No, sir.'

'Could you get a spot?'

'Certainly, sir.'

'Better bring the bottle.'

'Very good, sir.'

He melted away, and Gussie stared at me in honest amazement.

'What's all this? You can't start swigging brandy just before dinner.'

'I do not propose to. It is for you, my suffering old martyr at the stake, that I require the stuff.'

'I don't drink brandy.'

'I'll bet you drink this brandy — yes, and call for more. Sit down, Gussie, and let us chat awhile.'

And depositing him in the armchair, I engaged

him in desultory conversation about the weather and the crops. I didn't want to spring the thing on him till the restorative was handy. I prattled on, endeavouring to infuse into my deportment a sort of bedside manner which would prepare him for the worst, and it was not long before I noted that he was looking at me oddly.

'Bertie, I believe you're pie-eyed.'

'Not at all.'

'Then what are you babbling like this for?'

'Just filling in till Jeeves gets back with the fluid. Ah, thank you, Jeeves.'

I took the brimming beaker from his hand, and gently placed Gussie's fingers round the stem.

'You had better go and inform Aunt Dahlia that I shall not be able to keep our tryst, Jeeves. This is going to take some time.'

'Very good, sir.'

I turned to Gussie, who was now looking like a bewildered halibut.

'Gussie,' I said, 'drink that down, and listen. I'm afraid I have bad news for you. About that notebook.'

'About the notebook?'

'Yes.'

'You don't mean she hasn't got it?'

'That is precisely the nub or crux. She has, and she is going to give it to Pop Bassett.'

I had expected him to take it fairly substantially, and he did. His eyes, like stars, started from their spheres and he leaped from the chair, spilling the contents of the glass and causing the room to niff like the saloon bar of a pub on a Saturday night.

'What!'

'That is the posish, I fear.'

'But, my gosh!'

'Yes.'

'You don't really mean that?'

'I do.'

'But why?'

'She has her reasons.'

'But she can't realize what will happen.'

'Yes, she does.'

'It will mean ruin!'

'Definitely.'

'Oh, my gosh!'

It has often been said that disaster brings out the best in the Woosters. A strange calm descended on me. I patted his shoulder.

'Courage, Gussie! Think of Archimedes.'

'Why?'

'He was killed by a common soldier.'

'What of it?'

'Well, it can't have been pleasant for him, but I have no doubt he passed out smiling.'

My intrepid attitude had a good effect. He became more composed. I don't say that even now we were exactly like a couple of French aristocrats waiting for the tumbril, but there was a certain resemblance.

'When did she tell you this?'

'On the terrace not long ago.'

'And she really meant it?'

'Yes.'

'There wasn't — '

'A twinkle in her eyes? No. No twinkle.'

'Well, isn't there any way of stopping her?'

I had been expecting him to bring this up, but I was sorry he had done so. I foresaw a period of fruitless argument.

'Yes,' I said. 'There is. She says she will forgo her dreadful purpose if I steal old Bassett's cow-creamer.'

'You mean that silver cow thing he was showing us at dinner last night?'

'That's the one.'

'But why?'

I explained the position of affairs. He listened intelligently, his face brightening.

'Now I see! Now I understand! I couldn't imagine what her idea was. Her behaviour seemed so absolutely motiveless. Well, that's fine. That solves everything.'

I hated to put a crimp in his happy exuberance, but it had to be done.

'Not quite, because I'm jolly well not going to do it.'

'What! Why not?'

'Because, if I do, Roderick Spode says he will beat me to a jelly.'

'What's Roderick Spode got to do with it?'

'He appears to have espoused that cow-creamer's cause. No doubt from esteem for old Bassett.'

'H'm! Well, you aren't afraid of Roderick Spode.'

'Yes, I am.'

'Nonsense! I know you better than that.'

'No, you don't.'

He took a turn up and down the room.

'But, Bertie, there's nothing to be afraid of in a man like Spode, a mere mass of beef and brawn. He's bound to be slow on his feet. He would never catch you.'

'I don't intend to try out as a sprinter.'

'Besides, it isn't as if you had to stay on here. You can be off the moment you've put the thing through. Send a note down to this curate after dinner, telling him to be on the spot at midnight, and then go to it. Here is the schedule, as I see it. Steal cow-creamer — say, twelve-fifteen to twelve-thirty, or call it twelve-forty, to allow for accidents. Twelve-forty-five, be at stables, starting up your car. Twelve-fifty, out on the open road, having accomplished a nice, smooth job. I can't think what you're worrying about. The whole thing seems childishly simple to me.'

'Nevertheless — '

'You won't do it?'

'No.'

He moved to the mantelpiece, and began fiddling with a statuette of a shepherdess of sorts.

'Is this Bertie Wooster speaking?' he asked.

'It is.'

'Bertie Wooster whom I admired so at school — the boy we used to call 'Daredevil Bertie'?'

'That's right.'

'In that case, I suppose there is nothing more to be said.'

'No.'

'Our only course is to recover the book from the Byng.'

'How do you propose to do that?'

He pondered, frowning. Then the little grey cells seemed to stir.

'I know. Listen. That book means a lot to her, doesn't it?'

'It does.'

'This being so, she would carry it on her person, as I did.'

'I suppose so.'

'In her stocking, probably. Very well, then.'

'How do you mean, very well, then?'

'Don't you see what I'm driving at?'

'No.'

'Well, listen. You could easily engage her in a sort of friendly romp, if you know what I mean, in the course of which it would be simple to . . . well, something in the nature of a jocular embrace . . .'

I checked him sharply. There are limits, and we Woosters recognize them.

'Gussie, are you suggesting that I prod Stiffy's legs?'

'Yes.'

'Well, I'm not going to.'

'Why not?'

'We need not delve into my reasons,' I said, stiffly. 'Suffice it that the shot is not on the board.'

He gave me a look, a kind of wide-eyed, reproachful look, such as a dying newt might have given him, if he had forgotten to change its water regularly. He drew in his breath sharply.

'You certainly have altered completely from the boy I knew at school,' he said. 'You seem to have gone all to pieces. No pluck. No dash. No

124

enterprise. Alcohol, I suppose.'

He sighed and broke the shepherdess, and we moved to the door. As I opened it, he gave me another look.

'You aren't coming down to dinner like that, are you? What are you wearing a white tie for?'

'Jeeves recommended it, to keep up the spirits.'

'Well, you're going to feel a perfect ass. Old Bassett dines in a velvet smoking-jacket with soup stains across the front. Better change.'

There was a good deal in what he said. One does not like to look conspicuous. At the risk of lowering the morale, I turned to doff the tails. And as I did so there came to us from the drawing room below the sound of a fresh young voice chanting, to the accompaniment of a piano, what exhibited all the symptoms of being an old English folk song. The ear detected a good deal of 'Hey nonny nonny', and all that sort of thing.

This uproar had the effect of causing Gussie's eyes to smoulder behind the spectacles. It was as if he were feeling that this was just that little bit extra which is more than man can endure.

'Stephanie Byng!' he said bitterly. 'Singing at a time like this!'

He snorted, and left the room. And I was just finishing tying the black tie, when Jeeves entered.

'Mrs Travers,' he announced formally.

★   ★   ★

An 'Oh, golly!' broke from my lips. I had known, of course, hearing that formal announcement,

125

that she was coming, but so does a poor blighter taking a stroll and looking up and seeing a chap in an aeroplane dropping a bomb on his head know that that's coming, but it doesn't make it any better when it arrives.

I could see that she was a good deal stirred up — all of a doodah would perhaps express it better — and I hastened to bung her civilly into the armchair and make my apologies.

'Frightfully sorry I couldn't come and see you, old ancestor,' I said. 'I was closeted with Gussie Fink-Nottle upon a matter deeply affecting out mutual interests. Since we last met, there have been new developments, and my affairs have become somewhat entangled, I regret to say. You might put it that Hell's foundations are quivering. That is not overstating it, Jeeves?'

'No, sir.'

She dismissed my protestations with a wave of the hand.

'So you're having your troubles, too, are you? Well, I don't know what new developments there have been at your end, but there has been a new development at mine, and it's a stinker. That's why I've come down here in such a hurry. The most rapid action has got to be taken, or the home will be in the melting-pot.'

I began to wonder if even the Mona Lisa could have found the going so sticky as I was finding it. One thing after another, I mean to say.

'What is it?' I asked. 'What's happened?'

She choked for a moment, then contrived to utter a single word.

'Anatole!'

'Anatole?' I took her hand and pressed it soothingly. 'Tell me, old fever patient,' I said, 'what, if anything, are you talking about? How do you mean, Anatole?'

'If we don't look slippy, I shall lose him.'

A cold hand seemed to clutch at my heart.

'Lose him?'

'Yes.'

'Even after doubling his wages?'

'Even after doubling his wages. Listen, Bertie. Just before I left home this afternoon, a letter arrived for Tom from Sir Watkyn Bassett. When I say 'just before I left home', that was what made me leave home. Because do you know what was in it?'

'What?'

'It contained an offer to swap the cow-creamer for Anatole, and Tom is seriously considering it!'

I stared at her.

'What? Incredulous!'

'Incredible, sir.'

'Thank you, Jeeves. Incredible! I don't believe it. Uncle Tom would never contemplate such a thing for an instant.'

'Wouldn't he? That's all you know. Do you remember Pomeroy, the butler we had before Seppings?'

'I should say so. A noble fellow.'

'A treasure.'

'A gem. I never could think why you let him go.'

'Tom traded him to the Bessington-Copes for an oviform chocolate pot on three scroll feet.'

I struggled with a growing despair.

'But surely the delirious old ass — or, rather, Uncle Tom — wouldn't fritter Anatole away like that?'

'He certainly would.'

She rose, and moved restlessly to the mantelpiece. I could see that she was looking for something to break as a relief to her surging emotions — what Jeeves would have called a palliative — and courteously drew her attention to a terra cotta figure of the Infant Samuel at Prayer. She thanked me briefly, and hurled it against the opposite wall.

'I tell you, Bertie, there are no lengths to which a really loony collector will not go to secure a coveted specimen. Tom's actual words, as he handed me the letter to read, were that it would give him genuine pleasure to skin old Bassett alive and personally drop him into a vat of boiling oil, but that he saw no alternative but to meet his demands. The only thing that stopped him wiring him there and then that it was a deal was my telling him that you had gone to Totleigh Towers expressly to pinch the cow-creamer, and that he would have it in his hands almost immediately. How are you coming along in that direction, Bertie? Formed your schemes? All your plans cut and dried? We can't afford to waste time. Every moment is precious.'

I felt a trifle boneless. The news, I saw, would now have to be broken, and I hoped that that was all there would be. This aunt is a formidable old creature, when stirred, and I could not but recall what had happened to the Infant Samuel.

'I was going to talk to you about that,' I said.

128

'Jeeves, have you that document we prepared?'

'Here it is, sir.'

'Thank you, Jeeves. And I think it might be a good thing if you were to go and bring a spot more brandy.'

'Very good, sir.'

He withdrew, and I slipped her the paper, bidding her read it attentively. She gave it the eye.

'What's all this?'

'You will soon see. Note how it is headed. 'Wooster, B. — position of.' Those words tell the story. They explain,' I said, backing a step and getting ready to duck, 'why it is that I must resolutely decline to pinch that cow-creamer.'

'What!'

'I sent you a telegram to that effect this afternoon, but, of course, it missed you.'

She was looking at me pleadingly, like a fond mother at an idiot child who has just pulled something exceptionally goofy.

'But, Bertie, dear, haven't you been listening? About Anatole? Don't you realize the position?'

'Oh, quite.'

'Then have you gone cuckoo? When I say 'gone', of course — '

I held up a checking hand.

'Let me explain, aged r. You will recall that I mentioned to you that there had been some recent developments. One of these is that Sir Watkyn Bassett knows all about this cow-creamer-pinching scheme and is watching my every movement. Another is that he has confided his suspicions to a pal of his named Spode.

Perhaps on your arrival here you met Spode?'

'That big fellow?'

'Big is right, though perhaps 'supercolossal' would be more the *mot juste*. Well, Sir Watkyn, as I say, has confided his suspicions to Spode, and I have it from the latter personally that if that cow-creamer disappears, he will beat me to a jelly. That is why nothing constructive can be accomplished.'

A silence of some duration followed these remarks. I could see that she was chewing on the thing and reluctantly coming to the conclusion that it was no idle whim of Bertram's that was causing him to fail her in her hour of need. She appreciated the cleft stick in which he found himself and, unless I am vastly mistaken, shuddered at it.

This relative is a woman who, in the days of my boyhood and adolescence, was accustomed frequently to clump me over the side of the head when she considered that my behaviour warranted this gesture, and I have often felt in these days that she was on the point of doing it again. But beneath this earhole-sloshing exterior there beats a tender heart, and her love for Bertram is, I know, deep-rooted. She would be the last person to wish to see him get his eyes bunged up and have that well-shaped nose punched out of position.

'I see,' she said, at length. 'Yes. That makes things difficult, of course.'

'Extraordinarily difficult. If you care to describe the situation as an *impasse*, it will be all right with me.'

'Said he would beat you to a jelly, did he?'

'That was the expression he used. He repeated it, so that there should be no mistake.'

'Well, I wouldn't for the world have you manhandled by that big stiff. You wouldn't have a chance against a gorilla like that. He would tear the stuffing out of you before you could say 'Pip-pip'. He would rend you limb from limb and scatter the fragments to the four winds.'

I winced a little.

'No need to make a song about it, old flesh and blood.'

'You're sure he meant what he said?'

'Quite.'

'His bark may be worse than his bite.'

I smiled sadly.

'I see where you're heading, Aunt Dahlia,' I said. 'In another minute you will be asking if there wasn't a twinkle in his eye as he spoke. There wasn't. The policy which Roderick Spode outlined to me at our recent interview is the policy which he will pursue and fulfil.'

'Then we seem to be stymied. Unless Jeeves can think of something.' She addressed the man, who had just entered with the brandy — not before it was time. I couldn't think why he had taken so long over it. 'We are talking of Mr Spode, Jeeves.'

'Yes, madam?'

'Jeeves and I have already discussed the Spode menace,' I said moodily, 'and he confesses himself baffled. For once, that substantial brain has failed to click. He has brooded, but no formula.'

Aunt Dahlia had been swigging the brandy gratefully, and there now came into her face a thoughtful look.

'You know what has just occurred to me?' she said.

'Say on, old thicker than water,' I replied, still with that dark moodiness. 'I'll bet it's rotten.'

'It's not rotten at all. It may solve everything. I've been wondering if this man Spode hasn't some shady secret. Do you know anything about him, Jeeves?'

'No, madam.'

'How do you mean, a secret?'

'What I was turning over in my mind was the thought that, if he had some chink in his armour, one might hold him up by means of it, thus drawing his fangs. I remember, when I was a girl, seeing your Uncle George kiss my governess, and it was amazing how it eased the strain later on, when there was any question of her keeping me in after school to write out the principal imports and exports of the United Kingdom. You see what I mean? Suppose we knew that Spode had shot a fox, or something? You don't think much of it?' she said, seeing that I was pursing my lips dubiously.

'I can see it as an idea. But there seems to me to be one fatal snag — viz that we don't know.'

'Yes, that's true.' She rose. 'Oh well, it was just a random thought, I merely threw it out. And now I think I will be returning to my room and spraying my temples with *eau-de-Cologne*. My head feels as if it were about to burst like shrapnel.'

The door closed. I sank into the chair which she had vacated, and mopped the b.

'Well, that's over,' I said thankfully. 'She took the blow better than I had hoped, Jeeves. The Quorn trains its daughters well. But, stiff though her upper lip was, you could see that she felt it deeply, and that brandy came in handy. By the way, you were the dickens of a while bringing it. A St Bernard dog would have been there and back in half the time.'

'Yes, sir. I am sorry. I was detained in conversation by Mr Fink-Nottle.'

I sat pondering.

'You know, Jeeves,' I said, 'that wasn't at all a bad idea of Aunt Dahlia's about getting the goods on Spode. Fundamentally, it was sound. If Spode had buried the body and we knew where, it would unquestionably render him a negligible force. But you say you know nothing about him.'

'No, sir.'

'And I doubt if there is anything to know, anyway. There are some chaps, one look at whom is enough to tell you that they are pukka sahibs who play the game and do not do the things that aren't done, and prominent among these, I fear, is Roderick Spode. I shouldn't imagine that the most rigorous investigation would uncover anything about him worse than that moustache of his, and to the world's scrutiny of that he obviously has no objection, or he wouldn't wear the damned thing.'

'Very true, sir. Still, it might be worth while to institute inquiries.'

'Yes, but where?'

133

'I was thinking of the Junior Ganymede, sir. It is a club for gentlemen's personal gentlemen in Curzon Street, to which I have belonged for some years. The personal attendant of a gentleman of Mr Spode's prominence would be sure to be a member, and he would, of course, have confided to the secretary a good deal of material concerning him, for insertion in the club book.'

'Eh?'

'Under Rule Eleven, every new member is required to supply the club with full information regarding his employer. This not only provides entertaining reading, but serves as a warning to members who may be contemplating taking service with gentlemen who fall short of the ideal.'

A thought struck me, and I started. Indeed, I started rather violently.

'What happened when you joined?'

'Sir?'

'Did you tell them all about me?'

'Oh, yes, sir.'

'What, everything? The time when old Stoker was after me and I had to black up with boot polish in order to assume a rudimentary disguise?'

'Yes, sir.'

'And the occasion on which I came home after Pongo Twistleton's birthday-party and mistook the standard lamp for a burglar?'

'Yes, sir. The members like to have these things to read on wet afternoons.'

'They do, do they? And suppose some wet

134

afternoon Aunt Agatha reads them? Did that occur to you?'

'The contingency of Mrs Spenser Gregson obtaining access to the club book is a remote one.'

'I dare say. But recent events under this very roof will have shown you how women do obtain access to books.'

I relapsed into silence, pondering on this startling glimpse he had accorded me of what went on in institutions like the Junior Ganymede, of the existence of which I had previously been unaware. I had known, of course, that at nights, after serving the frugal meal, Jeeves would put on the old bowler hat and slip round the corner, but I had always supposed his destination to have been the saloon bar of some neighbouring pub. Of clubs in Curzon Street I had had no inkling.

Still less had I had an inkling that some of the fruitiest of Bertram Wooster's possibly ill-judged actions were being inscribed in a book. The whole thing to my mind smacked rather unpleasantly of Abou ben Adhem and Recording Angels, and I found myself frowning somewhat.

Still, there didn't seem much to be done about it, so I returned to what Constable Oates would have called the point at tissue.

'Then what's your idea? To apply to the Secretary for information about Spode?'

'Yes, sir.'

'You think he'll give it to you?'

'Oh, yes, sir.'

'You mean he scatters these data — these extraordinarily dangerous data — these data that

might spell ruin if they fell into the wrong hands
— broadcast to whoever asks for them?'

'Only to members, sir.'

'How soon could you get in touch with him?'

'I could ring him up on the telephone
immediately, sir.'

'Then do so, Jeeves, and if possible chalk the
call up to Sir Watkyn Bassett and don't lose your
nerve when you hear the girl say 'Three
minutes'. Carry on regardless. Cost what it may,
ye Sec. must be made to understand — and
understand thoroughly — that now is the time
for all good men to come to the aid of the party.'

'I think I can convince him that an emergency
exists, sir.'

'If you can't, refer him to me.'

'Very good, sir.'

He started off on his errand of mercy.

'Oh, by the way, Jeeves,' I said, as he was
passing through the door, 'did you say you had
been talking to Gussie?'

'Yes, sir.'

'Had he anything new to report?'

'Yes, sir. It appears that his relations with Miss
Bassett have been severed. The engagement is
broken off.'

He floated out, and I leaped three feet. A
dashed difficult thing to do, when you're sitting
in an armchair, but I managed it.

'Jeeves!' I yelled.

But he had gone, leaving not a wrack behind.

From downstairs there came the sudden
booming of the dinner gong.

6

It has always given me a bit of a pang to look back at that dinner and think that agony of mind prevented me sailing into it in the right carefree mood, for it was one which in happier circumstances I would have got my nose down to with a will. Whatever Sir Watkyn Bassett's moral shortcomings, he did his guests extraordinarily well at the festive board, and even in my preoccupied condition it was plain to me in the first five minutes that his cook was a woman who had the divine fire in her. From a Grade A soup we proceeded to a toothsome fish, and from the toothsome fish to a salmi of game which even Anatole might have been proud to sponsor. Add asparagus, a jam omelette and some spirited sardines on toast, and you will see what I mean.

All wasted on me, of course. As the fellow said, better a dinner of herbs when you're all buddies together than a regular blow-out when you're not, and the sight of Gussie and Madeline Bassett sitting side by side at the other end of the table turned the food to ashes in my m. I viewed them with concern.

You know what engaged couples are like in mixed company, as a rule. They put their heads together and converse in whispers. They slap and giggle. They pat and prod. I have even known the female member of the duo to feed her companion with a fork. There was none of this

137

sort of thing about Madeline Bassett and Gussie. He looked pale and corpse-like, she cold and proud and aloof. They put in the time for the most part making bread pills and, as far as I was able to ascertain, didn't exchange a word from start to finish. Oh, yes, once — when he asked her to pass the salt, and she passed the pepper, and he said 'I meant the salt,' and she said 'Oh, really?' and passed the mustard.

There could be no question whatever that Jeeves was right. Brass rags had been parted by the young couple, and what was weighing upon me, apart from the tragic aspect, was the mystery of it all. I could think of no solution, and I looked forward to the conclusion of the meal, when the women should have legged it and I would be able to get together with Gussie over the port and learn the inside dope.

To my surprise, however, the last female had no sooner passed through the door than Gussie, who had been holding it open, shot through after like a diving duck and did not return, leaving me alone with my host and Roderick Spode. And as they sat snuggled up together at the far end of the table, talking to one another in low voices, and staring at me from time to time as if I had been a ticket-of-leave man who had got in by crashing the gate and might be expected, unless carefully watched, to pocket a spoon or two, it was not long before I, too, left. Murmuring something about fetching my cigarette case, I sidled out and went up to my room. It seemed to me that either Gussie or Jeeves would be bound to look in their sooner or later.

A cheerful fire was burning in the grate, and to while away the time I pulled the armchair up and got out the mystery story I had brought with me from London. As my researches in it had already shown me, it was a particularly good one, full of crisp clues and meaty murders, and I was soon absorbed. Scarcely, however, had I really had time to get going on it, when there was a rattle at the door handle, and who should amble in but Roderick Spode.

I looked at him with not a little astonishment. I mean to say, the last chap I was expecting to invade my bedchamber. And it wasn't as if he had come to apologize for his offensive attitude on the terrace, when in addition to muttering menaces he had called me a miserable worm, or for those stares at the dinner table. One glance at his face told me that. The first thing a chap who has come to apologize does is to weigh in with an ingratiating simper, and of this there was no sign.

As a matter of fact, he seemed to me to be looking slightly more sinister than ever, and I found his aspect so forbidding that I dug up an ingratiating simper myself. I didn't suppose it would do much towards conciliating the blighter, but every little helps.

'Oh, hallo, Spode,' I said affably. 'Come on in. Is there something I can do for you?'

Without replying, he walked to the cupboard, threw it open with a brusque twiddle and glared into it. This done, he turned and eyed me, still in that unchummy manner.

'I thought Fink-Nottle might be here.'

'He isn't.'

'So I See.'

'Did you expect to find him in the cupboard?'

'Yes.'

'Oh?'

There was a pause.

'Any message I can give him if he turns up?'

'Yes. You can tell him that I am going to break his neck.'

'Break his neck?'

'Yes. Are you deaf? Break his neck.'

I nodded pacifically.

'I see. Break his neck. Right. And if he asks why?'

'He knows why. Because he is a butterfly who toys with women's hearts and throws them away like soiled gloves.'

'Right ho.' I hadn't had a notion that that was what butterflies did. Most interesting. 'Well, I'll let him know if I run across him.'

'Thank you.'

He withdrew, slamming the door, and I sat musing on the odd way in which history repeats itself. I mean to say, the situation was almost identical with the one which had arisen some few months earlier at Brinkley, when young Tuppy Glossop had come to my room with a similar end in view. True, Tuppy, if I remembered rightly, had wanted to pull Gussie inside out and make him swallow himself, while Spode had spoken of breaking his neck, but the principle was the same.

I saw what had happened, of course. It was a development which I had rather been anticipating. I had not forgotten what Gussie had told me earlier in the day about Spode informing him of his intention of leaving no stone unturned to dislocate his cervical vertebrae should he ever do Madeline Bassett wrong. He had doubtless learned the facts from her over the coffee, and was now setting out to put his policy into operation.

As to what these facts were, I still had not the remotest. But it was evident from Spode's manner that they reflected little credit on Gussie. He must, I realize, have been making an ass of himself in a big way.

A fearful situation, beyond a doubt, and if there had been anything I could have done about it, I would have done same without hesitation. But it seemed to me that I was helpless, and that Nature must take its course. With a slight sigh, I resumed my gooseflesher, and was making fair progress with it, when a hollow voice said: 'I say, Bertie!' and I sat up quivering in every limb. It was as if a family spectre had edged up and breathed down the back of my neck.

Turning, I observed Augustus Fink-Nottle appearing from under the bed.

★　★　★

Owing to the fact that the shock had caused my tongue to get tangled up with my tonsils, inducing an unpleasant choking sensation, I found myself momentarily incapable of speech. All I was able to do was goggle at Gussie, and it was immediately evident to me, as I did so, that he had been following the recent conversation closely. His whole demeanour was that of a man vividly conscious of being just about half a jump

141

ahead of Roderick Spode. The hair was ruffled, the eyes wild, the nose twitching. A rabbit pursued by a weasel would have looked just the same — allowing, of course, for the fact that it would not have been wearing tortoiseshell-rimmed spectacles.

'That was a close call, Bertie,' he said, in a low, quivering voice. He crossed the room, giving a little at the knees. His face was a rather pretty greenish colour. 'I think I'll lock the door, if you don't mind. He might come back. Why he didn't look under the bed, I can't imagine. I always thought these Dictators were so thorough.'

I managed to get the tongue unhitched.

'Never mind about beds and Dictators. What's all this about you and Madeline Bassett?'

He winced.

'Do you mind not talking about that?'

'Yes, I do mind not talking about it. It's the only thing I want to talk about. What on earth has she broken off the engagement for? What did you do to her?'

He winced again. I could see that I was probing an exposed nerve.

'It wasn't so much what I did to her — it was what I did to Stephanie Byng.'

'To Stiffy?'

'Yes.'

'What did you do to Stiffy?'

He betrayed some embarrassment.

'I — er . . . Well, as a matter of fact, I . . . Mind you, I can see now that it was a mistake, but it seemed a good idea at the time . . . You see, the fact is . . . '

'Get on with it.'

He pulled himself together with a visible effort.

'Well, I wonder if you remember, Bertie, what we were saying up here before dinner . . . about the possibility of her carrying that notebook on her person . . . I put forward the theory, if you recall, that it might be in her stocking . . . and I suggested if you recollect, that one might ascertain . . . '

I reeled. I had got the gist. 'You didn't — '

'Yes.'

'When?'

Again that look of pain passed over his face.

'Just before dinner. You remember we heard her singing folk songs in the drawing-room. I went down there, and there she was at the piano, all alone . . . At least, I thought she was alone . . . And it suddenly struck me that this would be an excellent opportunity to . . . What I didn't know, you see, was that Madeline, though invisible for the moment, was also present. She had gone behind the screen in the corner to get a further supply of folk songs from the chest in which they are kept . . . and . . . well, the long and short of it is that, just as I was . . . well, to cut a long story short, just as I was . . . How shall I put it? . . . Just as I was, so to speak, getting on with it, out she came . . . and . . . Well, you see what I mean . . . I mean, coming so soon after that taking-the-fly-out-of-the-girl's-eye-in-the-stable-yard business, it was not easy to pass it off. As a matter of fact, I didn't pass it off. That's the whole story. How are you on knotting sheets, Bertie?'

I could not follow what is known as the

transition of thought.

'Knotting sheets?'

'I was thinking it over under the bed, while you and Spode were chatting, and I came to the conclusion that the only thing to be done is for us to take the sheets off your bed and tie knots in them, and then you can lower me down from the window. They do it in books, and I have an idea I've seen it in the movies. Once outside, I can take your car and drive up to London. After that, my plans are uncertain. I may go to California.'

'California?'

'It's seven thousand miles away. Spode would hardly come to California.'

I stared at him aghast.

'You aren't going to do a bolt?'

'Of course I'm going to do a bolt. Immediately. You heard what Spode said?'

'You aren't afraid of Spode?'

'Yes, I am.'

'But you were saying yourself that he's a mere mass of beef and brawn, obviously slow on his feet.'

'I know. I remember. But that was when I thought he was after you. One's views change.'

'But, Gussie, pull yourself together. You can't just run away.'

'What else can I do?'

'Why, stick around and try to effect a reconciliation. You haven't had a shot at pleading with the girl yet.'

'Yes, I have. I did it at dinner. During the fish course. No good. She just gave me a cold look, and made bread pills.'

I racked the bean. I was sure there must be an avenue somewhere, waiting to be explored, and in about half a minute I spotted it.

'What you've got to do,' I said, 'is to get the notebook. If you secured that book and showed it to Madeline, its contents would convince her that your motives in acting as you did towards Stiffy were not what she supposed, but pure to the last drop. She would realize that your behaviour was the outcome of . . . it's on the tip of my tongue . . . of a counsel of desperation. She would understand and forgive.'

For a moment, a faint flicker of hope seemed to illumine his twisted features.

'It's a thought,' he agreed. 'I believe you've got something there, Bertie. That's not a bad idea.'

'It can't fail. *Tout comprendre, c'est tout pardonner* about sums it up.'

The flicker faded.

'But how can I get the book? Where is it?'

'It wasn't on her person?'

'I don't think so. Though my investigations were, in the circumstances, necessarily cursory.'

'Then it's probably in her room.'

'Well, there you are. I can't go searching a girl's room.'

'Why not? You see that book I was reading when you popped up. By an odd coincidence — I call it a coincidence, but probably these things are sent to us for a purpose — I had just come to a bit where a gang had been doing that very thing. Do it now, Gussie. She's probably fixed in the drawing-room for the next hour or so.'

'As a matter of fact, she's gone to the village. The curate is giving an address on the Holy Land with coloured slides to the Village Mothers at the Working Men's Labour Institute, and she is playing the piano accompaniment. But even so . . . No, Bertie, I can't do it. It may be the right thing to do . . . in fact, I can't do it. It might be the right to do . . . but I haven't the nerve. Suppose Spode came in and caught me.'

'Spode would hardly wander into a young girl's room.'

'I don't know so much. You can't form plans on any light-hearted assumption like that. I see him as a chap who wanders everywhere. No. My heart is broken, my future a blank, and there is nothing to be done but accept the fact and start knotting sheets. Let's get at it.'

'You don't knot any of my sheets.'

'But, dash it, my life is at stake.'

'I don't care. I decline to be a party to this craven scooting.'

'Is this Bertie Wooster speaking?'

'You said that before.'

'And I say it again. For the last time, Bertie, will you lend me a couple of sheets and help knot them?'

'No.'

'Then I shall just have to go off and hide somewhere till dawn, when the milk train leaves. Goodbye, Bertie. You have disappointed me.'

'You have disappointed *me*. I thought you had guts.'

'I have, and I don't want Roderick Spode fooling about with them.'

146

He gave me another of those dying-newt looks, and opened the door cautiously. A glance up and down the passage having apparently satisfied him that it was, for the moment, Spodeless, he slipped out and was gone. And I returned to my book. It was the only thing I could think of that would keep me from sitting torturing myself with agonizing broodings.

Presently I was aware that Jeeves was with me. I hadn't heard him come in, but you often don't with Jeeves. He just streams silently from spot A to spot B, like some gas.

7

I wouldn't say that Jeeves was actually smirking, but there was a definite look of quiet satisfaction on his face, and I suddenly remembered what this sickening scene with Gussie had caused me to forget — viz that the last time I had seen him he had been on his way to the telephone to ring up the Secretary of the Junior Ganymede Club. I sprang to my feet eagerly. Unless I had misread that look, he had something to report.

'Did you connect with the Sec., Jeeves?'

'Yes, sir. I have just finished speaking to him.'

'And did he dish the dirt?'

'He was most informative, sir.'

'Has Spode a secret?'

'Yes, sir.'

I smote the trouser leg emotionally.

'I should have known better than to doubt Aunt Dahlia. Aunts always know. It's a sort of intuition. Tell me all.'

'I fear I cannot do that, sir. The rules of the club regarding the dissemination of material recorded in the book are very rigid.'

'You mean your lips are sealed?'

'Yes, sir.'

'Then what was the use of telephoning?'

'It is only the details of the matter which I am precluded from mentioning, sir. I am at perfect liberty to tell you that it would greatly lessen Mr Spode's potentiality for evil, if you were to inform him that you know all about Eulalie, sir.'

'Eulalie?'

'Eulalie, sir.'

'That would really put the stopper on him?'

'Yes, sir.'

I pondered. It didn't sound much to go on.

'You're sure you can't go a bit deeper into the subject?'

'Quite sure, sir. Were I to do so, it is probable that my resignation would be called for.'

'Well, I wouldn't want that to happen, of course.' I hated to think of a squad of butlers forming a hollow square while the Committee snipped his buttons off. 'Still, you really are sure that if I look Spode in the eye and spring this gag, he will be baffled? Let's get this quite clear. Suppose you're Spode, and I walk up to you and say 'Spode, I know all about Eulalie,' that would make you wilt?'

'Yes, sir. The subject of Eulalie, sir, is one which the gentleman, occupying the position he does in the public eye, would, I am convinced, be most reluctant to have ventilated.'

I practised it for a bit. I walked up to the chest of drawers with my hands in my pockets, and said, 'Spode, I know all about Eulalie.' I tried it again, waggling my finger this time. I then had a go with folded arms, and I must say it still didn't sound too convincing.

However, I told myself that Jeeves always knew.

'Well, if you say so, Jeeves. Then the first thing I had better do is find Gussie and give him this life-saving information.'

'Sir?'

'Oh, of course, you don't know anything about that, do you? I must tell you, Jeeves, that, since we last met, the plot has thickened again. Were you aware that Spode has long loved Miss Bassett?'

'No, sir.'

'Well, such is the case. The happiness of Miss Bassett is very dear to Spode, and now that her engagement has gone phut for reasons highly discreditable to the male contracting party, he wants to break Gussie's neck.'

'Indeed, sir?'

'I assure you. He was in here just now, speaking of it, and Gussie, who happened to be under the bed at the time, heard him. With the result that he now talks of getting out of the window and going to California. Which, of course, would be fatal. It is imperative that he stays on and tries to effect a reconciliation.'

'Yes, sir.'

'He can't effect a reconciliation, if he is in California.'

'No, sir.'

'So I must go and try to find him. Though, mark you, I doubt if he will be easily found at this point in his career. He is probably on the roof, wondering how he can pull it up after him.'

My misgivings were proved abundantly justified. I searched the house assiduously, but there were no signs of him. Somewhere, no doubt, Totleigh Towers hid Augustus Fink-Nottle, but it kept its secret well. Eventually, I gave it up, and returned to my room, and stap my vitals if the

150

first thing I beheld on entering wasn't the man in person. He was standing by the bed, knotting sheets.

The fact that he had his back to the door and that the carpet was soft kept him from being aware of my entry till I spoke. My 'Hey!' — a pretty sharp one, for I was aghast at seeing my bed thus messed about — brought him spinning round, ashen to the lips.

'Woof!' he exclaimed. 'I thought you were Spode!'

Indignation succeeded panic. He gave me a hard stare. The eyes behind the spectacles were cold. He looked like an annoyed turbot.

'What do you mean, you blasted Wooster,' he demanded, 'by sneaking up on a fellow and saying 'Hey!' like that? You might have given me heart failure.'

'And what do you mean, you blighted Fink-Nottle,' I demanded in my turn, 'by mucking up my bed linen after I specifically forbade it? You have sheets of your own. Go and knot those.'

'How can I? Spode is sitting on my bed.'

'He is?'

'Certainly he is. Waiting for me. I went there after I left you, and there he was. If he hadn't happened to clear his throat, I'd have walked right in.'

I saw that it was high time to set this disturbed spirit at rest.

'You needn't be afraid of Spode, Gussie.'

'What do you mean, I needn't be afraid of Spode? Talk sense.'

'I mean just that. Spode, qua menace, if qua is the word I want, is a thing of the past. Owing to the extraordinary perfection of Jeeves's secret service system, I have learned something about him which he wouldn't care to have generally known.'

'What?'

'Ah, there you have me. When I said I had learned it, I should have said that Jeeves had learned it, and unfortunately Jeeves's lips are sealed. However, I am in a position to slip it across the man in no uncertain fashion. If he attempts any rough stuff, I will give him the works.' I broke off, listening. Footsteps were coming along the passage. 'Ah!' I said. 'Someone approaches. This may quite possibly be the blighter himself.'

An animal cry escaped Gussie.

'Lock that door!'

I waved a fairly airy hand.

'It will not be necessary,' I said. 'Let him come. I positively welcome this visit. Watch me deal with him, Gussie. It will amuse you.'

I had guessed correctly. It was Spode, all right. No doubt he had grown weary of sitting on Gussie's bed, and had felt that another chat with Bertram might serve to vary the monotony. He came in, as before, without knocking, and as he perceived Gussie, uttered a wordless exclamation of triumph and satisfaction. He then stood for a moment, breathing heavily through the nostrils.

He seemed to have grown a bit since our last meeting, being now about eight foot six, and had my advices *in re* getting the bulge on him proceeded from a less authoritative source, his aspect might have intimidated me quite a good deal. But so sedulously had I been trained through the years to rely on Jeeves's lightest word that I regarded him without a tremor.

Gussie, I was sorry to observe, did not share my sunny confidence. Possibly I had not given him a full enough explanation of the facts in the case, or it may have been that, confronted with Spode in the flesh, his nerve had failed him. At any rate, he now retreated to the wall and seemed, as far as I could gather, to be trying to get through it. Foiled in this endeavour, he stood looking as if he had been stuffed by some good taxidermist, while I turned to the intruder and gave him a long, level stare, in which surprise and hauteur were nicely blended.

'Well, Spode,' I said, 'what is it now?'

I had put a considerable amount of top spin on the final word, to indicate displeasure, but it was wasted on the man. Giving the question a miss like the deaf adder of Scripture, he began to advance slowly, his gaze concentrated on Gussie. The jaw muscles, I noted, were working as they had done on the occasion when he had come upon me toying with Sir Watkyn Bassett's collection of old silver: and something in his manner suggested that he might at any moment start beating his chest with a hollow drumming sound, as gorillas do in moments of emotion.

'Ha!' he said.

Well, of course, I was not going to stand any rot like that. This habit of his of going about the place saying 'Ha!' was one that had got to be checked, and checked promptly.

'Spode!' I said sharply, and I have an idea that I rapped the table.

He seemed for the first time to become aware of my presence. He paused for an instant, and gave me an unpleasant look.

'Well, what do *you* want?'

I raised an eyebrow or two.

'What do I want? I like that. That's good. Since you ask, Spode, I want to know what the devil you mean by keeping coming into my private apartment, taking up space which I require for other purposes and interrupting me when I am chatting with my personal friends. Really, one gets about as much privacy in this house as a strip-tease dancer. I assume that you have a room of your own. Get back to it, you fat slob, and stay there.'

I could not resist shooting a swift glance at Gussie, to see how he was taking all this, and was pleased to note on his face the burgeoning of a look of worshipping admiration, such as a distressed damsel of the Middle Ages might have directed at a knight on observing him getting down to brass tacks with the dragon. I could see that I had once more become to him the old Daredevil Wooster of our boyhood days, and I had no doubt that he was burning with shame and remorse as he recalled those sneers and jeers of his.

Spode, also, seemed a good deal impressed, though not so favourably. He was staring incredulously, like one bitten by a rabbit. He seemed to be asking himself if this could really

154

be the shrinking violet with whom he had conferred on the terrace.

He asked me if I had called him a slob, and I said I had.

'A fat slob?'

'A fat slob. It is about time,' I proceeded, 'that some public-spirited person came along and told you where you got off. The trouble with you, Spode, is that just because you have succeeded in inducing a handful of half-wits to disfigure the London scene by going about in black shorts, you think you're someone. You hear them shouting 'Heil, Spode!' and you imagine it is the Voice of the People. That is where you make your bloomer. What the Voice of the People is saying is: 'Look at that frightful ass Spode swanking about in footer bags! Did you ever in your puff see such a perfect perisher?''

He did what is known as struggling for utterance.

'Oh?' he said. 'Ha! Well, I will attend to you later.'

'And I,' I retorted, quick as a flash, 'will attend to you now.' I lit a cigarette. 'Spode,' I said, unmasking my batteries, 'I know your secret!'

'Eh?'

'I know all about — '

'All about what?'

It was to ask myself precisely that question that I had paused. For, believe me or believe me not, in this tense moment, when I so sorely needed it, the name which Jeeves had mentioned to me as the magic formula for coping with this blister had completely passed from my mind. I couldn't even remember what letter it began with.

It's an extraordinary thing about names. You've probably noticed it yourself. You think you've got them, I mean to say, and they simply slither away. I've often wished I had a quid for every time some bird with a perfectly familiar map has come up to me and Hallo-Woostered, and had me gasping for air because I couldn't put a label to him. This always makes one feel at a loss, but on no previous occasion had I felt so much at a loss as I did now.

'All about what?' said Spode.

'Well, as a matter of fact,' I had to confess, 'I've forgotten.'

A sort of gasping gulp from up-stage directed my attention to Gussie again, and I could see that the significance of my words had not been lost on him. Once more he tried to back: and as he realized that he had already gone as far as he could go, a glare of despair came into his eyes. And then, abruptly, as Spode began to advance upon him, it changed to one of determination and stern resolve.

I like to think of Augustus Fink-Nottle at the moment. He showed up well. Hitherto, I am bound to say, I had never regarded him highly as a man of action. Essentially the dreamer type, I should have said. But now he couldn't have smacked into it with a prompter gusto if he had been a rough-and-tumble fighter on the San Francisco waterfront from early childhood.

Above him, as he stood glued to the wall, there hung a fairish-sized oil painting of a chap in knee-breeches and a three-cornered hat gazing at a female who appeared to be chirruping to a bird of sorts — a dove, unless I am mistaken, or a pigeon. I had noticed it once or twice since I had been in the room, and had, indeed, thought of giving it to Aunt Dahlia to break instead of the Infant Samuel at Prayer. Fortunately, I had not done so, or Gussie would not now have been in a position to tear it from its moorings and bring it down with a nice wristy action on Spode's head.

I say 'fortunately', because if ever there was a fellow who needed hitting with oil paintings, that fellow was Roderick Spode. From the moment of our first meeting, his every word and action had proved abundantly that this was the stuff to give him. But there is always a catch in these good things, and it took me only an instant to see that this effort of Gussie's, though well meant, had achieved little of constructive importance. What he should have done, of course, was to hold the picture sideways, so as to get the best out of the stout frame. Instead of which, he had used the flat of the weapon, and Spode came through the canvas like a circus rider going through a paper hoop. In other words, what had promised to be a decisive blow had turned out to be merely what Jeeves would call a gesture.

It did, however, divert Spode from his purpose for a few seconds. He stood there blinking, with the thing round his neck like a ruff, and the pause was sufficient to enable me to get into action.

Give us a lead, make it quite clear to us that the party has warmed up and that from now on anything goes, and we Woosters do not hang back. There was a sheet lying on the bed where Gussie had dropped it when disturbed at his knotting, and to snatch this up and envelop Spode in it was with me the work of a moment. It is a long time since I studied the subject, and before committing myself definitely I should have to consult Jeeves, but I have an idea that ancient Roman gladiators used to do much the same sort of thing in the arena, and were rather well thought of in consequence.

I suppose a man who has been hit over the head with a picture of a girl chirruping to a pigeon and almost immediately afterwards enmeshed in a sheet can never really retain the cool, intelligent outlook. Any friend of Spode's, with his interests at heart, would have advised him at this juncture to keep quite still and not stir till he had come out of the cocoon. Only thus, in a terrain so liberally studded with chairs and things, could a purler have been avoided.

He did not do this. Hearing the rushing sound caused by Gussie exiting, he made a leap in its general direction and took the inevitable toss. At the moment when Gussie, moving well, passed through the door, he was on the ground, more inextricably entangled than ever.

My own friends, advising me, would undoubtedly have recommended an immediate departure at this point, and looking back, I can see that where I went wrong was in pausing to hit the bulge which, from the remarks that were coming through at that spot, I took to be Spode's head, with a china vase that stood on the mantelpiece not far from where the Infant Samuel had been. It was a strategical error. I got home all right and the vase broke into a dozen pieces, which was all to the good — for the more of the property of a man like Sir Watkyn Bassett that was destroyed, the better — but the action of dealing this buffet caused me to overbalance. The next moment, a hand coming out from under the sheet had grabbed my coat.

It was a serious disaster, of course, and one which might well have caused a lesser man to feel that it was no use going on struggling. But the whole point about the Woosters, as I have had occasion to remark before, is that they are not lesser men. They keep their heads. They think quickly, and they act quickly. Napoleon was the same. I have mentioned that at the moment when I was preparing to inform Spode that I knew his secret, I had lighted a cigarette. This cigarette, in its holder, was still between my lips. Hastily removing it, I pressed the glowing end on the ham-like hand which was impeding my getaway.

The results were thoroughly gratifying. You would have thought that the trend of recent events would have put Roderick Spode in a frame of mind to expect anything and be ready for it, but this simple manœuvre found him unprepared. With a sharp cry of anguish, he released the coat, and I delayed no longer. Bertram Wooster is a man who knows when and when not to be among those present. When Bertram Wooster sees a lion in his path, he ducks down a side street. I was off at an impressive speed, and would no doubt have crossed the threshold with a burst which would have clipped a second or two off Gussie's time, had I not experienced a head-on collision with a solid body which happened to be entering at the moment. I remember thinking, as we twined our arms about each other, that at Totleigh Towers, if it wasn't one thing, it was bound to be something else.

I fancy that it was the scent of *eau-de-Cologne* that still clung to her temples that enabled me to identify this solid body as that of Aunt Dahlia, though even without it the rich, hunting-field expletive which burst from her lips would have put me on the right track. We came down in a tangled heap, and must have rolled inwards to some extent, for the next thing I knew, we were colliding with the sheeted figure of Roderick Spode, who when last seen had been at the other end of the room. No doubt the explanation is that we had rolled nor'-nor'-east and he had been rolling sou'-sou'-west, with the result that we had come together somewhere in the middle.

Spode, I noticed, as Reason began to return to her throne, was holding Aunt Dahlia by the left leg, and she didn't seem to be liking it much. A good deal of breath had been knocked out of her by the impact of a nephew on her midriff, but enough remained to enable her to expostulate, and this she was doing with all the old fire.

'What is this joint?' she was demanding heatedly. 'A loony bin? Has everybody gone crazy? First I meet Spink-Bottle racing along the corridor like a mustang. Then you try to walk through me as if I were thistledown. And now the gentleman in the burnous has started tickling my ankle — a thing that hasn't happened to me since the York and Ainsty Hunt Ball of the year nineteen-twenty-one.'

These protests must have filtered through to Spode, and presumably stirred his better nature, for he let go, and she got up, dusting her dress.

'Now, then,' she said, somewhat calmer. 'An explanation, if you please, and a categorical one. What's the idea? What's it all about? Who the devil's that inside the winding-sheet?'

I made the introductions.

'You've met Spode, haven't you? Mr Roderick Spode, Mrs Travers.'

Spode had now removed the sheet, but the picture was still in position, and Aunt Dahlia eyed it wonderingly.

'What on earth have you got that thing round your neck for?' she asked. Then, in more tolerant vein: 'Wear it if you like, of course, but it doesn't suit you.'

Spode did not reply. He was breathing heavily. I didn't blame him, mind you — in his place, I'd have done the same — but the sound was not agreeable, and I wished he wouldn't. He was also gazing at me intently, and I wished he wouldn't do that, either. His face was flushed, his eyes were bulging, and one had the odd illusion that his hair was standing on end — like quills upon the fretful porpentine, as Jeeves once put it when describing to me the reactions of Barmy Fotheringay-Phipps on seeing a dead snip, on which he had invested largely, come in sixth in

161

the procession at the Newmarket Spring Meeting.

I remember once, during a temporary rift with Jeeves, engaging a man from the registry office to serve me in his stead, and he hadn't been with me a week when he got blotto one night and set fire to the house and tried to slice me up with a carving knife. Said he wanted to see the colour of my insides, of all bizarre ideas. And until this moment I had always looked on that episode as the most trying in my experience. I now saw that it must be ranked second.

This bird of whom I speak was a simple, untutored soul and Spode a man of good education and upbringing, but it was plain that there was one point at which their souls touched. I don't suppose they would have seen eye to eye on any other subject you could have brought up, but in the matter of wanting to see the colour of my insides their minds ran on parallel lines. The only difference seemed to be that whereas my employee had planned to use a carving knife for his excavations, Spode appeared to be satisfied that the job could be done all right with the bare hands.

'I must ask you to leave us, madam,' he said.

'But I've only just come,' said Aunt Dahlia.

'I am going to thrash this man within an inch of his life.'

It was quite the wrong tone to take with the aged relative. She has a very clannish spirit and, as I have said, is fond of Bertram. Her brow darkened.

'You don't touch a nephew of mine.'

'I am going to break every bone in his body.'

'You aren't going to do anything of the sort. The idea! . . . Here, you!'

She raised her voice sharply as she spoke the concluding words, and what had caused her to do so was the fact that Spode at this moment made a sudden move in my direction.

Considering the manner in which his eyes were gleaming and his moustache bristling, not to mention the gritting teeth and the sinister twiddling of the fingers, it was a move which might have been expected to send me flitting away like an adagio dancer. And had it occurred somewhat earlier, it would undoubtedly have done so. But I did not flit. I stood where I was, calm and collected. Whether I folded my arms or not, I cannot recall, but I remember that there was a faint, amused smile upon my lips.

For that brief monosyllable 'you' had accomplished what a quarter of an hour's research had been unable to do — viz the unsealing of the fount of memory. Jeeves's words came back to me with a rush. One moment, the mind a blank: the next, the fount of memory spouting like nobody's business. It often happens this way.

'One minute, Spode,' I said quietly. 'Just one minute. Before you start getting above yourself, it may interest you to learn that I know all about Eulalie.'

It was stupendous. I felt like one of those chaps who press buttons and explode mines. If it hadn't been that my implicit faith in Jeeves had led me to expect solid results, I should have been astounded at the effect of this pronouncement on the man. You could see that it had got right in amongst him and churned him up like an egg whisk. He recoiled as if he had run into something hot, and a look of horror and alarm spread slowly over his face.

The whole situation recalled irresistibly to my mind something that had happened to me once up at Oxford, when the heart was young. It was during Eights Week, and I was sauntering on the riverbank with a girl named something that has slipped my mind, when there was a sound of barking and a large, hefty dog came galloping up, full of beans and buck and obviously intent on mayhem. And I was just commending my soul to God, and feeling that this was where the old flannel trousers got about thirty bob's worth of value bitten out of them, when the girl, waiting till she saw the whites of its eyes, with extraordinary presence of mind suddenly opened a coloured Japanese umbrella in the animal's face. Upon which, it did three back somersaults and retired into private life.

Except that he didn't do any back somersaults, Roderick Spode's reactions were almost identical with those of this nonplussed hound. For a moment, he just stood gaping. Then he said 'Oh?' Then his lips twisted into what I took to be his idea of a conciliatory smile. After that, he swallowed six — or it may have been seven — times, as if he had taken aboard a fish bone. Finally, he spoke. And when he did so, it was the nearest thing to a cooing dove that I have ever heard — and an exceptionally mild-mannered dove, at that.

'Oh, do you?' he said.

'I do,' I replied.

If he had asked me what I knew about her, he would have had me stymied, but he didn't.

'Er — how did you find out?'

'I have my methods.'

'Oh?' he said.

'Ah,' I replied, and there was silence again for a moment.

I wouldn't have believed it possible for so tough an egg to sidle obsequiously, but that was how he now sidled up to me. There was a pleading look in his eyes.

'I hope you will keep this to yourself, Wooster? You will keep it to yourself, won't you, Wooster?'

'I will — '

'Thank you, Wooster.'

' — provided,' I continued, 'that we have no more of these extraordinary exhibitions on your part of — what's the word?'

He sidled a bit closer.

'Of course, of course. I'm afraid I have been acting rather hastily.' He reached out a hand and smoothed my sleeve. 'Did I rumple your coat, Wooster? I'm sorry. I forgot myself. It shall not happen again.'

'It had better not. Good Lord! Grabbing fellows' coats and saying you're going to break chaps' bones. I never heard of such a thing.'

'I know, I know. I was wrong.'

'You bet you were wrong. I shall be very sharp on that sort of thing in the future, Spode.'

'Yes, yes, I understand.'

'I have not been at all satisfied with your

behaviour since I came to this house. The way you were looking at me at dinner. You may think people don't notice these things, but they do.'

'Of course, of course.'

'And calling me a miserable worm.'

'I'm sorry I called you a miserable worm, Wooster. I spoke without thinking.'

'Always think, Spode. Well, that is all. You may withdraw.'

'Good night, Wooster.'

'Good night, Spode.'

He hurried out with bowed head, and I turned to Aunt Dahlia, who was making noises like a motor-bicycle in the background. She gazed at me with the air of one who has been seeing visions. And I suppose the whole affair must have been extraordinarily impressive to the casual bystander.

'Well, I'll be — '

Here she paused — fortunately, perhaps, for she is a woman who, when strongly moved, sometimes has a tendency to forget that she is no longer in the hunting-field, and the verb, had she given it utterance, might have proved a bit too fruity for mixed company.

'Bertie! What was all that about?'

I waved a nonchalant hand.

'Oh, I just put it across the fellow. Merely asserting myself. One has to take a firm line with chaps like Spode.'

'Who is this Eulalie?'

'Ah, there you've got me. For information on that point you will have to apply to Jeeves. And it won't be any good, because the club rules are rigid and members are permitted to go only just so far. Jeeves,' I went on, giving credit where credit was due, as is my custom, 'came to me some little while back and told me that I had only to inform Spode that I knew all about Eulalie to cause him to curl up like a burnt feather. And a burnt feather, as you have seen, was precisely what he did curl up like. As to who the above may be, I haven't the foggiest. All that one can say is that she is a chunk of Spode's past — and, one fears, a highly discreditable one.'

I sighed, for I was not unmoved.

'One can fill in the picture for oneself, I think, Aunt Dahlia? The trusting girl who learned too late that men betray . . . the little bundle . . . the last mournful walk to the riverbank . . . the splash . . . the bubbling cry . . . I fancy so, don't you? No wonder the man pales beneath the tan a bit at the idea of the world knowing of that.'

Aunt Dahlia drew a deep breath. A sort of Soul's Awakening look had come into her face.

'Good old blackmail! You can't beat it. I've always said so and I always shall. It works like magic in an emergency. Bertie,' she cried, 'do you realize what this means?'

'Means, old relative?'

'Now that you have got the goods on Spode, the only obstacle to your sneaking that cow-creamer has been removed. You can stroll down and collect it tonight.'

I shook my head regretfully. I had been afraid she was going to take that view of the matter. It compelled me to dash the cup of joy from her lips, always an unpleasant thing to have to do to an aunt who dandled one on her knee as a child.

'No,' I said. 'There you're wrong. There, if you will excuse me saying so, you are talking like a fathead. Spode may have ceased to be a danger to traffic, but that doesn't alter the fact that Stiffy still has the notebook. Before taking any steps in the direction of the cow-creamer, I have got to get it.'

'But why? Oh, but I suppose you haven't heard. Madeline Bassett has broken off her engagement with Spink-Bottle. She told me so in the strictest confidence just now. Well, then. The snag before was that young Stephanie might cause the engagement to be broken by showing old Bassett the book. But if it's broken already —'

I shook the bean again.

'My dear old faulty reasoner,' I said, 'you miss the gist by a mile. As long as Stiffy retains that book, it cannot be shown to Madeline Bassett. And only by showing it to Madeline Bassett can Gussie prove to her that his motive in pinching Stiffy's legs was not what she supposed. And only by proving to her that his motive was not what she supposed can he square himself and effect a reconciliation. And only if he squares himself and effects a reconciliation can I avoid the distasteful necessity of having to marry this bally Bassett myself. No, I repeat. Before doing anything else, I have got to have that book.'

My pitiless analysis of the situation had its effect. It was plain from her manner that she had got the strength. For a space, she sat chewing the lower lip in silence, frowning like an aunt who has drained the bitter cup.

'Well, how are you going to get it?'

'I propose to search her room.'

'What's the good of that?'

'My dear old relative, Gussie's investigations have already revealed that the thing is not on her person. Reasoning closely, we reach the conclusion that it must be in her room.'

'Yes, but, you poor ass, whereabouts in her room? It may be anywhere. And wherever it is, you can be jolly sure it's carefully hidden. I suppose you hadn't thought of that.'

As a matter of fact, I hadn't, and I imagine that my sharp 'Oh ah!' must have revealed this, for she snorted like a bison at the water trough.

'No doubt you thought it would be lying out on the dressing table. All right, search her room, if you like. There's no actual harm in it, I suppose. It will give you something to do and keep you out of the public houses. I, meanwhile, will be going off and starting to think of something sensible. It's time one of us did.'

Pausing at the mantelpiece to remove a china horse which stood there and hurl it to the floor and jump on it, she passed along. And I, somewhat discomposed, for I had thought I had got everything neatly planned out and it was a bit of a jar to find that I hadn't, sat down and began to bend the brain.

The longer I bent it the more I was forced to admit that the flesh and blood had been right. Looking round this room of my own, I could see at a glance a dozen places where, if I had had a small object to hide like a leather-covered

169

notebook full of criticisms of old Bassett's method of drinking soup, I could have done so with ease. Presumably, the same conditions prevailed in Stiffy's lair. In going thither, therefore, I should be embarking on a quest well calculated to baffle the brightest bloodhound, let alone a chap who from childhood up had always been rotten at hunt-the-slipper.

To give the brain a rest before having another go at the problem, I took up my gooseflesher again. And, by Jove, I hadn't read more than half a page when I uttered a cry. I had come upon a significant passage.

'Jeeves,' I said, addressing him as he entered a moment later, 'I have come upon a significant passage.'

'Sir?'

I saw that I had been too abrupt and that footnotes would be required.

'In this thriller I'm reading,' I explained. 'But wait. Before showing it to you, I would like to pay you a stately tribute on the accuracy of your information re Spode. A hearty vote of thanks, Jeeves. You said the name Eulalie would make him wilt, and it did. Spode, qua menace . . . is it qua?'

'Yes, sir. Quite correct.'

'I thought so. Well, Spode, qua menace, is a spent egg. He has dropped out and ceased to function.'

'That is very gratifying, sir.'

'Most. But we are still faced by this Becher's Brook, that young Stiffy continues in possession of the notebook. That notebook, Jeeves, must be located and re-snitched before we are free to move in any other direction. Aunt Dahlia has just left in despondent mood, because, while she concedes that the damned thing is almost certainly concealed in the little pimple's sleeping quarters, she sees no hope of fingers being able to be laid upon it. She says it may be anywhere and is undoubtedly carefully hidden.'

'That is the difficulty, sir.'

'Quite. But that is where this significant passage comes in. It points the way and sets the feet upon the right path. I'll read it to you. The detective is speaking to his pals, and the 'they' refers to some bounders at the present unidentified, who have been ransacking a girl's room, hoping to find the missing jewels. Listen attentively, Jeeves. 'They seem to have looked everywhere, my dear Postlethwaite, except in the one place where they might have expected to find something. Amateurs, Postlethwaite, rank amateurs. They never thought of the top of the cupboard, the thing any experienced crook thinks of at once, because' — note carefully what follows — 'because he knows it is every woman's favourite hiding-place.''

I eyed him keenly.

'You see the profound significance of that, Jeeves?'

'If I interpret your meaning aright, sir, you are suggesting that Mr Fink-Nottle's notebook may be concealed at the top of the cupboard in Miss Byng's apartment?'

'Not 'may', Jeeves, 'must'. I don't see how it can be concealed anywhere else but. That

171

detective is no fool. If he says a thing is so, it is so. I have the utmost confidence in the fellow, and am prepared to follow his lead without question.'

'But surely, sir, you are not proposing — '

'Yes, I am. I'm going to do it immediately. Stiffy has gone to the Working Men's Institute, and won't be back for ages. It's absurd to suppose that a gaggle of Village Mothers are going to be sated with coloured slides of the Holy Land, plus piano accompaniment, in anything under two hours. So now is the time to operate while the coast is clear. Gird up your loins, Jeeves, and accompany me.'

'Well, really, sir — '

'And don't say 'Well, really, sir'. I have had occasion to rebuke you before for this habit of yours of saying 'Well, really, sir' in a soupy sort of voice, when I indicate some strategic line of action. What I want from you is less of the 'Well, really, sir' and more of the buckling-to spirit. Think feudally, Jeeves. Do you know Stiffy's room?'

'Yes, sir.'

'Then Ho for it!'

I cannot say, despite the courageous dash which I had exhibited in the above slab of dialogue, that it was in any too bobbish a frame of mind that I made my way to our destination. In fact, the nearer I got, the less bobbish I felt. It had been just the same the time I allowed myself to be argued by Roberta Wickham into going and puncturing that hot-water bottle. I hate these surreptitious prowlings. Bertram Wooster is a man who likes to go through the world with his chin up and both feet on the ground, not to sneak about on tiptoe with his spine tying itself into reefer knots.

It was precisely because I had anticipated some such reactions that I had been so anxious that Jeeves should accompany me and lend moral support, and I found myself wishing that he would buck up and lend a bit more than he was doing. Willing service and selfless co-operation were what I had hoped for, and he was not giving me them. His manner from the very start betrayed an aloof disapproval. He seemed to be dissociating himself entirely from the proceedings, and I resented it.

Owing to this aloofness on his part and this resentment on mine, we made the journey in silence, and it was in silence that we entered the room and switched on the light.

The first impression I received on giving the apartment the once-over was that for a young shrimp of her shaky moral outlook Stiffy had been done pretty well in the matter of sleeping accommodation. Totleigh Towers was one of those country houses which had been built at a time when people planning a little nest had the idea that a bedroom was not a bedroom unless you could give an informal dance for about fifty couples in it, and this sanctum could have accommodated a dozen Stiffys. In the rays of the small electric light up in the ceiling, the bally thing seemed to stretch for miles in every direction, and the thought that if that detective had not called his shots correctly, Gussie's

173

notebook might be concealed anywhere in these great spaces, was a chilling one.

I was standing there, hoping for the best, when my meditations were broken in upon by an odd, gargling sort of noise, something like static and something like distant thunder, and to cut a long story short this proved to proceed from the larynx of the dog Bartholomew.

He was standing on the bed, stropping his front paws on the coverlet, and so easy was it to read the message in his eyes that we acted like two minds with but a single thought. At the exact moment when I soared like an eagle on to the chest of drawers, Jeeves was skimming like a swallow on to the top of the cupboard. The animal hopped from the bed and, advancing into the middle of the room, took a seat, breathing through the nose with a curious whistling sound, and looking at us from under his eyebrows like a Scottish elder rebuking sin from the pulpit.

And there for a while the matter rested.

8

Jeeves was the first to break a rather strained silence.

'The book does not appear to be here, sir.'

'Eh?'

'I have searched the top of the cupboard, sir, but I have not found the book.'

It may be that my reply erred a trifle on the side of acerbity. My narrow escape from those slavering jaws had left me a bit edgy.

'Blast the book, Jeeves! What about this dog?'

'Yes, sir.'

'What do you mean — 'Yes, sir'?'

'I was endeavouring to convey that I appreciate the point which you have raised, sir. The animal's unexpected appearance unquestionably presents a problem. While he continues to maintain his existing attitude, it will not be easy for us to prosecute the search for Mr Fink-Nottle's notebook. Our freedom of action will necessarily be circumscribed.'

'Then what's to be done?'

'It is difficult to say, sir.'

'You have no ideas?'

'No, sir.'

I could have said something pretty bitter and stinging at this — I don't know what, but something — but I refrained. I realized that it was rather tough on the man, outstanding though his gifts were, to expect him to ring the bell every time, without fail. No doubt that brilliant inspiration of his which had led to my signal victory over the forces of darkness as represented by R. Spode had taken it out of him a good deal, rendering the brain for the nonce a bit flaccid. One could wait and hope that the machinery would soon get going again, enabling him to seek new high levels of achievement.

And, I felt as I continued to turn the position of affairs over in my mind, the sooner, the better, for it was plain that nothing was going to budge this canine excrescence except an offensive on a major scale, dashingly conceived and skilfully carried out. I don't think I have ever seen a dog who conveyed more vididly the impression of being rooted to the spot and prepared to stay there till the cows — or, in this case, his propri-etress — came home. And what I was going to say to Stiffy if she returned and found me roost-ing on her chest of drawers was something I had not yet thought out in any exactness of detail.

Watching the animal sitting there like a bump on a log, I soon found myself chafing a good deal. I remember Freddie Widgeon, who was once chased on to the top of a wardrobe by an Alsatian during a country house visit, telling me that what he had disliked most about the thing was the indignity of it all — the blow to the proud spirit, if you know what I mean — the feeling, in fine, that he, the Heir of the Ages, as you might say, was camping out on a wardrobe at the whim of a bally dog.

It was the same with me. One doesn't want to make a song and dance about one's ancient lineage, of course, but after all the Woosters did come over with the Conqueror and were extremely pally with him: and a fat lot of good it is coming over with Conquerors, if you're simply going to wind up being given the elbow by Aberdeen terriers.

These reflections had the effect of making me rather peevish, and I looked down somewhat sourly at the animal.

'I call it monstrous, Jeeves,' I said, voicing my train of thought, 'that this dog should be lounging about in a bedroom. Most unhygienic.'

'Yes, sir.'

'Scotties are smelly, even the best of them. You will recall how my Aunt Agatha's McIntosh niffed to heaven while enjoying my hospitality. I frequently mentioned it to you.'

'Yes, sir.'

'And this one is even riper. He should obviously have been bedded out in the stables. Upon my Sam, what with Scotties in Stiffy's room and newts in Gussie's, Totleigh Towers is not far short of being a lazar house.'

'No, sir.'

'And consider the matter from another angle,' I said, warming to my theme. 'I refer to the danger of keeping a dog of this nature and disposition in a bedroom, where it can spring out ravening on anyone who enters. You and I happen to be able to take care of ourselves in an emergency such as has arisen, but suppose we had been some highly strung house-maid.'

'Yes, sir.'

'I can see her coming into the room to turn

down the bed. I picture her as a rather fragile girl with big eyes and a timid expression. She crosses the threshold. She approaches the bed. And out leaps this man-eating dog. One does not like to dwell upon the sequel.'

'No, sir.'

I frowned.

'I wish,' I said, 'that instead of sitting there saying 'Yes, sir' and 'No, sir', Jeeves, you would do something.'

'But what can I do, sir?'

'You can get action, Jeeves. That is what is required here — sharp, decisive action. I wonder if you recall a visit we once paid to the residence of my Aunt Agatha at Woollam Chersey in the county of Herts. To refresh your memory, it was the occasion on which, in company with the Right Honourable A. B. Filmer, the Cabinet Minister, I was chivvied on to the roof of a shack on the island in the lake by an angry swan.'

'I recall the incident vividly, sir.'

'So do I. And the picture most deeply imprinted on my mental retina — is that the correct expression?'

'Yes, sir.'

' — is of you facing that swan in the most intrepid 'You-can't-do-that-there-here' manner and bunging a raincoat over its head, thereby completely dishing its aims and plans and compelling it to revise its whole strategy from the bottom up. It was a beautiful bit of work. I don't know when I have seen a finer.'

'Thank you, sir. I am glad if I gave satisfaction.'

'You certainly did, Jeeves, in heaping measure. And what crossed my mind was that a similar operation would make this dog feel pretty silly.'

'No doubt, sir. But I have no raincoat.'

'Then I would advise seeing what you can do with a sheet. And in case you are wondering if a sheet would work as well, I may tell you that just before you came into my room I had had admirable results with one in the case of Mr Spode. He just couldn't seem to get out of the thing.'

'Indeed, sir?'

'I assure you, Jeeves. You could wish no better weapon than a sheet. There are some on the bed.'

'Yes, sir. On the bed.'

There was a pause. I was loath to wrong the man, but if this wasn't a *nolle prosequi*, I didn't know one when I saw one. The distant and unenthusiastic look on his face told me that I was right, and I endeavoured to sting his pride, rather as Gussie in our *pourparlers* in the matter of Spode had endeavoured to sting mine.

'Are you afraid of a tiny little dog, Jeeves?'

He corrected me respectfully, giving it as his opinion that the undersigned was not a tiny little dog, but well above the average in muscular development. In particular, he drew my attention to the animal's teeth.

I reassured him.

'I think you would find that if you were to make a sudden spring, his teeth would not enter into the matter. You could leap on to the bed, snatch up a sheet, roll him up in it before he

179

knew what was happening, and there we would be.'

'Yes, sir.'

'Well, are you going to make a sudden spring?'

'No, sir.'

A rather stiff silence ensued, during which the dog Bartholomew continued to gaze at me unwinkingly, and once more I found myself noticing — and resenting — the superior, sanctimonious expression on his face. Nothing can ever render the experience of being treed on top of a chest of drawers by an Aberdeen terrier pleasant, but it seemed to me that the least you can expect on such an occasion is that the animal will meet you half-way and not drop salt into the wound by looking at you as if he were asking if you were saved.

It was in the hope of wiping this look off his face that I now made a gesture. There was a stump of candle standing in the parent candlestick beside me, and I threw this at the little blighter. He ate it with every appearance of relish, took time out briefly in order to be sick, and resumed his silent stare. And at this moment the door opened and in came Stiffy — hours before I had expected her.

The first thing that impressed itself upon one on seeing her was that she was not in her customary buoyant spirits. Stiffy, as a rule, is a girl who moves jauntily from spot to spot — youthful elasticity is, I believe, the expression — but she entered now with a slow and dragging step like a Volga boatman. She cast a dull eye at us, and after a brief 'Hallo, Bertie. Hallo, Jeeves,' seemed to dismiss us from her thoughts. She made for the dressing table and having removed her hat, sat looking at herself in the mirror with sombre eyes. It was plain that for some reason the soul had got a flat tyre, and seeing that unless I opened the conversation there was going to be one of those awkward pauses, I did so.

'What ho, Stiffy.'

'Hallo.'

'Nice evening. Your dog's just been sick on the carpet.'

All this, of course, was merely by way of leading into the main theme, which I now proceeded to broach.

'Well, Stiffy, I suppose you're surprised to see us here?'

'No, I'm not. Have you been looking for that book?'

'Why, yes. That's right. We have. Though, as a matter of fact, we hadn't got really started. We were somewhat impeded by the bow-wow.' (Keeping it light, you notice. Always the best way on these occasions.) 'He took our entrance in the wrong spirit.'

'Oh?'

'Yes. Would it be asking too much of you to attach a stout lead to his collar, thus making the world safe for democracy?'

'Yes, it would.'

'Surely you wish to save the lives of two fellow creatures?'

'No, I don't. Not if they're men. I loathe all men. I hope Bartholomew bites you to the bone.'

I saw that little was to be gained by

approaching the matter from this angle. I switched to another *point d'appui*.

'I wasn't expecting you,' I said. 'I thought you had gone to the Working Men's Institute, to tickle the ivories in accompaniment to old Stinker's coloured lecture on the Holy Land.'

'I did.'

'Back early, aren't you?'

'Yes. The lecture was off. Harold broke the slides.'

'Oh?' I said, feeling that he was just the sort of chap who would break slides. 'How did that happen?'

She passed a listless hand over the brow of the dog Bartholomew, who had stepped up to fraternize.

'He dropped them.'

'What made him do that?'

'He had a shock, when I broke off our engagement.'

'What!'

'Yes.' A gleam came into her eyes, as if she were reliving unpleasant scenes, and her voice took on the sort of metallic sharpness which I have so often noticed in that of my Aunt Agatha during our get-togethers. Her listlessness disappeared, and for the first time she spoke with a girlish vehemence. 'I got to Harold's cottage, and I went in, and after we'd talked of this and that for a while, I said 'When are you going to pinch Eustace Oates's helmet, darling?' And would you believe it, he looked at me in a horrible, sheepish, hang-dog way and said that he had been wrestling with his conscience in the hope of

182

getting its OK, but that it simply wouldn't hear of him pinching Eustace Oates's helmet, so it was all off. 'Oh?' I said, drawing myself up. 'All off, is it? Well, so is our engagement,' and he dropped a double handful of coloured slides of the Holy Land, and I came away.'

'You don't mean that?'

'Yes, I do. And I consider that I have had a very lucky escape. If he is the sort of man who is going to refuse me every little thing I ask, I'm glad I found out in time. I'm delighted about the whole thing.'

Here, with a sniff like the tearing of a piece of calico, she buried the bean in her hands, and broke into what are called uncontrollable sobs.

Well, dashed painful, of course, and you wouldn't be far wrong in saying that I ached in sympathy with her distress. I don't suppose there is a man in the W1 postal district of London more readily moved by a woman's grief than myself. For two pins, if I'd been a bit nearer, I would have patted her head. But though there is this kindly streak in the Woosters, there is also a practical one, and it didn't take me long to spot the bright side to all this.

'Well, that's too bad,' I said. 'The heart bleeds. Eh, Jeeves?'

'Distinctly, sir.'

'Yes, by Jove, it bleeds profusely, and I suppose that all one can say is that one hopes that Time, the great healer, will eventually stitch up the wound. However, as in these circs you will, of course, no longer have any use for that notebook of Gussie's, how about handing it over?'

'What?'

'I said that if your projected union with Stinker is off, you will, of course, no longer wish to keep that notebook of Gussie's among your effects — '

'Oh, don't bother me about notebooks now.'

'No, no, quite. Not for the world. All I'm saying is that if — at your leisure — choose the time to suit yourself — you wouldn't mind slipping it across — '

'Oh, all right. I can't give it you now, though. It isn't here.'

'Not here?'

'No. I put it . . . Hallo, what's that?'

What had caused her to suspend her remarks just at the point when they were becoming fraught with interest was a sudden tapping sound. A sort of tap-tap-tap. It came from the direction of the window.

This room of Stiffy's, I should have mentioned, in addition to being equipped with four-poster beds, valuable pictures, richly upholstered chairs and all sorts of things far too good for a young squirt who went about biting the hand that had fed her at luncheon at its flat by causing it the utmost alarm and despondency, had a balcony outside its window. It was from this balcony that the tapping sound proceeded, leading one to infer that someone stood without.

That the dog Bartholomew had reached this conclusion was shown immediately by the lissom agility with which he leaped at the window and starting trying to bite his way through. Up till this moment he had shown himself a dog of strong reserves, content merely to sit and stare, but now he was full of strange oaths. And I confess that as I watched his champing and listened to his observations I congratulated myself on the promptitude with which I had breezed on to that chest of drawers. A bone-crusher, if ever one drew breath, this Bartholomew Byng. Reluctant as one always is to criticize the acts of an all-wise Providence, I was dashed if I could see why a dog of his size should have been fitted out with the jaws and teeth of a crocodile. Still, too late of course to do anything about it now.

Stiffy, after that moment of surprised inaction which was to be expected in a girl who hears tapping sounds at her window, had risen and gone to investigate. I couldn't see a thing from where I was sitting, but she was evidently more fortunately placed. As she drew back the curtain, I saw her clap a hand to her throat, like someone in a play, and a sharp cry escaped her, audible even above the ghastly row which was proceeding from the lips of the frothing terrier.

'Harold!' she yipped, and putting two and two together I gathered that the bird on the balcony must be old Stinker Pinker, my favourite curate.

It was with a sort of joyful yelp, like that of a woman getting together with her demon lover, that the little geezer had spoken his name, but it was evident that reflection now told her that after what had occurred between this man of God and herself this was not quite the tone. Her next words were uttered with a cold, hostile intonation. I was able to hear them, because she had stooped and picked up the bounder Bartholomew, clamping a hand over his mouth to still his cries — a thing I wouldn't have done for a goodish bit of money.

'What do you want?'

Owing to the lull in Bartholomew, the stuff was coming through well now. Stinker's voice was a bit muffled by the intervening sheet of glass, but I got it nicely.

'Stiffy!'

'Well?'

'Can I come in?'

'No, you can't.'

'But I've brought you something.'

A sudden howl of ecstasy broke from the young pimple.

'Harold! You angel lamb! You haven't got it, after all?'

'Yes.'

'Oh, Harold, my dream of joy!'

She opened the window with eager fingers, and a cold draught came in and played about my ankles. It was not followed, as I had supposed it would be, by old Stinker. He continued to hang about on the outskirts, and a moment later his motive in doing so was made clear.

'I say, Stiffy, old girl, is that hound of yours under control?'

'Yes, rather. Wait a minute.'

She carried the animal to the cupboard and bunged him in, closing the door behind him. And from the fact that no further bulletins were received from him, I imagine he curled up and went to sleep. These Scotties are philosophers, well able to adapt themselves to changing conditions. They can take it as well as dish it out.

'All clear, angel,' she said, and returned to the window, arriving there just in time to be folded in the embrace of the incoming Stinker.

It was not easy for some moments to sort out the male from the female ingredients in the ensuing tangle, but eventually he disengaged himself and I was able to see him steadily and see him whole. And when I did so, I noticed that there was rather more of him than there had been when I had seen him last. Country butter and the easy life these curates lead had added a pound or two to an always impressive figure. To find the lean, finely trained Stinker of my nonage, I felt that one would have to catch him in Lent.

But the change in him, I soon perceived, was purely superficial. The manner in which he now tripped over a rug and cannoned into an occasional table, upsetting it with all the old thoroughness, showed me that at heart he still remained the same galumphing man with two left feet, who had always been constitutionally incapable of walking through the great Gobi desert without knocking something over.

Stinker's was a face which in the old College days had glowed with health and heartiness. The health was still there — he looked like a clerical beetroot — but of heartiness at this moment one noted rather a shortage. His features were drawn, as if Conscience were gnawing at his vitals. And no doubt it was, for in one hand he was carrying the helmet which I had last

187

observed perched on the dome of Constable Eustace Oates. With a quick, impulsive movement, like that of a man trying to rid himself of a dead fish, he thrust it at Stiffy, who received it with a soft, tender squeal of ecstasy.

'I brought it,' he said dully.

'Oh, Harold!'

'I brought your gloves, too. You left them behind. At least, I've brought one of them. I couldn't find the other.'

'Thank you, darling. But never mind about gloves, my wonder man. Tell me everything that happened.'

He was about to do so, when he paused, and I saw that he was staring at me with a rather feverish look in his eyes. Then he turned and stared at Jeeves. One could read what was passing in his mind. He was debating within himself whether we were real, or whether the nervous strain to which he had been subjected was causing him to see things.

'Stiffy,' he said, lowering his voice, 'don't look now, but is there something on top of that chest of drawers?'

'Eh? Oh, yes, that's Bertie Wooster.'

'Oh, it is?' said Stinker, brightening visibly. 'I wasn't quite sure. Is that somebody on the cupboard, too?'

'That's Bertie's man Jeeves.'

'How do you do?' said Stinker.

'How do you do, sir?' said Jeeves.

We climbed down, and I came forward with outstretched hand, anxious to get the reunion going.

'What ho, Stinker.'

'Hallo, Bertie.'

'Long time since we met.'

'It is a bit, isn't it?'

'I hear you're a curate now.'

'Yes, that's right.'

'How are the souls?'

'Oh, fine, thanks.'

There was a pause, and I suppose I would have gone on to ask him if he had seen anything of old So-and-so lately or knew what had become of old What's-his-name, as one does when the conversation shows a tendency to drag on these occasions of ancient College chums meeting again after long separation, but before I could do so, Stiffy, who had been crooning over the helmet like a mother over the cot of her sleeping child, stuck it on her head with a merry chuckle, and the spectacle appeared to bring back to Stinker like a slosh in the waistcoat the realization of what he had done. You've probably heard the expression 'The wretched man seemed fully conscious of his position.' That was Harold Pinker at this juncture. He shied like a startled horse, knocked over another table, tottered to a chair, knocked that over, picked it up and sat down, burying his face in his hands.

'If the Infants' Bible Class should hear of this!' he said, shuddering strongly.

I saw what he meant. A man in his position has to watch his step. What people expect from a curate is a zealous performance of his parochial duties. They like to think of him as a chap who preaches about Hivites, Jebusites and what not, speaks the word in season to the backslider, conveys soup and blankets to the deserving bedridden, and all that sort of thing. When they find him de-helmeting policemen, they look at one another with the raised eyebrow of censure, and ask themselves if he is quite the right man for the job. That was what was bothering Stinker and preventing him being the old effervescent curate whose jolly laugh had made the last School Treat go with such a bang.

Stiffy endeavoured to hearten him.

'I'm sorry, darling. If it upsets you, I'll put it away.' She crossed to the chest of drawers, and did so. 'But why it should,' she said, returning, 'I can't imagine. I should have thought it would have made you so proud and happy. And now tell me everything that happened.'

'Yes,' I said. 'One would like the first-hand story.'

'Did you creep up behind him like a leopard?' asked Stiffy.

'Of course he did,' I said, admonishing the silly young shrimp. 'You don't suppose he pranced up in full view of the fellow? No doubt you trailed him with unremitting snakiness, eh, Stinker, and did the deed when he was relaxing on a stile or somewhere over a quiet pipe?'

Stinker sat staring straight before him, that drawn look still on his face.

'He wasn't on the stile. He was leaning against it. After you left me, Stiffy, I went for a walk, to think things over, and I had just crossed Plunkett's meadow and was going to climb the stile into the next one, when I saw something

190

dark in front of me, and there he was.'

I nodded. I could visualize the scene.

'I hope,' I said, 'that you remembered to give the forward shove before the upwards lift?'

'It wasn't necessary. The helmet was not on his head. He had taken it off and put it on the ground. And I just crept up and grabbed it.'

I started, pursing the lips a bit.

'Not quite playing the game, Stinker.'

'Yes, it was,' said Stiffy, with a good deal of warmth. 'I call it very clever of him.'

I could not recede from my position. At the Drones, we hold strong views on these things.

'There is a right way and a wrong way of pinching policemen's helmets,' I said firmly.

'You're talking absolute nonsense,' said Stiffy. 'I think you were wonderful, darling.'

I shrugged my shoulders.

'How do you feel about it, Jeeves?'

'I scarcely think that it would be fitting for me to offer an opinion, sir.'

'No,' said Stiffy. 'And it jolly well isn't fitting for you to offer an opinion, young pie-faced Bertie Wooster. Who do you think you are,' she demanded, with renewed warmth, 'coming strolling into a girl's bedroom, sticking on dog about the right way and wrong way of pinching helmets? It isn't as if you were such a wonder at it yourself, considering that you got collared and hauled up next morning at Bosher Street, where you had to grovel to Uncle Watkyn in the hope of getting off with a fine.'

I took this up promptly.

'I did not grovel to the old disease. My

191

manner throughout was calm and dignified, like that of a Red Indian at the stake. And when you speak of me hoping to get off with a fine — '

Here Stiffy interrupted, to beg me to put a sock in it.

'Well, all I was about to say was that the sentence stunned me. I felt so strongly that it was a case for a mere reprimand. However, this is beside the point — which is that Stinker in the recent encounter did not play to the rules of the game. I consider his behaviour morally tantamount to shooting a sitting bird. I cannot alter my opinion.'

'And I can't alter my opinion that you have no business in my bedroom. What are you doing here?'

'Yes, I was wondering that,' said Stinker, touching on the point for the first time. And I could see, of course, how he might quite well be surprised at finding this mob scene in what he had supposed the exclusive sleeping apartment of the loved one.

I eyed her sternly.

'You know what I am doing here. I told you. I came — '

'Oh, yes. Bertie came to borrow a book, darling. But' — here her eyes lingered on mine in a cold and sinister manner — 'I'm afraid I can't let him have it just yet. I have not finished with it myself. By the way,' she continued, still holding me with that compelling stare, 'Bertie says he will be delighted to help us with that cow-creamer scheme.'

'Will you, old man?' said Stinker eagerly.

'Of course he will,' said Stiffy. 'He was saying only just now what a pleasure it would be.'

'You won't mind me hitting you on the nose?'

'Of course he won't.'

'You see, we must have blood. Blood is of the essence.'

'Of course, of course, of course,' said Stiffy. Her manner was impatient. She seemed in a hurry to terminate the scene. 'He quite understands that.'

'When would you feel like doing it, Bertie?'

'He feels like doing it tonight,' said Stiffy. 'No sense in putting things off. Be waiting outside at midnight, darling. Everybody will have gone to bed by then. Midnight will suit you, Bertie? Yes, Bertie says it will suit him splendidly. So that's all settled. And now you really must be going, precious. If somebody came in and found you here, they might think it odd. Good night, darling.'

'Good night, darling.'

'Good night, darling.'

'Good night, darling.'

'Wait!' I said, cutting in on these revolting exchanges, for I wished to make a last appeal to Stinker's finer feelings.

'He can't wait. He's got to go. Remember, angel. On the spot, ready to the last button, at twelve pip emma. Good night, darling.'

'Good night, darling.'

'Good night, darling.'

'Good night, darling.'

They passed on to the balcony, the nauseous endearments receding in the distance, and I turned to Jeeves, my face stern and hard.

'Faugh, Jeeves!'

'Sir?'

'I said 'Faugh!' I am a pretty broadminded man, but this has shocked me — I may say to the core. It is not so much the behaviour of Stiffy that I find so revolting. She is a female, and the tendency of females to be unable to distinguish between right and wrong is notorious. But that Harold Pinker, a clerk in Holy Orders, a chap who buttons his collar at the back, should countenance this thing appals me. He knows she has got that book. He knows that she is holding me up with it. But does he insist on her returning it? No! He lends himself to the raw work with open enthusiasm. A nice look-out for the Totleigh-in-the-Wold flock, trying to keep on the straight and narrow path with a shepherd like that! A pretty example he sets to this Infants' Bible Class of which he speaks! A few years of sitting at the feet of Harold Pinker and imbibing his extraordinary views on morality and ethics, and every bally child on the list will be serving a long stretch at Wormwood Scrubs for blackmail.'

I paused, much moved. A bit out of breath, too.

'I think you do the gentleman an injustice, sir.'

'Eh?'

'I am sure that he is under the impression that your acquiescence in the scheme is due entirely to goodness of heart and a desire to assist an old friend.'

'You think she hasn't told him about the notebook?'

'I am convinced of it, sir. I could gather that

194

from the lady's manner.'

'I didn't notice anything about her manner.'

'When you were about to mention the notebook, it betrayed embarrassment, sir. She feared lest Mr Pinker might inquire into the matter and, learning the facts, compel her to make restitution.'

'By Jove, Jeeves, I believe you're right.'

I reviewed the recent scene. Yes, he was perfectly correct. Stiffy, though one of those girls who enjoy in equal quantities the gall of an army mule and the calm *insouciance* of a fish on a slab of ice, had unquestionably gone up in the air a bit when I had seemed about to explain to Stinker my motives for being in the room. I recalled the rather feverish way in which she had hustled him out, like a small bouncer at a pub ejecting a large customer.

'Egad, Jeeves!' I said, impressed.

There was a muffled crashing sound from the direction of the balcony. A few moments later, Stiffy returned.

'Harold fell off the ladder,' she explained, laughing heartily. 'Well, Bertie, you've got the programme all clear? Tonight's the night!'

I drew out a gasper and lit it.

'Wait!' I said. 'Not so fast. Just one moment, young Stiffy.'

*   *   *

The ring of quiet authority in my tone seemed to take her aback. She blinked twice, and looked at me questioningly, while I, drawing in a cargo of smoke, expelled it nonchalantly through the nostrils.

'Just one moment,' I repeated.

In the narrative of my earlier adventures with Augustus Fink-Nottle at Brinkley Court, with which you may or may not be familiar, I mentioned that I had once read a historical novel about a Buck or Beau or some such cove who, when it became necessary for him to put people where they belonged, was in the habit of laughing down from lazy eyelids and flicking a speck of dust from the irreproachable Mechlin lace at his wrists. And I think I stated that I had had excellent results from modelling myself on this bird.

I did so now.

'Stiffy,' I said, laughing down from my lazy eyelids and flicking a speck of cigarette ash from my irreproachable cuff, 'I will trouble you to disgorge that book.'

The questioning look became intensified. I could see that all this was perplexing her. She had supposed that she had Bertram nicely ground beneath the iron heel, and here he was, popping up like a two-year-old, full of the fighting spirit.

'What do you mean?'

I laughed down a bit more.

'I should have supposed,' I said, flicking, 'that my meaning was quite clear. I want that notebook of Gussie's, and I want it immediately, without any more back chat.'

Her lips tightened.

'You will get it tomorrow — if Harold turns in a satisfactory report.'

'I shall get it now.'

'Ha jolly ha!'

' 'Ha jolly ha!' to you, young Stiffy, with knobs on,' I retorted with quiet dignity. 'I repeat, I shall get it now. If I don't, I shall go to old Stinker and tell him all about it.'

'All about what?'

'All about everything. At present, he is under the impression that my acquiescence in your scheme is due entirely to goodness of heart and a desire to assist an old friend. You haven't told him about the notebook. I am convinced of it. I could gather that from your manner. When I was about to mention the notebook, it betrayed embarrassment. You feared lest Stinker might inquire into the matter and, learning the facts, compel you to make restitution.'

Her eyes flickered. I saw that Jeeves had been correct in his diagnosis.

'You're talking absolute rot,' she said, but it was with a quaver in the v.

'All right. Well, toodle-oo. I'm off to find Stinker.'

I turned on my heel and, as I expected, she stopped me with a pleading yowl.

'No, Bertie, don't! You mustn't!'

I came back.

'So! You admit it? Stinker knows nothing of your . . . ' The powerful phrase which Aunt Dahlia had employed when speaking of Sir Watkyn Bassett occurred to me — 'of your underhand skulduggery.'

'I don't see why you call it underhand skulduggery.'

197

'I call it underhand skulduggery because that is what I consider it. And that is what Stinker, dripping as he is with high principles, will consider it when the facts are placed before him.' I turned on the h. again. 'Well, toodle-oo once more.'

'Bertie, wait!'

'Well?'

'Bertie, darling —— '

I checked her with a cold wave of the cigarette-holder.

'Less of the 'Bertie, darling'. 'Bertie, darling', forsooth! Nice time to start the 'Bertie, darling'-ing.'

'But, Bertie darling, I want to explain. Of course I didn't dare tell Harold about the book. He would have had a fit. He would have said it was a rotten trick, and of course I knew it was. But there was nothing else to do. There didn't seem any other way of getting you to help us.'

'There wasn't.'

'But you are going to help us, aren't you?'

'I am not.'

'Well, I do think you might.'

'I dare say you do, but I won't.'

Somewhere about the first or second line of this chunk of dialogue, I had observed her eyes begin to moisten and her lips to tremble, and a pearly one had started to steal down the cheek. The bursting of the dam, of which that pearly one had been the first preliminary trickle, now set in with great severity. With a brief word to the effect that she wished she were dead and that I would look pretty silly when I gazed down at her coffin, knowing that my inhumanity had put her there, she flung herself on the bed and started going *oomp*.

It was the old uncontrollable sob-stuff which she had pulled earlier in the proceedings, and once more I found myself a bit unmanned. I stood there irresolute, plucking nervously at the cravat. I had already alluded to the effect of a woman's grief on the Woosters.

'Oomp,' she went.

'But, Stiffy — ' I said.

'Oomp . . . Oomp . . . '

'But, Stiffy, old girl, be reasonable. Use the bean. You can't seriously expect me to pinch that cow-creamer.'

'It oomps everything to us.'

'Very possibly. But listen. You haven't envisaged the latent snags. Your blasted uncle is watching my every move, just waiting for me to start something. And even if he wasn't, the fact that I would be co-operating with Stinker renders the thing impossible. I have already given you my views on Stinker as a partner in crime. Somehow, in some manner, he would muck everything up. Why, look at what happened just now. He couldn't even climb down a ladder without falling off.'

'Oomp.'

'And, anyway, just examine this scheme of yours in pitiless analysis. You tell me the wheeze is for Stinker to stroll in all over blood and say he hit the marauder on the nose. Let us suppose he does so. What ensues? 'Ha!' says your uncle, who doubtless knows a clue as well as the next man.

'Hit him on the nose, did you? Keep your eyes skinned, everybody, for a bird with a swollen nose.' And the first thing he sees is me with a beezer twice the proper size. Don't tell me he wouldn't draw conclusions.'

I rested my case. It seemed to me that I had made out a pretty good one, and I anticipated the resigned 'Right ho. Yes, I see what you mean. I suppose you're right.' But she merely oomped the more, and I turned to Jeeves, who hitherto had not spoken.

'You follow my reasoning, Jeeves?'

'Entirely, sir.'

'You agree with me, that the scheme, as planned, would merely end in disaster?'

'Yes, sir. It undoubtedly presents certain grave difficulties. I wonder if I might be permitted to suggest an alternative one.'

I stared at the man.

'You mean you have found a formula?'

'I think so, sir.'

His words had de-oomped Stiffy. I don't think anything else in the world would have done it. She sat up, looking at him with a wild surmise.

'Jeeves! Have you really?'

'Yes, miss.'

'Well, you certainly are the most wonderful wooly baa-lamb that ever stepped.'

'Thank you, miss.'

'Well, let us have it, Jeeves,' I said, lighting another cigarette and lowering self into a chair. 'One hopes, of course, that you are right, but I should have thought personally that there were no avenues.'

'I think we can find one, sir, if we approach the matter from the psychological angle.'

'Oh, psychological?'

'Yes, sir.'

'The psychology of the individual?'

'Precisely, sir.'

'I see. Jeeves,' I explained to Stiffy, who, of course, knew the man only slightly, scarcely more, indeed, than as a silent figure that had done some smooth potato-handing when she had lunched at my flat, 'is and always has been a whale on the psychology of the individual. He eats it alive. What individual, Jeeves?'

'Sir Watkyn Bassett, sir.'

I frowned doubtfully.

'You propose to try to soften that old public enemy? I don't think it can be done, except with a knuckleduster.'

'No, sir. It would not be easy to soften Sir Watkyn, who, as you imply, is a man of strong character, not easily moulded. The idea I have in mind is to endeavour to take advantage of his attitude towards yourself. Sir Watkyn does not like you, sir.'

'I don't like him.'

'No, sir. But the important thing is that he has conceived a strong distaste for you, and would consequently sustain a severe shock, were you to inform him that you and Miss Byng were betrothed and were anxious to be united in matrimony.'

'What! You want me to tell him that Stiffy and I are that way?'

'Precisely, sir.'

I shook the head.

'I see no percentage in it, Jeeves. All right for a laugh, no doubt — watching the old bounder's reactions I mean — but of little practical value.'

Stiffy, too, seemed disappointed. It was plain that she had been hoping for better things.

'It sounds goofy to me,' she said. 'Where would that get us, Jeeves?'

'If I might explain, miss. Sir Watkyn's strong reactions would, as Mr Wooster suggests, be of a strongly defined character.'

'He would hit the ceiling.'

'Exactly, miss. A very colourful piece of imagery. And if you were then to assure him that there was no truth in Mr Wooster's statement, adding that you were, in actual fact, betrothed to Mr Pinker, I think the overwhelming relief which he would feel at the news would then lead him to look with a kindly eye on your union with that gentleman.'

Personally, I had never heard anything so potty in my life, and my manner indicated as much. Stiffy, on the other hand, was all over it. She did the first few steps of a spring dance.

'Why, Jeeves, that's marvellous!'

'I think it would prove effective, miss.'

'Of course, it would. It couldn't fail. Just imagine, Bertie, darling, how he would feel if you told him I wanted to marry you. Why, if after that I said 'Oh, no, it's all right, Uncle Watky. The chap I really want to marry is the boy who cleans the boots,' he would fold me in his arms and promise to come and dance at the wedding. And when he finds that the real fellow is a splendid, wonderful, terrific man like Harold, the thing will be a walk-over. Jeeves, you really are a specific dream-rabbit.'

'Thank you, miss. I am glad to have given satisfaction.'

I rose. It was my intention to say goodbye to all this. I don't mind people talking rot in my presence, but it must not be utter rot. I turned to Stiffy, who was now in the later stages of her spring dance, and addressed her with curt severity.

'I will now take the book, Stiffy.'

She was over by the cupboard, strewing roses. She paused for a moment.

'Oh, the book. You want it?'

'I do. Immediately.'

'I'll give it to you after you've seen Uncle Watkyn.'

'Oh?'

'Yes. It isn't that I don't trust you, Bertie, darling, but I should feel much happier if I knew that you knew I had still got it, and I'm sure you want me to feel happy. You toddle off and beard him, and then we'll talk.'

I frowned.

'I will toddle off,' I said coldly, 'but beard him, no. I don't seem to see myself bearding him!'

She stared.

'But, Bertie, this sounds as if you weren't going to sit in.'

'It was how I meant it to sound.'

'You wouldn't fail me, would you?'

'I would. I would fail you like billy-o.'

'Don't you like the scheme?'

'I do not. Jeeves spoke a moment ago of his gladness at having given satisfaction. He has given me no satisfaction whatsoever. I consider that the idea he has advanced marks the absolute zero in human goofiness, and I am surprised that he should have entertained it. The book, Stiffy, if you please — and slippily.'

She was silent for a space.

'I was rather asking myself,' she said, 'if you might not take this attitude.'

'And now you know the answer,' I riposted. 'I have. The book, if you please.'

'I'm not going to give you any book.'

'Very well. Then I go to Stinker and tell him all.'

'All right. Do. And before you can get within a mile of him, I shall be up in the library, telling Uncle Watkyn all.'

She waggled her chin, like a girl who considers that she has put over a swift one: and, examining what she had said, I was compelled to realize that this was precisely what she had put over. I had overlooked this contingency completely. Her words gave me pause. The best I could do in the way of a come-back was to utter a somewhat baffled 'H'm!' There is no use attempting to disguise the fact — Bertram was nonplussed.

'So there you are. Now, how about it?'

It is never pleasant for a chap who has been doing the dominant male to have to change his stance and sink to ignoble pleadings, but I could see no other course. My voice, which had been firm and resonant, took on a melting tremolo.

'But, Stiffy, dash it! You wouldn't do that?'

'Yes, I would, if you don't go and sweeten Uncle Watkyn.'

'But how can I go and sweeten him? Stiffy, you can't subject me to this fearful ordeal.'

'Yes, I can. And what's so fearful about it? He can't eat you.'

I conceded this.

'True. But that's about the best you can say.'

'It won't be any worse than a visit to the dentist.'

'It'll be worse than six visits to six dentists.'

'Well, think how glad you will be when it's over.'

I drew little consolation from this. I looked at her closely, hoping to detect some signs of softening. Not one. She had been as tough as a restaurant steak, and she continued as tough as a restaurant steak. Kipling was right. D. than the m. No getting round it.

I made one last appeal.

'You won't recede from your position?'

'Not a step.'

'In spite of the fact — excuse me mentioning it — that I gave you a dashed good lunch at my flat, no expense spared?'

'No.'

I shrugged my shoulders, as some Roman gladiator — one of those chaps who threw knotted sheets over people, for instance — might have done on hearing the call-boy shouting his number in the wings.

'Very well, then,' I said.

She beamed at me maternally.

'That's the spirit. That's my brave little man.'

At a less preoccupied moment, I might have resented her calling me her brave little man, but in this grim hour it scarcely seemed to matter.

'Where is this frightful uncle of yours?'

'He's bound to be in the library now.'

'Very good. Then I will go to him.'

I don't know if you were ever told as a kid that story about the fellow whose dog chewed up the priceless manuscript of the book he was writing. The blow-out, if you remember, was that he gave the animal a pained look and said: 'Oh, Diamond, Diamond, you — or it may have been thou — little know — or possibly knowest — what you — or thou — has — or hast — done.' I heard it in the nursery, and it has always lingered in my mind. And why I bring it up now is that this was how I looked at Jeeves as I passed from the room. I didn't actually speak the gag, but I fancy he knew what I was thinking.

I could have wished that Stiffy had not said 'Yoicks! Tally-ho!' as I crossed the threshold. It seemed to me in the circumstances flippant and in dubious taste.

9

It has been well said of Bertram Wooster by those who know him best that there is a certain resilience in his nature that enables him as a general rule to rise on stepping-stones of his dead self in the most unfavourable circumstances. It isn't often that I fail to keep my chin up and the eye sparkling. But as I made my way to the library in pursuance of my dreadful task, I freely admit that Life had pretty well got me down. It was with leaden feet, as the expression is, that I tooled along.

Stiffy had compared the binge under advisement to a visit to the dentist, but as I reached journey's end I was feeling more as I had felt in the old days of school when going to keep a tryst with the headmaster in his study. You will recall my telling you of the time I sneaked down by night to the Rev. Aubrey Upjohn's lair in quest of biscuits and found myself unexpectedly cheek by jowl with the old bird, I in striped non-shrinkable pyjamas, he in tweeds and a dirty look. On that occasion, before parting, we had made a date for half-past-four next day at the same spot, and my emotions now were almost exactly similar to those which I had experienced on that far-off afternoon, as I tapped on the door and heard a scarcely human voice invite me to enter.

The only difference was that while the Rev.

Aubrey had been alone, Sir Watkyn Bassett appeared to be entertaining company. As my knuckles hovered over the panel, I seemed to hear the rumble of voices, and when I went in I found that my ears had not deceived me. Pop Bassett was seated at the desk, and by his side stood Constable Eustace Oates.

It was a spectacle that rather put the lid on the shrinking feeling from which I was suffering. I don't know if you have ever been jerked before a tribunal of justice, but if you have you will bear me out when I say that the memory of such an experience lingers, with the result that when later you are suddenly confronted by a sitting magistrate and a standing policeman, the association of ideas gives you a bit of a shock and tends to unman.

A swift, keen glance from old B. did nothing to still the fluttering pulse.

'Yes, Mr Wooster?'

'Oh — ah — could I speak to you for a moment?'

'Speak to me?' I could see that a strong distaste for having his sanctum cluttered up with Woosters was contending in Sir Watkyn Bassett's bosom with a sense of the obligations of a host. After what seemed a nip-and-tuck struggle, the latter got its nose ahead. 'Why, yes . . . That is . . . If you really . . . Oh, certainly . . . Pray take a seat.'

I did so, and felt a good deal better. In the dock, you have to stand. Old Bassett, after a quick look in my direction to see that I wasn't stealing the carpet, turned to the constable again.

'Well, I think that is all, Oates.'

'Very good, Sir Watkyn.'

'You understand what I wish you to do?'

'Yes, sir.'

'And with regard to that other matter, I will look into it very closely, bearing in mind what you have told me of your suspicions. A most rigorous investigation shall be made.'

The zealous officer clumped out. Old Bassett fiddled for a moment with the papers on his desk. Then he cocked an eye at me.

'That was Constable Oates, Mr Wooster.'

'Yes.'

'You know him?'

'I've seen him.'

'When?'

'This afternoon.'

'Not since then?'

'No.'

'You are quite sure?'

'Oh, quite.'

'H'm.'

He fiddled with the papers again, then touched on another topic.

'We were all disappointed that you were not with us in the drawing-room after dinner, Mr Wooster.'

This, of course, was a bit embarrassing. The man of sensibility does not like to reveal to his host that he has been dodging him like a leper.

'You were much missed.'

'Oh, was I? I'm sorry. I had a bit of a headache, and went and ensconced myself in my room.'

'I see. And you remained there?'

'Yes.'

'You did not by any chance go for a walk in the fresh air, to relieve your headache?'

'Oh, no. Ensconced all the time.'

'I see. Odd. My daughter Madeline tells me that she went twice to your room after the conclusion of dinner, but found it unoccupied.'

'Oh, really? Wasn't I there?'

'You were not.'

'I suppose I must have been somewhere else.'

'The same thought had occurred to me.'

'I remember now. I did saunter out on two occasions.'

'I see.'

He took up a pen and leaned forward, tapping it against his left forefinger.

'Somebody stole Constable Oates's helmet tonight,' he said, changing the subject.

'Oh, yes.'

'Yes. Unfortunately he was not able to see the miscreant.'

'No?'

'No. At the moment when the outrage took place, his back was turned.'

'Dashed difficult, of course, to see miscreants, if your back's turned.'

'Yes.'

'Yes.'

There was a pause. And as, in spite of the fact that we seemed to be agreeing on every point, I continued to sense a strain in the atmosphere, I tried to lighten things with a gag which I remembered from the old *in statu pupillari* days.

'Sort of makes you say to yourself *Quis custodiet ipsos custodes*, what?'

'I beg your pardon?'

'Latin joke,' I explained. '*Quis* — who — *custodiet* — shall guard — *ipsos custodes* — the guardians themselves? Rather funny, I mean to say,' I proceeded, making it clear to the meanest intelligence, 'a chap who's supposed to stop chaps pinching things from chaps having a chap come along and pinch something from him.'

'Ah, I see your point. Yes, I can conceive that a certain type of mind might detect a humorous side to the affair. But I can assure you, Mr Wooster, that that is not the side which presents itself to me as a Justice of the Peace. I take the very gravest view of the matter, and this, when once he is apprehended and placed in custody, I shall do my utmost to persuade the culprit to share.'

I didn't like the sound of this at all. A sudden alarm for old Stinker's well-being swept over me.

'I say, what do you think he would get?'

'I appreciate your zeal for knowledge, Mr Wooster, but at the moment I am not prepared to confide in you. In the words of the late Lord Asquith, I can only say 'Wait and see'. I think it is possible that your curiosity may be gratified before long.'

I didn't want to rake up old sores, always being a bit of a lad for letting the dead past bury its dead, but I thought it might be as well to give him a pointer.

'You fined me five quid,' I reminded him.

'So you informed me this afternoon,' he said,

pince-nezing me coldly. 'But if I understood correctly what you were saying, the outrage for which you were brought before me at Bosher Street was perpetrated on the night of the annual boat race between the Universities of Oxford and Cambridge, when a certain licence is tradition-ally granted by the authorities. In the present case, there are no such extenuating circum-stances. I should certainly not punish the wanton stealing of Government property from the person of Constable Oates with a mere fine.'

'You don't mean it would be chokey?'

'I said that I was not prepared to confide in you, but having gone so far I will. The answer to your question, Mr Wooster, is in the affirmative.'

There was a silence. He sat tapping his finger with the pen. I, if memory serves me correctly, straightening my tie. I was deeply concerned. The thought of poor old Stinker being bunged into the Bastille was enough to disturb anyone with a kindly interest in his career and prospects. Nothing retards a curate's advancement in his chosen profession more surely than a spell in the jug.

He lowered the pen.

'Well, Mr Wooster, I think that you were about to tell me what brings you here?'

I started a bit. I hadn't actually forgotten my mission, of course, but all this sinister stuff had caused me to shove it away at the back of my mind, and the suddenness with which it now came popping out gave me a bit of a jar.

I saw that there would have to be a few preliminary *pourparlers* before I got down to the nub. When relations between a bloke and another bloke are of a strained nature, the second bloke can't charge straight into the topic of wanting to marry the first bloke's niece. Not, that is to say, if he has a nice sense of what is fitting, as the Woosters have.

'Oh, ah, yes. Thanks for reminding me.'

'Not at all.'

'I just thought I'd drop in and have a chat.'

'I see.'

What the thing wanted, of course, was edging into, and I found I had got the approach. I teed up with a certain access of confidence.

'Have you ever thought about love, Sir Watkyn?'

'I beg your pardon?'

'About love. Have you ever brooded on it to any extent?'

'You have not come here to discuss love?'

'Yes, I have. That's exactly it. I wonder if you have noticed a rather rummy thing about it — viz that it is everywhere. You can't get away from it. Love, I mean. Wherever you go, there it is, buzzing along in every class of life. Quite remarkable. Take newts, for instance.'

'Are you quite well, Mr Wooster?'

'Oh, fine, thanks. Take newts, I was saying. You wouldn't think it, but Gussie Fink-Nottle tells me they get it right up their noses in the mating season. They stand in line by the hour, waggling their tails at the local belles. Starfish, too. Also undersea worms.'

'Mr Wooster — '

'And, according to Gussie, even ribbonlike

seaweed. That surprises you, eh? It did me. But he assures me that it is so. Just where a bit of ribbonlike seaweed thinks it is going to get by pressing its suit is more than I can tell you, but at the time of the full moon it hears the voice of Love all right and is up and doing with the best of them. I suppose it builds on the hope that it will look good to other bits of ribbonlike seaweed, which, of course, would also be affected by the full moon. Well, be that as it may, what I'm working round to is that the moon is pretty full now, and if that's how it affects seaweed you can't very well blame a chap like me for feeling the impulse, can you?'

'I am afraid — '

'Well, can you?' I repeated, pressing him strongly. And I threw in an 'Eh, what?' to clinch the thing.

But there was no answering spark of intelligence in his eye. He had been looking like a man who had missed the finer shades, and he still looked like a man who had missed the finer shades.

'I am afraid, Mr Wooster, that you will think me dense, but I have not the remotest notion what you are talking about.'

Now that the moment for letting him have it in the eyeball had arrived, I was pleased to find that the all-of-a-twitter feeling which had gripped me at the outset had ceased to function. I don't say that I had become exactly debonair and capable of flicking specks of dust from the irreproachable Mechlin lace at my wrists, but I felt perfectly calm.

What had soothed the system was the realization that in another half-jiffy I was about to slip a stick of dynamite under this old buster which would teach him that we are not put into the world for pleasure alone. When a magistrate has taken five quid off you for what, properly looked at, was a mere boyish pecadillo which would have been amply punished by a waggle of the forefinger and a brief 'Tut, tut!' it is always agreeable to make him jump like a pea on a hot shovel.

'I'm talking about me and Stiffy.'

'Stiffy?'

'Stephanie.'

'Stephanie? My niece?'

'That's right. Your niece. Sir Watkyn,' I said, remembering a good one, 'I have the honour to ask you for your niece's hand.'

'You — what?'

'I have the honour to ask you for your niece's hand.'

'I don't understand.'

'It's quite simple. I want to marry young Stiffy. She wants to marry me. Surely you've got it now? Take a line through that ribbonlike seaweed.'

There was no question as to its being value for money. On the cue 'niece's hand', he had come out of his chair like a rocketing pheasant. He now sank back, fanning himself with the pen. He seemed to have aged quite a lot.

'She wants to marry you?'

'That's the idea.'

'But I was not aware that you knew my niece.'

'Oh, rather. We two, if you care to put it that way, have plucked the gowans fine. Oh, yes, I know Stiffy, all right. Well, I mean to say, if I didn't, I shouldn't want to marry her, should I?'

He seemed to see the justice of this. He became silent, except for a soft, groaning noise. I remembered another good one.

'You will not be losing a niece. You will be gaining a nephew.'

'But I don't want a nephew, damn it!'

Well, there was that, of course.

He rose, and muttering something which sounded like 'Oh, dear! Oh, dear!' went to the fireplace and pressed the bell with a weak finger. Returning to his seat, he remained holding his head in his hands until the butler blew in.

'Butterfield,' he said in a low, hoarse voice, 'find Miss Stephanie and tell her that I wish to speak to her.'

A stage wait then occurred, but not such a long one as you might have expected. It was only about a minute before Stiffy appeared. I imagine she had been lurking in the offing, expectant of this summons. She tripped in, all merry and bright.

'You want to see me, Uncle Watkyn? Oh, hallo, Bertie.'

'Hallo.'

'I didn't know you were here. Have you and Uncle Watkyn been having a nice talk?'

Old Bassett, who had gone into a coma again, came out of it and uttered a sound like the death-rattle of a dying duck.

' 'Nice',' he said, 'is not the adjective I would

216

have selected.' He moistened his ashen lips. 'Mr Wooster has just informed me that he wishes to marry you.'

I must say that young Stiffy gave an extremely convincing performance. She stared at him. She stared at me. She clasped her hands. I rather think she blushed.

'Why Bertie!'

Old Bassett broke the pen. I had been wondering when he would.

'Oh, Bertie! You have made me very proud.'

'Proud?' I detected an incredulous note in old Bassett's voice. 'Did you say 'proud'?'

'Well, it's the greatest compliment a man can pay a woman, you know. All the nibs are agreed on that. I'm tremendously flattered and grateful . . . and, well, all that sort of thing. But, Bertie dear, I'm terribly sorry. I'm afraid it's impossible.'

I hadn't supposed that there was anything in the world capable of jerking a man from the depths so effectively as one of those morning mixtures of Jeeves's, but these words acted on old Bassett with an even greater promptitude and zip. He had been sitting in his chair in a boneless, huddled sort of way, a broken man. He now started up, with gleaming eyes and twitching lips. You could see that hope had dawned.

'Impossible? Don't you want to marry him?'

'No.'

'He said you did.'

'He must have been thinking of a couple of other fellows. No, Bertie, darling, it cannot be.

You see, I love somebody else.'

Old Bassett started.

'Eh? Who?'

'The most wonderful man in the world.'

'He has a name, I presume?'

'Harold Pinker.'

'Harold Pinker? ... Pinker ... The only Pinker I know is — '

'The curate. That's right. He's the chap.'

'You love the curate?'

'Ah!' said Stiffy, rolling her eyes up and looking like Aunt Dahlia when she had spoken of the merits of blackmail. 'We've been secretly engaged for weeks.'

It was plain from old Bassett's manner that he was not prepared to classify this under the heading of tidings of great joy. His brows were knitted, like those of some diner in a restaurant who, sailing into his dozen oysters, finds that the first one to pass his lips is a wrong 'un. I saw that Stiffy had shown a shrewd knowledge of human nature, if you could call his that, when she had told me that this man would have to be heavily sweetened before the news could be broken. You could see that he shared the almost universal opinion of parents and uncles that curates were nothing to start strewing roses out of a hat about.

'You know that vicarage that you have in your gift, Uncle Watkyn? What Harold and I were thinking was that you might give him that, and then we could get married at once. You see, apart from the increased dough, it would start him off on the road to higher things. Up till now, Harold has been working under wraps. As a curate, he

218

has no scope. But slip him a vicarage, and watch him let himself out. There is literally no eminence to which that boy will not rise, once he spits on his hands and starts in.'

She wiggled from base to apex with girlish enthusiasm, but there was no girlish enthusiasm in old Bassett's demeanour. Well, there wouldn't be, of course, but what I mean is there wasn't.

'Ridiculous!'

'Why?'

'I could not dream — '

'Why not?'

'In the first place, you are far too young — '

'What nonsense. Three of the girls I was at school with were married last year. I'm senile compared with some of the infants you see toddling up the aisle nowadays.'

Old Bassett thumped the desk — coming down, I was glad to see, on an upturned paper fastener. The bodily anguish induced by this lent vehemence to his tone.

'The whole thing is quite absurd and utterly out of the question. I refuse to consider the idea for an instant.'

'But what have you got against Harold?'

'I have nothing, as you put it, against him. He seems zealous in his duties and popular in the parish — '

'He's a baa-lamb.'

'No doubt.'

'He played football for England.'

'Very possibly.'

'And he's marvellous at tennis.'

'I dare say he is. But that is not a reason why

219

he should marry my niece. What means has he, if any, beyond his stipend?'

'About five hundred a year.'

'Tchah!'

'Well, I don't call that bad. Five hundred's pretty good sugar, if you ask me. Besides, money doesn't matter.'

'It matters a great deal.'

'You really feel that, do you?'

'Certainly. You must be practical.'

'Right ho, I will. If you'd rather I married for money, I'll marry for money. Bertie, it's on. Start getting measured for the wedding trousers.'

Her words created what is known as a genuine sensation. Old Bassett's 'What!' and my 'Here, I say, dash it!' popped out neck and neck and collided in mid air, my heart-cry having, perhaps, an even greater horse-power than his. I was frankly appalled. Experience has taught me that you never know with girls, and it might quite possibly happen, I felt, that she would go through with this frightful project as a gesture. Nobody could teach me anything about gestures. Brinkley Court in the preceding summer had crawled with them.

'Bertie is rolling in the stuff and, as you suggest, one might do worse than take a whack at the Wooster millions. Of course, Bertie dear, I am only marrying you to make you happy. I can never love you as I love Harold. But as Uncle Watkyn has taken this violent prejudice against him — '

Old Bassett hit the paper fastener again, but this time didn't seem to notice it.

'My dear child, don't talk such nonsense. You are quite mistaken. You must have completely misunderstood me. I have no prejudice against this young man Pinker. I like and respect him. If you really think your happiness lies in becoming his wife, I would be the last man to stand in your way. By all means, marry him. The alternative — '

He said no more, but gave me a long, shuddering look. Then, as if the sight of me were more than his frail strength could endure, he removed his gaze, only to bring it back again and give me a short, quick one. He then closed his eyes and leaned back in his chair, breathing stertorously. And as there didn't seem anything to keep me, I sidled out. The last I saw of him, he was submitting without any great animation to a niece's embrace.

I suppose that when you have an uncle like Sir Watkyn Bassett on the receiving end, a niece's embrace is a thing you tend to make pretty snappy. It wasn't more than about a minute before Stiffy came out and immediately went into her dance.

'What a man! What a man! What a man! What a man! What a man!' she said, waving her arms and giving other indications of *bien-être*. 'Jeeves,' she explained, as if she supposed that I might imagine her to be alluding to the recent Bassett. 'Did he say it would work? He did. And was he right? He was. Bertie, could one kiss Jeeves?'

'Certainly not.'

'Shall I kiss you?'

'No, thank you. All I require from you, young

Byng, is that notebook.'

'Well I must kiss someone, and I'm dashed if I'm going to kiss Eustace Oates.'

She broke off. A graver look came into her dial.

'Eustace Oates!' she repeated meditatively. 'That reminds me. In the rush of recent events, I had forgotten him. I exchanged a few words with Eustace Oates just now, Bertie, while I was waiting on the stairs for the balloon to go up, and he was sinister to a degree.'

'Where's that notebook?'

'Never mind about the notebook. The subject under discussion is Eustace Oates and his sinisterness. He's on my trail about that helmet.'

'What!'

'Absolutely. I'm Suspect Number One. He told me that he reads a lot of detective stories, and he says that the first thing a detective makes a bee-line for is motive. After that, opportunity. And finally clues. Well, as he pointed out, with that high-handed behaviour of his about Bartholomew rankling in my bosom, I had a motive all right, and seeing that I was going out and about at the time of the crime I had the opportunity, too. And as for clues, what do you think he had with him, when I saw him? One of my gloves! He had picked it up on the scene of the outrage — while measuring footprints or looking for cigar ash, I suppose. You remember when Harold brought me back my gloves, there was only one of them. The other he apparently dropped while scooping in the helmet.'

A sort of dull, bruised feeling weighed me

down as I mused on this latest manifestation of Harold Pinker's goofiness, as if a strong hand had whanged me over the cupola with a blackjack. There was such a sort of hideous ingenuity in the way he thought up new methods of inviting ruin.

'He would!'

'What do you mean, he would?'

'Well, he did, didn't he?'

'That's not the same as saying he would — in a beastly, sneering, supercilious tone, as if you were so frightfully hot yourself. I can't understand you, Bertie — the way you're always criticizing poor Harold. I thought you were so fond of him.'

'I love him like a b. But that doesn't alter my opinion that of all the pumpkin-headed foozlers who ever preached about Hivites and Jebusites, he is the foremost.'

'He isn't half as pumpkin-headed as you.'

'He is, at a conservative estimate, about twenty-seven times as pumpkin-headed as me. He begins where I leave off. It may be a strong thing to say, but he's more pumpkin-headed than Gussie.'

With a visible effort, she swallowed the rising choler.

'Well, never mind about that. The point is that Eustace Oates is on my trail, and I've got to look slippy and find a better safe-deposit vault for that helmet than my chest of drawers. Before I know where I am, the Ogpu will be searching my room. Where would be a good place, do you think?'

I dismissed the thing wearily.

'Oh, dash it, use your own judgement. To return to the main issue, where is that notebook?'

'Oh, Bertie, you're a perfect bore about that notebook. Can't you talk of anything else?'

'No, I can't. Where is it?'

'You're going to laugh when I tell you.'

I gave her an austere look.

'It is possible that I may some day laugh again — when I have got well away from this house of terror, but there is a fat chance of my doing so at this early date. Where is that book?'

'Well, if you really must know, I hid it in the cow-creamer.'

Everyone, I imagine, has read stories in which things turned black and swam before people. As I heard these words, Stiffy turned black and swam before me. It was as if I had been looking at a flickering negress.

'You — what?'

'I hid it in the cow-creamer.'

'What on earth did you do that for?'

'Oh, I thought I would.'

'But how am I to get it?'

A slight smile curved the young pimple's mobile lips.

'Oh, dash it, use your own judgement,' she said. 'Well, see you soon, Bertie.'

She biffed off, and I leaned limply against the banisters, trying to rally from this frightful wallop. But the world still flickered, and a few moments later I became aware that I was being addressed by a flickering butler.

'Excuse me, sir. Miss Madeline desired me to say that she would be glad if you could spare her a moment.'

I gazed at the man dully, like someone in a prison cell when the jailer has stepped in at dawn to notify him that the firing squad is ready. I knew what this meant, of course. I had recognized this butler's voice for what it was — the voice of doom. There could be only one thing that Madeline Bassett would be glad if I could spare her a moment about.

'Oh, did she?'

'Yes, sir.'

'Where is Miss Bassett?'

'In the drawing-room, sir.'

'Right ho.'

I braced myself with the old Wooster grit. Up came the chin, back went the shoulders.

'Lead on,' I said to the butler, and the butler led on.

10

The sound of soft and wistful music percolating
through the drawing-room door as I approached
did nothing to brighten the general outlook: and
when I went in and saw Madeline Bassett seated
at the piano, drooping on her stem a goodish
deal, the sight nearly caused me to turn and leg
it. However, I fought down the impulse and
started things off with a tentative 'What ho.'

The observation elicited no immediate response. She had risen, and for perhaps half a
minute stood staring at me in a sad sort of way,
like the Mona Lisa on one of the mornings when
the sorrows of the world had been coming over
the plate a bit too fast for her. Finally, just as I
was thinking I had better try to fill in with
something about the weather, she spoke.

'Bertie — '

It was, however, only a flash in the pan. She
blew a fuse, and silence supervened again.

'Bertie — '

No good. Another wash-out.

I was beginning to feel the strain a bit. We had
had one of these deaf-mutes-getting-together
sessions before, at Brinkley Court, in the
summer, but on that occasion I had been able to
ease things along by working in a spot of stage
business during the awkward gaps in the
conversation. Our previous chat as you may or
possibly may not recall, had taken place in the

226

Brinkley dining-room in the presence of a cold collation, and it had helped a lot being in a position to bound forward at intervals with a curried egg or a cheese straw. In the absence of these foodstuffs, we were thrown back a good deal on straight staring, and this always tends to embarrass.

Her lips parted. I saw that something was coming to the surface. A couple of gulps, and she was off to a good start.

'Bertie, I wanted to see you . . . I asked you to come . . . because I wanted to say . . . I wanted to tell you . . . Bertie, my engagement to Augustus is at an end.'

'Yes.'

'You knew?'

'Oh, rather. He told me.'

'Then you know why I asked you to come here. I wanted to say — '

'Yes.'

'That I'm willing — '

'Yes.'

'To make you happy.'

She appeared to be held up for a moment by a slight return of the old tonsil trouble, but after another brace of gulps she got it out.

'I will be your wife, Bertie.'

I suppose that after this most chaps would have thought it scarcely worthwhile to struggle against the inev., but I had a dash at it. With such vital issues at stake, one would have felt a chump if one had left any stone unturned.

'Awfully decent of you,' I said civilly. 'Deeply sensible of the honour, and what not. But have you thought? Have you reflected? Don't you feel you're being a bit rough on poor old Gussie?'

'What! After what happened this evening?'

'Ah, I wanted to talk to you about that. I always think, don't you, that it is as well on these occasions, before doing anything drastic, to have a few words with a seasoned man of the world and get the real low-down. You wouldn't like later on to have to start wringing your hands and saying 'Oh, if I had only known!' In my opinion, the whole thing should be re-examined with a view to threshing out. If you care to know what I think, you're wronging Gussie.'

'Wronging him? When I saw him with my own eyes — '

'Ah, but you haven't got the right angle. Let me explain.'

'There can be no explanation. We will not talk about it any more, Bertie. I have blotted Augustus from my life. Until tonight I saw him only through the golden mist of love, and thought him the perfect man. This evening he revealed himself as what he really is — a satyr.'

'But that's just what I'm driving at. That's just where you're making your bloomer. You see — '

'We will not talk about it any more.'

'But — '

'Please!'

'Oh, right ho.'

I tuned out. You can't make any headway with that *tout comprendre, c'est tout pardonner* stuff if the girl won't listen.

She turned the bean away, no doubt to hide a silent tear, and there ensued a brief interval during which she swabbed the eyes with a pocket handkerchief and I, averting my gaze, dipped the beak into a jar of *pot-pourri* which stood on the piano.

Presently, she took the air again.

'It is useless, Bertie. I know, of course, why you are speaking like this. It is that sweet, generous nature of yours. There are no lengths to which you will not go to help a friend, even though it may mean the wrecking of your own happiness. But there is nothing you can say that will change me. I have finished with Augustus. From tonight he will be to me merely a memory — a memory that will grow fainter and fainter through the years as you and I draw ever closer together. You will help me to forget. With you beside me, I shall be able in time to exorcize Augustus's spell . . . And now I suppose I had better go and tell Daddy.'

I started. I could still see Pop Bassett's face when he had thought that he was going to draw me for a nephew. It would be a bit thick, I felt, while he was still quivering to the roots of the soul at the recollection of that hair's-breadth escape, to tell him that I was about to become his son-in-law. I was not fond of Pop Bassett, but one has one's humane instincts.

'Oh, my aunt!' I said. 'Don't do that!'

'But I must. He will have to know that I am to be your wife. He is expecting me to marry Augustus three weeks from tomorrow.'

I chewed this over. I saw what she meant, of course. You've got to keep a father posted about these things. You can't just let it all slide and have the poor old egg rolling up to the church in a topper and a buttonhole, to find that the wedding is off and nobody bothered to mention it to him.

'Well, don't tell him tonight,' I urged. 'Let him simmer a bit. He's just had a pretty testing shock.'

'A shock?'

'Yes. He's not quite himself.'

A concerned look came into her eyes, causing them to bulge a trifle.

'So I was right. I thought he was not himself, when I met him coming out of the library just now. He was wiping his forehead and making odd little gasping noises. And when I asked him if anything was the matter, he said that we all had our cross to bear in this world, but that he supposed he ought not to complain, because things were not so bad as they might have been. I couldn't think what he meant. He then said he was going to have a warm bath and take three aspirins and go to bed. What was it? What had happened?'

I saw that to reveal the full story would be to complicate an already fairly well complicated situation. I touched, accordingly, on only one aspect of it.

'Stiffy had just told him she wanted to marry the curate.'

'Stephanie? The curate? Mr Pinker?'

'That's right. Old Stinker Pinker. And it churned him up a good deal. He appears to be a bit allergic to curates.'

She was breathing emotionally, like the dog

230

Bartholomew just after he had finished eating the candle.

'But . . . But . . . '

'Yes?'

'But does Stephanie love Mr Pinker?'

'Oh, rather. No question about that.'

'But then — '

I saw what was in her mind, and nipped in promptly.

'Then there can't be anything between her and Gussie, you were going to say? Exactly. This proves it, doesn't it? That's the very point I've been trying to work the conversation round to from the start.'

'But he — '

'Yes, I know he did. But his motives in doing so were as pure as the driven snow. Purer, if anything. I'll tell you all about it, and I am prepared to give you a hundred to eight that when I have finished you will admit that he was more to be pitied than censured.'

Give Bertram Wooster a good, clear story to unfold, and he can narrate it well. Starting at the beginning with Gussie's aghastness at the prospect of having to make a speech at the wedding breakfast, I took her step by step through the subsequent developments, and I may say that I was as limpid as dammit. By the time I had reached the final chapter, I had her a bit squiggle-eyed but definitely wavering on the edge of conviction.

'And you say Stephanie has hidden this notebook in Daddy's cow-creamer?'

'Plumb spang in the cow-creamer.'

'But I never heard such an extraordinary story in my life.'

'Bizarre, yes, but quite capable of being swallowed, don't you think? What you have got to take into consideration is the psychology of the individual. You may say that you wouldn't have a psychology like Stiffy's if you were paid for it, but it's hers all right.'

'Are you sure you are not making all this up, Bertie?'

'Why on earth?'

'I know your altruistic nature so well.'

'Oh, I see what you mean. No, rather not. This is the straight official stuff. Don't you believe it?'

'I shall, if I find the notebook where you say Stephanie put it. I think I had better go and look.'

'I would.'

'I will.'

'Fine.'

She hurried out, and I sat down at the piano and began to play 'Happy Days are Here Again' with one finger. It was the only method of self-expression that seemed to present itself. I would have preferred to get outside a curried egg or two, for the strain had left me weak, but, as I have said, there were no curried eggs present.

I was profoundly braced. I felt like some Marathon runner who, after sweating himself to the bone for hours, at length breasts the tape. The only thing that kept my bracedness from being absolutely unmixed was the lurking thought that in this ill-omened house there was always the chance of something unforeseen

232

suddenly popping up to mar the happy ending. I somehow couldn't see Totleigh Towers throwing in the towel quite so readily as it appeared to be doing. It must, I felt, have something up its sleeve.

Nor was I wrong. When Madeline Bassett returned a few minutes later, there was no notebook in her hand. She reported total inability to discover so much as a trace of a notebook in the spot indicated. And, I gathered from her remarks, she had ceased entirely to be a believer in that notebook's existence.

I don't know if you have ever had a bucket of cold water right in the mazzard. I received one once in my boyhood through the agency of a groom with whom I had had some difference of opinion. That same feeling of being knocked endways came over me now.

I was at a loss and nonplussed. As Constable Oates had said, the first move the knowledgeable bloke makes when rummy goings-on are in progress is to try to spot the motive, and what Stiffy's motive could be for saying the notebook was in the cow-creamer, when it wasn't, I was unable to fathom. With a firm hand this girl had pulled my leg, but why — that was the point that baffled — why had she pulled my leg?

I did my best.

'Are you sure you really looked?'

'Perfectly sure.'

'I mean, carefully.'

'Very carefully.'

'Stiffy certainly swore it was there.'

'Indeed?'

'How do you mean, indeed?'

'If you want to know what I mean, I do not believe there ever was a notebook.'

'You don't credit my story?'

'No, I do not.'

Well, after that, of course, there didn't seem much to say. I may have said 'Oh?' or something along those lines — I'm not sure — but if I did, that let me out. I edged to the door, and pushed off in a sort of daze, pondering.

You know how it is when you ponder. You become absorbed, concentrated. Outside phenomena do not register on the what-is-it. I suppose I was fully half-way along the passage leading to my bedroom before the beastly row that was going on there penetrated to my consciousness, causing me to stop, look and listen.

★ ★ ★

This row to which I refer was a kind of banging row, as if somebody were banging on something. And I had scarcely said to myself 'What ho, a banger!' when I saw who this banger was. It was Roderick Spode, and what he was banging on was the door of Gussie's bedroom. As I came up, he was in the act of delivering another buffet on the woodwork.

The spectacle had an immediate tranquillizing effect on my jangled nervous system. I felt a new man. And I'll tell you why.

Everyone, I suppose, has experienced the sensation of comfort and relief which comes when you are being given the run-around by forces beyond your control and suddenly discover someone on whom you can work off the pent-up feelings. The merchant prince, when things are going wrong, takes it out of the junior clerk. The junior clerk goes and ticks off the office boy. The office boy kicks the cat. The cat steps down the street to find a smaller cat, which in its turn, the interview concluded, starts scouring the countryside for a mouse.

It was so with me now. Snootered to bursting point by Pop Bassetts and Madeline Bassetts and Stiffy Byngs and what not, and hounded like the dickens by a remorseless Fate, I found solace in the thought that I could still slip it across Roderick Spode.

'Spode!' I cried sharply.

He paused with lifted fist and turned an inflamed face in my direction. Then, as he saw who had spoken, the red light died out of his eyes. He wilted obsequiously.

'Well, Spode, what is all this?'

'Oh, hallo, Wooster. Nice evening.'

I proceeded to work off the pent-up f.

'Never mind what sort of an evening it is,' I said. 'Upon my word, Spode, this is too much. This is just that little bit above the odds which compels a man to take drastic steps.'

'But, Wooster — '

'What do you mean by disturbing the house with this abominable uproar? Have you forgotten already what I told you about checking this disposition of yours to run amok like a raging hippopotamus? I should have thought that after what I said you would have spent the remainder of the evening curled up with a good book. But no. I find you renewing your efforts to assault and batter my friends. I must warn you, Spode, that my patience is not inexhaustible.'

'But, Wooster, you don't understand.'

'What don't I understand?'

'You don't know the provocation I have received from this pop-eyed Fink-Nottle.' A wistful look came into his face. 'I must break his neck.'

'You are not going to break his neck.'

'Well, shake him like a rat.'

'Nor shake him like a rat.'

'But he says I'm a pompous ass.'

'When did Gussie say that to you?'

'He didn't exactly say it. He wrote it. Here it is.'

Before my bulging eyes he produced from his pocket a small, brown, leather-covered notebook.

Harking back to Archimedes just once more, Jeeves's description of him discovering the principle of displacement, though brief, had made a deep impression on me, bringing before my eyes a very vivid picture of what must have happened on that occasion. I had been able to see the man testing the bath water with his toe . . . stepping in . . . immersing the frame. I had accompanied him in spirit through all the subsequent formalities — the soaping of the loofah, the shampooing of the head, the burst of song . . .

And then, abruptly, as he climbs towards the high note, there is a silence. His voice has died away. Through the streaming suds you can see that his eyes are glowing with a strange light. The loofah falls from his grasp, disregarded. He utters a triumphant cry. 'Got it! What ho! The principle of displacement!' And he leaps, feeling like a million dollars.

In precisely the same manner did the miraculous appearance of this notebook affect me. There was that identical moment of stunned silence, followed by the triumphant cry. And I have no doubt that, as I stretched out a compelling hand, my eyes were glowing with a strange light.

'Give me that book, Spode!'

'Yes, I would like you to look at it, Wooster. Then you will see what I mean. I came upon this,' he said, 'in rather a remarkable way. The thought crossed my mind that Sir Watkyn might feel happier if I were to take charge of that cow-creamer of his. There have been a lot of burglaries in the neighbourhood,' he added hastily, 'a lot of burglaries, and those french windows are never really safe. So I — er — went to the collection-room, and took it out of its case. I was surprised to hear something bumping about inside it. I opened it, and found this book. Look,' he said, pointing a banana-like finger over my shoulder. 'There is what he says about the way I eat asparagus.'

I think Roderick Spode's idea was that we were going to pore over the pages together. When he saw me slip the volume into my pocket, I sensed the feeling of bereavement.

'Are you going to keep the book, Wooster?'

'I am.'

'But I wanted to show it to Sir Watkyn. There's a lot about him in it, too.'

'We will not cause Sir Watkyn needless pain, Spode.'

'Perhaps you're right. Then I'll be getting on with breaking this door down?'

'Certainly not,' I said sternly. 'All you do is pop off.'

'Pop off?'

'Pop off. Leave me, Spode. I would be alone.'

I watched him disappear round the bend, then rapped vigorously on the door.

'Gussie.'

No reply.

'Gussie, come out.'

'I'm dashed if I do.'

'Come out, you ass. Wooster speaking.'

But even this did not produce immediate results. He explained later that he was under the impression that it was Spode giving a cunning imitation of my voice. But eventually I convinced him that this was indeed the boyhood friend and no other, and there came the sound of furniture being dragged away, and presently the door opened and his head emerged cautiously, like that of a snail taking a look round after a thunderstorm.

Into the emotional scene which followed I need not go in detail. You will have witnessed much the same sort of thing in the pictures, when the United States Marines arrive in the nick of time to relieve the beleaguered garrison. I may sum it up by saying that he fawned upon me. He seemed to be under the impression that I had worsted Roderick Spode in personal combat and it wasn't worthwhile to correct it. Pressing the notebook into his hand, I sent him off to show it to Madeline Bassett, and proceeded to my room.

Jeeves was there, messing about at some professional task.

It had been my intention, on seeing this man again, to put him through it in no uncertain fashion for having subjected me to the tense nervous strain of my recent interview with Pop Bassett. But now I greeted him with the cordial smile rather than the acid glare. After all, I told myself, his scheme had dragged home the gravy, and in any case this was no moment for recriminations. Wellington didn't go about ticking people off after the battle of Waterloo. He slapped their backs and stood them drinks.

'Aha, Jeeves! You're there, are you?'

'Yes, sir.'

'Well, Jeeves, you may start packing the effects.'

'Sir?'

'For the homeward trip. We leave tomorrow.'

'You are not proposing, then, sir, to extend your stay at Totleigh Towers?'

I laughed one of my gay, jolly ones.

'Don't ask foolish questions, Jeeves. Is Totleigh Towers a place where people extend their stays, if they haven't got to? And there is now no longer any necessity for me to linger on the premises. My work is done. We leave first thing tomorrow morning. Start packing, therefore, so that we shall be in a position to get off the mark without an instant's delay. It won't take you long?'

'No, sir. There are merely two suitcases.'

He hauled them from beneath the bed, and opening the larger of the brace began to sling coats and things into it, while I, seating myself in the armchair, proceeded to put him abreast of recent events.

'Well, Jeeves, that plan of yours worked all right.'

'I am most gratified to hear it, sir.'

'I don't say that the scene won't haunt me in my dreams for some little time to come. I make no comment on your having let me in for such a thing. I merely state that it proved a winner. An uncle's blessing came popping out like a cork out of a champagne bottle, and Stiffy and Stinker are headed for the altar rails with no more fences ahead.'

'Extremely satisfactory, sir. Then Sir Watkyn's reactions were as we had anticipated?'

'If anything, more so. I don't know if you have ever seen a stout bark buffeted by the waves?'

'No, sir. My visits to the seaside have always been made in clement weather.'

'Well, that was what he resembled on being informed by me that I wanted to become his nephew by marriage. He looked and behaved like the Wreck of the *Hesperus*. You remember? It sailed the wintry sea, and the skipper had taken his little daughter to bear him company.'

'Yes, sir. Blue were her eyes as the fairy-flax, her cheeks like the dawn of day, and her bosom was white as the hawthorn buds that open in the month of May.'

'Quite. Well, as I was saying, he reeled beneath the blow and let water in at every seam. And when Stiffy appeared, and told him that it was all a mistake and that the *promesso sposo* was in reality old Stinker Pinker, his relief knew no bounds. He instantly gave his sanction to their union. Could hardly get the words out quick enough. But why am I wasting time telling you all this, Jeeves? A mere side issue. Here's the real front-page stuff. Here's the news that will shock the *chancelleries*. I've got that notebook.'

'Indeed, sir?'

'Yes, absolutely got it. I found Spode with it and took it away from him, and Gussie is even now showing it to Miss Bassett and clearing his name of the stigma that rested upon it. I shouldn't be surprised if at this very moment they were locked in a close embrace.'

'A consummation devoutly to be wished, sir.'

'You said it, Jeeves.'

'Then you have nothing to cause you further concern, sir.'

'Nothing. The relief is stupendous. I feel as if a great weight had been rolled from my shoulders. I could dance and sing. I think there can be no question that exhibiting that notebook will do the trick.'

'None, I should imagine, sir.'

'I say, Bertie,' said Gussie, trickling in at this juncture with the air of one who has been passed through a wringer, 'a most frightful thing has happened. The wedding's off.'

11

I stared at the man, clutching the brow and rocking on my base.

'Off?'

'Yes.'

'Your wedding?'

'Yes.'

'It's off?'

'Yes.'

'What — off?'

'Yes.'

I don't know what the Mona Lisa would have done in my place. Probably just what I did.

'Jeeves,' I said. 'Brandy.'

'Very good, sir.'

He rolled away on his errand of mercy, and I turned to Gussie, who was tacking about the room in a dazed manner, as if filling in the time before starting to pluck straws from his hair.

'I can't bear it!' I heard him mutter. 'Life without Madeline won't be worth living.'

It was an astounding attitude, of course, but you can't argue about fellows' tastes. One man's peach is another man's poison, and *vice versa*. Even my Aunt Agatha, I remembered, had roused the red-hot spark of pash in the late Spenser Gregson.

His wandering had taken him to the bed, and I saw that he was looking at the knotted sheet which lay there.

'I suppose,' he said, in an absent, soliloquizing voice, 'a chap could hang himself with that.'

I resolved to put a stopper on this trend of thought promptly. I had got more or less used by now to my bedroom being treated as a sort of meeting-place of the nations, but I was dashed if I was going to have it turned into the spot marked with an X. It was a point on which I felt strongly.

'You aren't going to hang yourself here.'

'I shall have to hang myself somewhere.'

'Well, you don't hang yourself in my bedroom.'

He raised his eyebrows.

'Have you any objection to my sitting in your armchair?'

'Go ahead.'

'Thanks.'

He seated himself, and stared before him with glazed eyes.

'Now, then, Gussie,' I said, 'I will take your statement. What is all this rot about the wedding being off?'

'It is off.'

'But didn't you show her the notebook?'

'Yes. I showed her the notebook.'

'Did she read its contents?'

'Yes.'

'Well, didn't she *tout comprendre*?'

'Yes.'

'And *tout pardonner*?'

'Yes.'

'Then you must have got your facts twisted. The wedding can't be off.'

'It is, I tell you. Do you think I don't know when a wedding's off and when it isn't? Sir Watkyn has forbidden it.'

This was an angle I had not foreseen.

'Why? Did you have a row or something?'

'Yes. About newts. He didn't like me putting them in the bath.'

'You put newts in the bath?'

'Yes.'

Like a keen cross-examining counsel, I swooped on the point.

'Why?'

His hand fluttered, as if about to reach for a straw.

'I broke the tank. The tank in my bedroom. The glass tank I keep my newts in. I broke the glass tank in my bedroom, and the bath was the only place to lodge the newts. The basin wasn't large enough. Newts need elbow room. So I put them in the bath. Because I had broken the tank. The glass tank in my bedroom. The glass tank I keep my newts in — '

I saw that if allowed to continue in this strain he might go on practically indefinitely, so I called him to order with a sharp rap of a china vase on the mantelpiece.

'I get the idea,' I said, brushing the fragments into the fire-place. 'Proceed. How does Pop Bassett come into the picture?'

'He went to take a bath. It never occurred to me that anyone would be taking a bath as late as this. And I was in the drawing-room, when he burst in shouting: 'Madeline, that blasted Fink-Nottle has been filling my bathtub with tadpoles!' And I lost my head a little, I'm afraid. I yelled: 'Oh, my gosh, you silly old ass, be careful what you're doing with those newts. Don't touch them. I'm in the middle of a most important experiment.''

'I see. And then — '

'I went on to tell him how I wished to ascertain whether the full moon affected the love life of newts. And a strange look came into his face, and he quivered a bit, and then he told me that he had pulled out the plug and all my newts had gone down the waste pipe.'

I think he would have preferred at this point to fling himself on the bed and turn his face to the wall, but I headed him off. I was resolved to stick to the *res*.

'Upon which you did what?'

'I ticked him off properly. I called him every name I could think of. In fact, I called him names that I hadn't a notion I knew. They just seemed to come bubbling up from my subconsciousness. I was hampered a bit at first by the fact that Madeline was there, but it wasn't long before he told her to go to bed, and then I was really able to express myself. And when I finally paused for breath, he forbade the banns and pushed off. And I rang the bell and asked Butterfield to bring me a glass of orange juice.'

I started.

'Orange juice?'

'I wanted picking up.'

'But orange juice? At such a time?'

'It was what I felt I needed.'

I shrugged my shoulders.

'Oh, well,' I said.

Just another proof, of course, of what I often say — that it takes all sorts to make a world.

'As a matter of fact, I could do with a good long drink now.'

'The tooth-bottle is at your elbow.'

'Thanks . . . Ah! That's the stuff!'

'Have a go at the jug.'

'No, thanks. I know when to stop. Well, that's the position, Bertie. He won't let Madeline marry me, and I'm wondering if there is any possible way of bringing him round. I'm afraid there isn't. You see, it wasn't only that I called him names — '

'Such as?'

'Well, louse, I remember was one of them. And skunk, I think. Yes, I'm pretty sure I called him a wall-eyed skunk. But he might forgive that. The real trouble is that I mocked at that cow-creamer of his.'

'Cow-creamer!'

I spoke sharply. He had started a train of thought. An idea had begun to burgeon. For some little time I had been calling on all the resources of the Wooster intellect to help me to solve this problem, and I don't often do that without something breaking loose. At this mention of the cow-creamer, the brain seemed suddenly to give itself a shake and start off across country with its nose to the ground.

'Yes. Knowing how much he loved and admired it, and searching for barbed words that would wound him, I told him it was modern Dutch. I had gathered from his remarks at the dinner table last night that that was the last thing it ought to be. 'You and your eighteenth-century cow-creamers!' I said. 'Pah! Modern Dutch!' or words to that effect. The thrust got home. He turned purple, and broke off the wedding.'

'Listen, Gussie,' I said. 'I think I've got it.'

His face lit up. I could see that optimism had stirred and was shaking a leg. This Fink-Nottle has always been of an optimistic nature. Those who recall his address to the boys of Market Snodsbury Grammar School will remember that it was largely an appeal to the little blighters not to look on the dark side.

'Yes, I believe I see the way. What you have got to do, Gussie, is pinch that cow-creamer.'

His lips parted, and I thought an 'Eh, what?' was coming through, but it didn't. Just silence and a couple of bubbles.

'That is the first, essential step. Having secured the cow-creamer, you tell him it is in your possession and say: 'Now, how about it?' I feel convinced that in order to recover that foul cow he would meet any terms you care to name. You know what collectors are like. Practically potty, every one of them. Why, my Uncle Tom wants the thing so badly that he is actually prepared to yield up his supreme cook, Anatole, in exchange for it.'

'Not the fellow who was functioning at Brinkley when I was there?'

'That's right.'

'The chap who dished up those *nonettes de poulet Agnes Sorel?*'

'That very artist.'

'You really mean that your uncle would consider Anatole well lost if he could secure this cow-creamer?'

'I have it from Aunt Dahlia's own lips.'

He drew a deep breath.

'Then you're right. This scheme of yours would certainly solve everything. Assuming, of course, that Sir Watkyn values the thing equally highly.'

'He does. Doesn't he Jeeves?' I said, putting it up to him, as he trickled in with the brandy. 'Sir Watkyn Bassett has forbidden Gussie's wedding,' I explained, 'and I've been telling him that all he has to do in order to make him change his mind is to get hold of that cow-creamer and refuse to give it back until he coughs up a father's blessing. You concur?'

'Undoubtedly, sir. If Mr Fink-Nottle possesses himself of the *objet d'art* in question, he will be in a position to dictate. A very shrewd plan, sir.'

'Thank you, Jeeves. Yes, not bad, considering that I had to think on my feet and form my strategy at a moment's notice. If I were you, Gussie, I would put things in train immediately.'

'Excuse me, sir.'

'You spoke, Jeeves?'

'Yes, sir. I was about to say that before Mr Fink-Nottle can put the arrangements in operation there is an obstacle to be surmounted.'

'What's that?'

'In order to protect his interests, Sir Watkyn has posted Constable Oates on guard in the collection-room.'

'What!'

'Yes, sir.'

The sunshine died out of Gussie's face, and he uttered a stricken sound like a gramophone record running down.

'However, I think that with a little finesse it will be perfectly possible to eliminate this factor. I wonder if you recollect, sir, the occasion at Chuffnell Hall, when Sir Roderick Glossop had become locked up in the potting-shed, and your efforts to release him appeared likely to be foiled by the fact that Police Constable Dobson had been stationed outside the door?'

'Vividly, Jeeves.'

'I ventured to suggest that it might be possible to induce him to leave his post by conveying word to him that the parlourmaid Mary, to whom he was betrothed, wished to confer with him in the raspberry bushes. The plan was put into effect and proved successful.'

'True, Jeeves. But,' I said dubiously, 'I don't see how anything like that could be worked here. Constable Dobson, you will recall, was young, ardent, romantic — just the sort of chap who would automatically go leaping into raspberry bushes if you told him there were girls in there. Eustace Oates has none of the Dobson fire. He is well stricken in years and gives the impression of being a settled married man who would rather have a cup of tea.'

'Yes, sir, Constable Oates is, as you say, of a more sober temperament. But it is merely the principle of the thing which I would advocate applying to the present emergency. It would be necessary to provide a lure suited to the psychology of the individual. What I would suggest is that Mr Fink-Nottle should inform the officer that he has seen his helmet in your possession.'

'Egad, Jeeves!'

'Yes, sir.'

'I see the idea. Yes, very hot. Yes, that would do it.'

Gussie's glassy eye indicating that all this was failing to register, I explained.

'Earlier in the evening, Gussie, a hidden hand snitched this *gendarme's* lid, cutting him to the quick. What Jeeves is saying is that a word from you to the effect that you have seen it in my room will bring him bounding up here like a tigress after its lost cub, thus leaving you a clear field in which to operate. That is your idea in essence, is it not, Jeeves?'

'Precisely, sir.'

Gussie brightened visibly.

'I see. It's a ruse.'

'That's right. One of the ruses, and not the worst of them. Nice work, Jeeves.'

'Thank you, sir.'

'That will do the trick, Gussie. Tell him I've got his helmet, wait while he bounds out, nip to the glass case and trouser the cow. A simple programme. A child could carry it out. My only regret, Jeeves, is that this appears to remove any chance Aunt Dahlia might have had of getting the thing. A pity there has been such a wide popular demand for it.'

'Yes, sir. But possibly Mrs Travers, feeling that Mr Fink-Nottle's need is greater than hers, will accept the disappointment philosophically.'

'Possibly. On the other hand, possibly not. Still, there it is. On these occasions when individual interests clash, somebody has got to draw the short straw.'

'Very true, sir.'

'You can't be expected to dish out happy endings all round — one per person, I mean.'

'No, sir.'

'The great thing is to get Gussie fixed. So buzz off, Gussie, and Heaven speed your efforts.'

I lit a cigarette.

'A very sound idea, that, Jeeves. How did you happen to think of it?'

'It was the officer himself who put it into my head, sir, when I was chatting with him not long ago. I gathered from what he said that he actually does suspect you of being the individual who purloined his helmet.'

'Me? Why on earth? Dash it, I scarcely know the man. I thought he suspected Stiffy.'

'Originally, yes, sir. And it is still his view that Miss Byng was the motivating force behind the theft. But he now believes that the young lady must have had a male accomplice, who did the rough work. Sir Watkyn, I understand, supports him in this theory.'

I suddenly remembered the opening passages of my interview with Pop Bassett in the library, and at last got on to what he had been driving at. Those remarks of his which had seemed to me then mere idle gossip had had, I now perceived, a sinister under-current of meaning. I had supposed that we were just two of the boys chewing over the latest bit of hot news, and all the time the thing had been a probe or quiz.

'But what makes them think that I was the male accomplice?'

'I gather that the officer was struck by the cordiality which he saw to exist between Miss Byng and yourself, when he encountered you in the road this afternoon, and his suspicions became strengthened when he found the young lady's glove on the scene of the outrage.'

'I don't get you, Jeeves.'

'He supposes you to be enamoured of Miss Byng, sir, and thinks that you were wearing her glove next to your heart.'

'If it had been next my heart, how could I have dropped it?'

'His view is that you took it out to press to your lips, sir.'

'Come, come, Jeeves. Would I start pressing gloves to my lips at the moment when I was about to pinch a policeman's helmet?'

'Apparently Mr Pinker did, sir.'

I was on the point of explaining to him that what old Stinker would do in any given situation and what the ordinary, normal person with a couple of ounces more brain than a cuckoo clock would do were two vastly different things, when I was interrupted by the re-entrance of Gussie. I could see by the buoyancy of his demeanour that matters had been progressing well.

'Jeeves was right, Bertie,' he said. 'He read Eustace Oates like a book.'

'The information stirred him up?'

'I don't think I have ever seen a more

252

thoroughly roused policeman. His first impulse was to drop everything and come dashing up here right away.'

'Why didn't he?'

'He couldn't quite bring himself to, in view of the fact that Sir Watkyn had told him to stay there.'

I followed the psychology. It was the same as that of the boy who stood on the burning deck, whence all but he had fled.

'Then the procedure, I take it, will be that he will send word to Pop Bassett, notifying him of the facts and asking permission to go ahead?'

'Yes. I expect you will have him with you in a few minutes.'

'Then you ought not to be here. You should be lurking in the hall.'

'I'm going there at once. I only came to report.'

'Be ready to slip in the moment he is gone.'

'I will. Trust me. There won't be a hitch. It was a wonderful idea of yours, Jeeves.'

'Thank you, sir.'

'You can imagine how relieved I'm feeling, knowing that in about five minutes everything will be all right. The only thing I'm a bit sorry for now,' said Gussie thoughtfully, 'is that I gave the old boy that notebook.'

He threw out this appalling statement so casually that it was a second or two before I got its import. When I did, a powerful shock permeated my system. It was as if I had been reclining in the electric chair and the authorities had turned on the juice.

'You gave him the notebook!'

'Yes. Just as he was leaving. I thought there might be some names in it which I had forgotten to call him.'

I supported myself with a trembling hand on the mantelpiece.

'Jeeves!'

'Sir?'

'More brandy!'

'Yes, sir.'

'And stop doling it out in those small glasses, as if it were radium. Bring the cask.'

Gussie was regarding me with a touch of surprise.

'Something the matter, Bertie?'

'Something the matter?' I let out a mirthless l. 'Ha! Well, this has torn it.'

'How do you mean? Why?'

'Can't you see what you've done, you poor chump! It's no use pinching that cow-creamer now. If old Bassett has read the contents of that notebook, nothing will bring him round.'

'Why not?'

'Well, you saw how they affected Spode. I don't suppose Pop Bassett is any fonder of reading home truths about himself than Spode is.'

'But he's had the home truths already. I told you how I ticked him off.'

'Yes, but you could have got away with that. Overlook it, please . . . spoken in hot blood . . . strangely forgot myself . . . all that sort of stuff. Coldly reasoned opinions, carefully inscribed day by day in a notebook, are a very different thing.'

I saw that it had penetrated at last. The

greenish tinge was back in his face. His mouth opened and shut like that of a goldfish which sees another goldfish nip in and get away with the ant's egg which it had been earmarking for itself.

'Oh, gosh!'

'Yes.'

'What can I do?'

'I don't know.'

'Think, Bertie, think!'

I did so, tensely, and was rewarded with an idea.

'Tell me,' I said, 'what exactly occurred at the conclusion of the vulgar brawl? You handed him the book. Did he dip into it on the spot?'

'No. He shoved it away in his pocket.'

'And did you gather that he still intended to take a bath?'

'Yes.'

'Then answer me this. What pocket? I mean the pocket of what garment? What was he wearing?'

'A dressing gown.'

'Over — think carefully, Fink-Nottle, for everything hangs on this — over shirt and trousers and things?'

'Yes, he had his trousers on. I remember noticing.'

'Then there is still hope. After leaving you, he would have gone to his room to shed the upholstery. He was pretty steamed up, you say?'

'Yes, very much.'

'Good. My knowledge of human nature, Gussie, tells me that a steamed-up man does not loiter about feeling in his pocket for notebooks and steeping himself in their contents. He flings off the garments, and legs it to the *salle de bain*. The book must still be in the pocket of his dressing gown — which, no doubt, he flung on the bed or over a chair — and all you have to do is nip into his room and get it.'

I had anticipated that this clear thinking would produce the joyous cry and the heartfelt burst of thanks. Instead of which, he merely shuffled his feet dubiously.

'Nip into his room?

'Yes.'

'But dash it!'

'Now, what?'

'You're sure there isn't some other way?'

'Of course there isn't.'

'I see . . . You wouldn't care to do it for me, Bertie?'

'No, I would not.'

'Many fellows would, to help an old school friend.'

'Many fellows are mugs.'

'Have you forgotten those days at the dear old school?'

'Yes.'

'You don't remember the time I shared my last bar of milk chocolate with you?'

'No.'

'Well, I did, and you told me then that if ever you had an opportunity of doing anything for me . . . However, if these obligations — sacred, some people might consider them — have no weight with you, I suppose there is nothing more to be said.'

He pottered about for a while, doing the old cat-in-an-adage stuff: then, taking from his breast pocket a cabinet photograph of Madeline Bassett, he gazed at it intently. It seemed to be the bracer he required. His eyes lit up. His face lost its fishlike look. He strode out, to return immediately, slamming the door behind him.

'I say, Bertie, Spode's out there!'

'What of it?'

'He made a grab at me.'

'Made a grab at you?'

I frowned. I am a patient man, but I can be pushed too far. It seemed incredible, after what I had said to him, that Roderick Spode's hat was still in the ring. I went to the door, and threw it open. It was even as Gussie had said. The man was lurking.

He sagged a bit, as he saw me. I addressed him with cold severity.

'Anything I can do for you, Spode?'

'No. No, nothing, thanks.'

'Push along, Gussie,' I said, and stood watching him with a protective eye as he sidled round the human gorilla and disappeared along the passage. Then I turned to Spode.

'Spode,' I said in a level voice, 'did I or did I not tell you to leave Gussie alone?'

He looked at me pleadingly.

'Couldn't you possibly see your way to letting me do something to him, Wooster? If it was only to kick his spine up through his hat?'

'Certainly not.'

'Well, just as you say, of course.' He scratched his cheek discontentedly. 'Did you read that notebook, Wooster?'

'No.'

'He says my moustache is like the faint discoloured smear left by a squashed blackbeetle on the side of a kitchen sink.'

'He always was a poetic sort of chap.'

'And that the way I eat asparagus alters one's whole conception of Man as Nature's last word.'

'Yes, he told me that, I remember. He's about right, too. I was noticing at dinner. What you want to do, Spode, in future is lower the vegetable gently into the abyss. Take it easy. Don't snap at it. Try to remember that you are a human being and not a shark.'

'Ha, ha! 'A human being and not a shark.' Cleverly put, Wooster. Most amusing.'

He was still chuckling, though not frightfully heartily I thought, when Jeeves came along with a decanter on a tray.

'The brandy, sir.'

'And about time, Jeeves.'

'Yes, sir. I must once more apologize for my delay. I was detained by Constable Oates.'

'Oh? Chatting with him again?'

'Not so much chatting, sir, as staunching the flow of blood.'

'Blood?'

'Yes, sir. The officer had met with an accident.'

My momentary pique vanished, and in its place there came a stern joy. Life at Totleigh Towers had hardened me, blunting the gentler emotions, and I derived nothing but gratification from the news that Constable Oates had been meeting with accidents. Only one thing, indeed, could have pleased me more — if I had been informed that Sir Watkyn Bassett had trodden on the soap and come a purler in the bathtub.

'How did that happen?'

'He was assaulted while endeavouring to recover Sir Watkyn's cow-creamer from a midnight marauder, sir.'

Spode uttered a cry.

'The cow-creamer has not been stolen?'

'Yes, sir.'

It was evident that Roderick Spode was deeply affected by the news. His attitude towards the cow-creamer had, if you remember, been fatherly from the first. Not lingering to hear more, he galloped off, and I accompanied Jeeves into the room, agog for details.

'What happened, Jeeves?'

'Well, sir, it was a little difficult to extract a coherent narrative from the officer, but I gather that he found himself restless and fidgety — '

'No doubt owing to his inability to get in touch with Pop Bassett, who, as we know, is in his bath, and receive permission to leave his post and come up here after his helmet.'

'No doubt, sir. And being restless, he experienced a strong desire to smoke a pipe. Reluctant, however, to run the risk of being found to have smoked while on duty — as might have been the case had he done so in an enclosed room, where the fumes would have lingered — he stepped out into the garden.'

'A quick thinker, this Oates.'

'He left the french window open behind him. And some little time later his attention was arrested by a sudden sound from within.'

'What sort of sound?'

'The sound of stealthy footsteps, sir.'

'Someone stepping stealthily, as it were?'

'Precisely, sir. Followed by the breaking of glass. He immediately hastened back to the room — which was, of course, in darkness.'

'Why?'

'Because he had turned the light out, sir.'

I nodded. I followed the idea.

'Sir Watkyn's instructions to him had been to keep his vigil in the dark, in order to convey to a marauder the impression that the room was unoccupied.'

I nodded again. It was a dirty trick, but one which would spring naturally to the mind of an ex-magistrate.

'He hurried to the case in which the cow-creamer had been deposited, and struck a match. This almost immediately went out, but not before he had been able to ascertain that the *objet d'art* had disappeared. And he was still in the process of endeavouring to adjust himself to the discovery, when he heard a movement and, turning, perceived a dim figure stealing out through the french window. He pursued it into the garden, and was overtaking it and might shortly have succeeded in effecting an arrest, when there sprang from the darkness a dim figure —'

'The same dim figure?'

'No, sir. Another one.'

'A big night for dim figures.'

'Yes, sir.'

260

'Better call them Pat and Mike, or we shall be getting mixed.'

'A and B perhaps, sir?

'If you prefer it, Jeeves. He was overtaking dim figure A, you say, when dim figure B sprang from the darkness — '

' — and struck him upon the nose.'

I uttered an exclamash. The thing was a mystery no longer.

'Old Stinker!'

'Yes, sir. No doubt Miss Byng inadvertently forgot to apprise him that there had been a change in the evening's arrangement.'

'And he was lurking there, waiting for me.'

'So one would be disposed to imagine, sir.'

I inhaled deeply, my thoughts playing about the constable's injured beezer. There, I was feeling, but for whatever it is, went Bertram Wooster, as the fellow said.

'This assault diverted the officer's attention, and the object of his pursuit was enabled to escape.'

'What became of Stinker?'

'On becoming aware of the officer's identity, he apologized, sir. He then withdrew.'

'I don't blame him. A pretty good idea, at that. Well, I don't know what to make of this, Jeeves. This dim figure. I am referring to dim figure A. Who could it have been? Had Oates any views on the subject?'

'Very definite views, sir. He is convinced that it was you.'

I stared.

'Me? Why the dickens has everything that

happens in this ghastly house got to be me?'

'And it is his intention, as soon as he is able to secure Sir Watkyn's co-operation, to proceed here and search your room.'

'He was going to do that, anyway, for the helmet.'

'Yes, sir.'

I couldn't help smiling. The thing tickled me.

'This is going to be rather funny, Jeeves. It will be entertaining to watch these two blighters ferret about, feeling sillier and sillier asses as each moment goes by and they find nothing.'

'Most diverting, sir.'

'And when the search is over and they are standing there baffled, stammering out weak apologies, I shall get a bit of my own back. I shall fold my arms and draw myself up to my full height — '

There came from without the hoof beats of a galloping relative, and Aunt Dahlia whizzed in.

'Here, shove this away somewhere, young Bertie,' she panted, seeming touched in the wind.

And so saying, she thrust the cow-creamer into my hands.

12

In my recent picture of Sir Watkyn Bassett reeling beneath the blow of hearing that I wanted to marry into his family, I compared his garglings, if you remember, to the death-rattle of a dying duck. I might now have been this duck's twin brother, equally stricken. For some moments I stood there, quacking feebly: then with a powerful effort of the will I pulled myself together and cheesed the bird imitation. I looked at Jeeves. He looked at me. I did not speak, save with the language of the eyes, but his trained senses enabled him to read my thoughts unerringly.

'Thank you, Jeeves.'

I took the tumbler from him, and lowered perhaps half an ounce of the raw spirit. Then, the dizzy spell overcome, I transferred my gaze to the aged relative, who was taking an easy in the armchair.

It is pretty generally admitted, both in the Drones Club and elsewhere, that Bertram Wooster in his dealings with the opposite sex invariably shows himself a man of the nicest chivalry — what you sometimes hear described as a *parfait gentil* knight. It is true that at the age of six, when the blood ran hot, I once gave my nurse a juicy one over the top knot with a porringer, but the lapse was merely a temporary one. Since then, though few men have been more sorely tried by the sex, I have never raised a hand against a woman. And I can give no better indication of my emotions at this moment than by saying that, *preux chevalier* though I am, I came within the veriest toucher of hauling off and letting a revered aunt have it on the side of the head with a *papier mâché* elephant — the only object on the mantelpiece which the fierce rush of life at Totleigh Towers had left still unbroken.

She, while this struggle was proceeding in my bosom, was at her chirpiest. Her breath recovered, she had begun to prattle with a carefree gaiety which cut me like a knife. It was obvious from her demeanour that, stringing along with the late Diamond, she little knew what she had done.

'As nice a run,' she was saying, 'as I have had since the last time I was out with the Berks and Bucks. Not a check from start to finish. Good clean British sport at its best. It was a close thing though, Bertie. I could feel that cop's hot breath on the back of my neck. If a posse of curates hadn't popped up out of a trap and lent a willing hand at precisely the right moment, he would have got me. Well, God bless the clergy, say I. A fine body of men. But what on earth were policemen doing on the premises? Nobody ever mentioned policemen to me.'

'That was Constable Oates, the vigilant guardian of the peace of Totleigh-in-the-Wold,' I replied, keeping a tight hold on myself lest I should howl like a banshee and shoot up to the ceiling. 'Sir Watkyn had stationed him in the room to watch over his belongings. He was lying in wait. I was the visitor he expected.'

'I'm glad you weren't the visitor he got. The situation would have been completely beyond you, my poor lamb. You would have lost your head and stood there like a stuffed wombat, to fall an easy prey. I don't mind telling you that when that man suddenly came in through the window, I myself was for a moment paralysed. Still, all's well that ends well.'

I shook a sombre head.

'You err, my misguided old object. This is not an end, but a beginning. Pop Bassett is about to spread a drag-net.'

'Let him.'

'And when he and the constable come and search this room?'

'They wouldn't do that.'

'They would and will. In the first place, they think the Oates helmet is here. In the second place, it is the officer's view, relayed to me by Jeeves, who had it from him first hand as he was staunching the flow of blood, that it was I whom he pursued.'

Her chirpiness waned. I had expected it would. She had been beaming. She beamed no longer. Eyeing her steadily, I saw that the native hue of resolution had become sicklied o'er with the pale cast of thought.

'H'm! This is awkward.'

'Most.'

'If they find the cow-creamer here, it may be a little difficult to explain.'

She rose, and broke the elephant thoughtfully.

'The great thing,' she said, 'is not to lose our heads. We must say to ourselves: 'What would

Napoleon have done?' He was the boy in a crisis. He knew his onions. We must do something very clever, very shrewd, which will completely baffle these bounders. Well, come on, I'm waiting for suggestions.'

'Mine is that you pop off without delay, taking that beastly cow with you.'

'And run into the search party on the stairs! Not if I know it. Have you any ideas, Jeeves?'

'Not at the moment, madam.'

'You can't produce a guilty secret of Sir Watkyn's out of the hat, as you did with Spode?'

'No, madam.'

'No, I suppose that's too much to ask. Then we've got to hide the thing somewhere. But where? It's the old problem, of course — the one that makes life so tough for murderers — what to do with the body. I suppose the old Purloined Letter stunt wouldn't work?'

'Mrs Travers is alluding to the well-known story by the late Edgar Allan Poe, sir,' said Jeeves, seeing that I was not abreast. 'It deals with the theft of an important document, and the character who had secured it foiled the police by placing it in full view in a letter-rack, his theory being that what is obvious is often overlooked. No doubt Mrs Travers wishes to suggest that we deposit the object on the mantelpiece.'

I laughed a hollow one.

'Take a look at the mantelpiece! It is as bare as a windswept prairie. Anything placed there would stick out like a sore thumb.'

'Yes, that's true,' Aunt Dahlia was forced to admit.

266

'Put the bally thing in the suitcase, Jeeves.'

'That's no good. They're bound to look there.'

'Merely as a palliative,' I explained. 'I can't stand the sight of it any longer. In with it, Jeeves.'

'Very good, sir.'

A silence ensued, and it was just after Aunt Dahlia had broken it to say how about barricading the door and standing a siege that there came from the passage the sound of approaching footsteps.

'Here they are,' I said.

'They seem in a hurry,' said Aunt Dahlia.

She was correct. These were running foot-steps. Jeeves went to the door and looked out.

'It is Mr Fink-Nottle, sir.'

And the next moment Gussie entered, going strongly.

A single glance at him was enough to reveal to the discerning eye that he had not been running just for the sake of the exercise. His spectacles were glittering in a hunted sort of way, and there was more than a touch of the fretful porpentine about his hair.

'Do you mind if I hide here till the milk train goes, Bertie?' he said. 'Under the bed will do. I shan't be in your way.'

'What's the matter?'

'Or, still better, the knotted sheet. That's the stuff.'

A snort like a minute-gun showed that Aunt Dahlia was in no welcoming mood.

'Get out of here, you foul Spink-Bottle,' she said curtly. 'We're in conference. Bertie, if an aunt's wishes have any weight with you, you will stamp on this man with both feet and throw him out on his ear.'

I raised a hand.

'Wait! I want to get the strength of this. Stop messing about with those sheets, Gussie and explain. Is Spode after you again? Because, if so — '

'Not Spode. Sir Watkyn.'

Aunt Dahlia snorted again, like one giving an encore in response to a popular demand.

'Bertie — '

I raised another hand.

'Half a second, old ancestor. How do you mean Sir Watkyn? Why Sir Watkyn? What on earth is he chivvying you for?'

'He's read the notebook.'

'What!'

'Yes.'

'Bertie, I am only a weak woman — '

I raised a third hand. This was no time for listening to aunts.

'Go on, Gussie,' I said dully.

He took off his spectacles and wiped them with a trembling handkerchief. You could see that he was a man who had passed through the furnace.

'When I left you, I went to his room. The door was ajar, and I crept in. And when I had got in, I found that he hadn't gone to have a bath, after all. He was sitting on the bed in his underwear, reading the notebook. He looked up, and our eyes met. You've no notion what a frightful shock it gave me.'

'Yes, I have. I once had a very similar

268

experience with the Rev. Aubrey Upjohn.'

'There was a long, dreadful pause. Then he uttered a sort of gurgling sound and rose, his face contorted. He made a leap in my direction. I pushed off. He followed. It was neck and neck down the stairs, but as we passed through the hall he stopped to get a hunting crop, and this enabled me to secure a good lead, which I — '

'Bertie,' said Aunt Dahlia, 'I am only a weak woman, but if you won't tread on this insect and throw the remains outside, I shall have to see what I can do. The most tremendous issues hanging in the balance . . . Our plan of action still to be decided on . . . Every second of priceless importance . . . and he comes in here, telling us the story of his life. Spink-Bottle, you ghastly goggle-eyed piece of gorgonzola, will you hop it or will you not?'

There is a compelling force about the old flesh and blood, when stirred, which generally gets her listened to. People have told me that in her hunting days she could make her wishes respected across two ploughed fields and a couple of spinneys. The word 'not' had left her lips like a high-powered shell, and Gussie, taking it between the eyes, rose some six inches into the air. When he returned to terra firma, his manner was apologetic and conciliatory.

'Yes, Mrs Travers. I'm just going, Mrs Travers. The moment we get the sheet working, Mrs Travers. If you and Jeeves will just hold this end, Bertie — '

'You want them to let you down from the window with a sheet?'

'Yes, Mrs Travers. Then I can borrow Bertie's car and drive to London.'

'It's a long drop.'

'Oh, not so very, Mrs Travers.'

'You may break your neck.'

'Oh, I don't think so, Mrs Travers.'

'But you may,' argued Aunt Dahlia. 'Come on, Bertie,' she said, speaking with real enthusiasm, 'hurry up. Let the man down with the sheet, can't you? What are you waiting for?'

I turned to Jeeves. 'Ready, Jeeves?'

'Yes, sir.' He coughed gently. 'And perhaps if Mr Fink-Nottle is driving your car to London, he might take your suitcase with him and leave it at the flat.'

I gasped. So did Aunt Dahlia. I stared at him. Aunt Dahlia the same. Our eyes met, and I saw in hers the same reverent awe which I have no doubt she viewed in mine.

I was overcome. A moment before, I had been dully conscious that nothing could save me from the soup. Already I had seemed to hear the beating of its wings. And now this!

Aunt Dahlia, speaking of Napoleon, had claimed that he was pretty hot in an emergency, but I was prepared to bet that not even Napoleon could have topped this superb effort. Once more, as so often in the past, the man had rung the bell and was entitled to the cigar or coconut.

'Yes, Jeeves,' I said, speaking with some difficulty, 'that is true. He might, mightn't he?'

'Yes, sir.'

'You won't mind taking my suitcase, Gussie. If

you're borrowing the car, I shall have to go by train. I'm leaving in the morning myself. And it's a nuisance hauling about a lot of luggage.'

'Of course.'

'We'll just loose you down on the sheet and drop the suitcase after you. All set, Jeeves?'

'Yes, sir.'

'Then upsy-daisy!'

I don't think I have ever assisted at a ceremony which gave such universal pleasure to all concerned. The sheet didn't split, which pleased Gussie. Nobody came to interrupt us, which pleased me. And when I dropped the suitcase, it hit Gussie on the head, which delighted Aunt Dahlia. As for Jeeves, one could see that the faithful fellow was tickled pink at having been able to cluster round and save the young master in his hour of peril. His motto is 'Service'.

The stormy emotions through which I had been passing had not unnaturally left me weak, and I was glad when Aunt Dahlia, after a powerful speech in which she expressed her gratitude to our preserver in well-phrased terms, said that she would hop along and see what was going on in the enemy's camp. Her departure enabled me to sink into the armchair in which, had she remained, she would unquestionably have parked herself indefinitely. I flung myself on the cushioned seat and emitted a woof that came straight from the heart.

'So that's that, Jeeves!'

'Yes, sir.'

'Once again your swift thinking has averted disaster as it loomed.'

'It is very kind of you to say so, sir.'

'Not kind, Jeeves. I am merely saying what any thinking man would say. I didn't chip in while Aunt Dahlia was speaking, for I saw that she wished to have the floor, but you may take it that I was silently subscribing to every sentiment she uttered. You stand alone, Jeeves. What size hat do you take?'

'A number eight, sir.'

'I should have thought larger. Eleven or twelve.'

I helped myself to a spot of brandy, and sat rolling it round my tongue luxuriantly. It was delightful to relax after the strain and stress I had been through.

'Well, Jeeves, the going has been pretty tough, what?'

'Extremely, sir.'

'One begins to get some idea of how the skipper of the *Hesperus's* little daughter must have felt. Still, I suppose these tests and trials are good for the character.'

'No doubt, sir.'

'Strengthening.'

'Yes, sir.'

'However, I can't say I'm sorry it's all over. Enough is always enough. And it is all over, one feels. Even this sinister house can surely have no further shocks to offer.'

'I imagine not, sir.'

'No, this is the finish. Totleigh Towers has shot its bolt, and at long last we are sitting pretty. Gratifying, Jeeves.'

'Most gratifying, sir.'

'You bet it is. Carry on with the packing. I want to get it done and go to bed.'

He opened the small suitcase, and I lit a cigarette and proceeded to stress the moral lesson to be learned from all this rannygazoo.

'Yes, Jeeves, 'gratifying' is the word. A short while ago, the air was congested with V-shaped depressions, but now one looks north, south, east and west and descries not a single cloud on the horizon — except the fact that Gussie's wedding is still off, and that can't be helped. Well, this should certainly teach us, should it not, never to repine, never to despair, never to allow the upper lip to unstiffen, but always to remember that, no matter how dark the skies may be, the sun is shining somewhere and will eventually come smiling through.'

I paused. I perceived that I was not securing his attention. He was looking down with an intent, thoughtful expression on his face.

'Something the matter, Jeeves?'

'Sir?'

'You appear preoccupied.'

'Yes, sir. I have just discovered that there is a policeman's helmet in this suitcase.'

13

I had been right about the strengthening effect on the character of the vicissitudes to which I had been subjected since clocking in at the country residence of Sir Watkyn Bassett. Little by little, bit by bit, they had been moulding me, turning me from a sensitive clubman and *boulevardier* to a man of chilled steel. A novice to conditions in this pest house, abruptly handed the news item which I had just been handed, would, I imagine, have rolled up the eyeballs and swooned where he sat. But I, toughened and fortified by the routine of one damn thing after another which constituted life at Totleigh Towers, was enabled to keep my head and face the issue.

I don't say I didn't leave my chair like a jack-rabbit that has sat on a cactus, but having risen I wasted no time in fruitless twitterings. I went to the door and locked it. Then, tight-lipped and pale, I came back to Jeeves, who had now taken the helmet from the suitcase and was oscillating it meditatively by its strap.

His first words showed me that he had got the wrong angle on the situation.

'It would have been wiser, sir,' he said with faint reproach, 'to have selected some more adequate hiding-place.'

I shook my head. I may even have smiled — wanly, of course. My swift intelligence had enabled me to probe to the bottom of this thing.

'Not me, Jeeves. Stiffy.'

'Sir?'

'The hand that placed that helmet there was not mine, but that of S. Byng. She had it in her room. She feared lest a search might be instituted, and when I last saw her was trying to think of a safer spot. This is her idea of one.'

I sighed.

'How do you imagine a girl gets a mind like Stiffy's, Jeeves?'

'Certainly the young lady is somewhat eccentric in her actions, sir.'

'Eccentric? She could step straight into Colney Hatch, and no questions asked. They would lay down the red carpet for her. The more the thoughts dwell on that young shrimp, the more the soul sickens in horror. One peers into the future, and shudders at what one sees there. One has to face it, Jeeves — Stiffy, who is pure padded cell from the foundations up, is about to marry the Rev. H. P. Pinker, himself about as pronounced a goop as ever broke bread, and there is no reason to suppose — one has to face this, too — that their union will not be blessed. There will, that is to say, 'ere long be little feet pattering about the home. And what one asks oneself is — Just how safe will human life be in the vicinity of those feet, assuming — as one is forced to assume — that they will inherit the combined loopiness of two such parents? It is with a sort of tender pity, Jeeves, that I think of the nurses, the governesses, the private-school masters and the public-school masters who will lightly take on the responsibility of looking after a blend of Stephanie Byng and Harold Pinker, little knowing that they are coming up against something hotter than mustard. However,' I went on, abandoning these speculations, 'all this, though of absorbing interest, is not really germane to the issue. Contemplating that helmet and bearing in mind the fact that the Oates-Bassett comedy duo will be arriving at any moment to start their search, what would you recommend?'

'It is a little difficult to say, sir. A really effective hiding place for so bulky an object does not readily present itself.'

'No. The damn thing seems to fill the room, doesn't it?'

'It unquestionably takes the eye, sir.'

'Yes. The authorities wrought well when they shaped this helmet for Constable Oates. They aimed to finish him off impressively, not to give him something which would balance on top of his head like a peanut, and they succeeded. You couldn't hide a lid like this in an impenetrable jungle. Ah, well,' I said, 'we will just have to see what tact and suavity will do. I wonder when these birds are going to arrive. I suppose we may expect them very shortly. Ah! That would be the hand of doom now, if I mistake not, Jeeves.'

But in assuming that the knocker who had just knocked on the door was Sir Watkyn Bassett, I had erred. It was Stiffy's voice that spoke.

'Bertie, let me in.'

There was nobody I was more anxious to see, but I did not immediately fling wide the gates. Prudence dictated a preliminary inquiry.

'Have you got that bally dog of yours with you?'

'No. He's being aired by the butler.'

'In that case, you may enter.'

When she did so, it was to find Bertram confronting her with folded arms and a hard look. She appeared, however, not to note my forbidding exterior.

'Bertie, darling — '

She broke off, checked by a fairly animal snarl from the Wooster lips.

'Not so much of the 'Bertie, darling'. I have just one thing to say to you, young Stiffy, and it is this: Was it you who put that helmet in my suitcase?'

'Of course it was. That's what I was coming to talk to you about. You remember I was trying to think of a good place. I racked the brain quite a bit, and then suddenly I got it.'

'And now I've got it.'

The acidity of my tone seemed to surprise her. She regarded me with girlish wonder — the wide-eyed kind.

'But you don't mind, do you, Bertie, darling?'

'Ha!'

'But why? I thought you would be so glad to help me out.'

'Oh, yes?' I said, and I meant it to sting.

'I couldn't risk having Uncle Watkyn find it in my room.'

'You preferred to have him find it in mine?'

'But how can he? He can't come searching your room.'

'He can't, eh?'

'Of course not. You're his guest.'

'And you suppose that that will cause him to

hold his hand?' I smiled one of those bitter, sardonic smiles. 'I think you are attributing to the old poison germ a niceness of feeling and a respect for the laws of hospitality which nothing in his record suggests that he possesses. You can take it from me that he definitely is going to search the room, and I imagine that the only reason he hasn't arrived already is that he is still scouring the house for Gussie.'

'Gussie?'

'He is at the moment chasing Gussie with a hunting crop. But a man cannot go on doing that indefinitely. Sooner or later he will give it up, and then we shall have him here, complete with magnifying glass and bloodhounds.'

The gravity of the situash had at last impressed itself upon her. She uttered a squeak of dismay, and her eyes became a bit soup-platey.

'Oh, Bertie! Then I'm afraid I've put you in rather a spot.'

'That covers the facts like a dust-sheet.'

'I'm sorry now I ever asked Harold to pinch the thing. It was a mistake. I admit it. Still, after all, even if Uncle Watkyn does come here and find it, it doesn't matter much, does it?'

'Did you hear that, Jeeves?'

'Yes, sir.'

'So did I. I see. It doesn't matter, you feel?'

'Well, what I mean is your reputation won't really suffer much, will it? Everybody knows that you can't keep your hands off policemen's helmets. This'll be just another one.'

'Ha! And what leads you to suppose, young Stiffy, that when the Assyrian comes down like a

278

wolf on the fold I shall meekly assume the guilt and not blazon the truth — what, Jeeves?'

'Forth to the world, sir.'

'Thank you, Jeeves. What makes you suppose that I shall meekly assume the guilt and not blazon the truth forth to the world?'

I wouldn't have supposed that her eyes could have widened any more, but they did perceptibly. Another dismayed squeak escaped her. Indeed, such was its volume that it might perhaps be better to call it a squeal.

'But, Bertie!'

'Well?'

'Bertie, listen!'

'I'm listening.'

'Surely you will take the rap? You can't let Harold get it in the neck. You were telling me this afternoon that he would be unfrocked. I won't have him unfrocked. Where is he going to get if they unfrock him? That sort of thing gives a curate a frightful black eye. Why can't you say you did it? All it would mean is that you would be kicked out of the house, and I don't suppose you're so anxious to stay on, are you?'

'Possibly you are not aware that your bally uncle is proposing to send the perpetrator of this outrage to chokey.'

'Oh, no. At the worst, just a fine.'

'Nothing of the kind. He specifically told me chokey.'

'He didn't mean it. I expect there was — '

'No, there was not a twinkle in his eye.'

'Then that settles it. I can't have my precious, angel Harold doing a stretch.'

279

'How about your precious, angel Bertram?'

'But Harold's so sensitive.'

'So am I sensitive.'

'Not half so sensitive as Harold. Bertie, surely you aren't going to be difficult about this? You're much too good a sport. Didn't you tell me once that the Code of the Woosters was 'Never let a pal down'?'

She had found the talking point. People who appeal to the Code of the Woosters rarely fail to touch a chord in Bertram. My iron front began to crumble.

'That's all very fine — '

'Bertie, darling!'

'Yes, I know, but, dash it all — '

'Bertie!'

'Oh, well!'

'You will take the rap?'

'I suppose so.'

She yodelled ecstatically, and I think that if I had not sidestepped she would have flung her arms about my neck. Certainly she came leaping forward with some such purpose apparently in view. Foiled by my agility, she began to tear off a few steps of that spring dance to which she was so addicted.

'Thank you, Bertie, darling. I knew you would be sweet about it. I can't tell you how grateful I am, and how much I admire you. You remind me of Carter Paterson . . . no, that's not it . . . Nick Carter . . . no, not Nick Carter . . . Who does Mr Wooster remind me of, Jeeves?'

'Sidney Carton, miss.'

'That's right. Sidney Carton. But he was

smalltime stuff compared with you, Bertie. And, anyway, I expect we are getting the wind up quite unnecessarily. Why are we taking it for granted that Uncle Watkyn will find the helmet, if he comes and searches the room? There are a hundred places where you can hide it.'

And before I could say 'Name three!' she had pirouetted to the door and pirouetted out. I could hear her dying away in the distance with a song on her lips.

My own, as I turned to Jeeves, were twisted in a bitter smile.

'Women, Jeeves!'

'Yes, sir.'

'Well, Jeeves,' I said, my hand stealing towards the decanter, 'this is the end!'

'No, sir.'

I started with a violence that nearly unshipped my front uppers.

'Not the end?'

'No, sir.'

'You don't mean you have an idea?'

'Yes, sir.'

'But you told me just now you hadn't.'

'Yes, sir. But since then I have been giving the matter some thought, and am now in a position to say "Eureka!"'

'Say what?'

'Eureka, sir. Like Archimedes.'

'Did he say Eureka? I thought it was Shakespeare.'

'No, sir. Archimedes. What I would recommend is that you drop the helmet out of the window. It is most improbable that it will occur to Sir Watkyn to search the exterior of the premises, and we shall be able to recover it at our leisure.' He paused, and stood listening. 'Should this suggestion meet with your approval, sir, I feel that a certain haste would be advisable. I fancy I can hear the sound of approaching footsteps.'

He was right. The air was vibrant with their clumping. Assuming that a herd of bison was not making its way along the second-floor passage of Totleigh Towers, the enemy were upon us. With the nippiness of a lamb in the fold on observing the approach of Assyrians, I snatched up the helmet, bounded to the window and loosed the thing into the night. And scarcely had I done so, when the door opened, and through it came — in the order named — Aunt Dahlia, wearing an amused and indulgent look, as if she were joining in some game to please the children, Pop Bassett, in a purple dressing gown, and Police Constable Oates, who was dabbing at his nose with a pocket-handkerchief.

'So sorry to disturb you, Bertie,' said the aged relative courteously.

'Not at all,' I replied with equal suavity. 'Is there something I can do for the multitude?'

'Sir Watkyn has got some extraordinary idea into his head about wanting to search your room.'

'Search my room?'

'I intend to search it from top to bottom,' said old Bassett, looking very Bosher Street-y.

I glanced at Aunt Dahlia, raising the eyebrows.

'I don't understand. What's all this about?'

She laughed indulgently.

'You will scarcely believe it, Bertie, but he thinks that cow-creamer is here.'

'Is it missing?'

'It's been stolen.'

'You don't say!'

'Yes.'

'Well, well, well.'

'He's very upset about it.'

'I don't wonder.'

'Most distressed.'

'Poor old bloke.'

I placed a kindly hand on Pop Bassett's shoulder. Probably the wrong thing to do, I can see, looking back, for it did not soothe.

'I can do without your condolences, Mr Wooster, and I should be glad if you would not refer to me as a bloke. I have every reason to believe that not only is my cow-creamer in your possession, but Constable Oates's helmet, as well.'

A cheery guffaw seemed in order. I uttered it.

'Ha, ha!'

Aunt Dahlia came across with another.

'Ha, ha!'

'How dashed absurd!'

'Perfectly ridiculous.'

'What on earth would I be doing with cow-creamers?'

'Or policemen's helmets?'

'Quite.'

'Did you ever hear such a weird idea?'

'Never. My dear old host,' I said, 'let us keep perfectly calm and cool and get all this straightened out. In the kindliest spirit, I must point out that you are on the verge — if not slightly past the verge — of making an ass of yourself. This sort of thing won't do, you know. You can't dash about accusing people of nameless crimes without a shadow of evidence.'

'I have all the evidence I require, Mr Wooster.'

'That's what you think. And that, I maintain, is where you are making the floater of a lifetime. When was this modern Dutch gadget of yours abstracted?'

He quivered beneath the thrust, pinkening at the tip of the nose.

'It is not modern Dutch!'

'Well, we can thresh that out later. The point is: When did it leave the premises?'

'It has not left the premises.'

'That, again, is what you think. Well, when was it stolen?'

'About twenty minutes ago.'

'Then there you are. Twenty minutes ago I was up here in my room.'

This rattled him. I had thought it would.

'You were in your room?'

'In my room.'

'Alone?'

'On the contrary. Jeeves was here.'

'Who is Jeeves?'

'Don't you know Jeeves? This is Jeeves. Jeeves . . . Sir Watkyn Bassett.'

'And who may you be, my man?'

'That's exactly what he is — my man. May I say my right-hand man?'

'Thank you, sir.'

'Not at all, Jeeves. Well-earned tribute.'

Pop Bassett's face was disfigured, if you could disfigure a face like his, by an ugly sneer.

'I regret, Mr Wooster, that I am not prepared to accept as conclusive evidence of your innocence the unsupported word of your manservant.'

'Unsupported, eh? Jeeves, go and page Mr Spode. Tell him I want him to come and put a bit of stuffing into my alibi.'

'Very good, sir.'

He shimmered away, and Pop Bassett seemed to swallow something hard and jagged.

'Was Roderick Spode with you?'

'Certainly he was. Perhaps you will believe him?'

'Yes, I would believe Roderick Spode.'

'Very well, then. He'll be here in a moment.'

He appeared to muse.

'I see. Well, apparently I was wrong, then, in supposing that you are concealing my cow-creamer. It must have been purloined by somebody else.'

'Outside job, if you ask me,' said Aunt Dahlia.

'Possibly the work of an international gang,' I hazarded.

'Very likely.'

'I expect it was all over the place that Sir Watkyn had bought the thing. You remember Uncle Tom had been counting on getting it, and no doubt he told all sorts of people where it had gone. It wouldn't take long for the news to filter through to the international gangs. They keep their ear to the ground.'

'Damn clever, those gangs,' assented the aged relative.

Pop Bassett had seemed to me to wince a trifle at the mention of Uncle Tom's name. Guilty conscience doing its stuff, no doubt — gnawing, as these guilty consciences do.

'Well, we need not discuss the matter further,' he said. 'As regards the cow-creamer, I admit that you have established your case. We will now turn to Constable Oates's helmet. That, Mr Wooster, I happen to know positively, is in your possession.'

'Oh, yes?'

'Yes. The constable received specific information on the point from an eyewitness. I will proceed, therefore, to search your room without delay.'

'You really feel you want to?'

'I do.'

I shrugged the shoulders.

'Very well,' I said, 'very well. If that is the spirit in which you interpret the duties of a host, carry on. We invite inspection. I can only say that you appear to have extraordinarily rummy views on making your guests comfortable over the weekend. Don't count on my coming here again.'

I had expressed the opinion to Jeeves that it would be entertaining to stand by and watch this blighter and his colleague ferret about, and so it proved. I don't know when I have extracted more solid amusement from anything. But all these good things have to come to an end at last. About ten minutes later, it was plain that the bloodhounds were planning to call it off and pack up.

To say that Pop Bassett was wry, as he desisted from his efforts and turned to me, would be to understate it.

'I appear to owe you an apology, Mr Wooster,' he said.

'Sir W. Bassett,' I rejoined, 'you never spoke a truer word.'

And folding my arms and drawing myself up to my full height, I let him have it.

The exact words of my harangue have, I am sorry to say, escaped my memory. It is a pity that there was nobody taking them down in shorthand, for I am not exaggerating when I say that I surpassed myself. Once or twice, when a bit lit at routs and revels, I have spoken with an eloquence which, rightly or wrongly, has won the plaudits of the Drones Club, but I don't think that I have ever quite reached the level to which I now soared. You could see the stuffing trickling out of old Bassett in great heaping handfuls.

But as I rounded into my peroration, I suddenly noticed that I was failing to grip. He had ceased to listen, and was staring past me at something out of my range of vision. And so worth looking at did this spectacle, judging from his expression, appear to be that I turned in order to take a dekko.

It was the butler who had so riveted Sir Watkyn Bassett's attention. He was standing in the doorway, holding in his right hand a silver salver. And on that salver was a policeman's helmet.

14

I remember old Stinker Pinker, who towards the end of his career at Oxford used to go in for social service in London's tougher districts, describing to me once in some detail the sensations he had experienced one afternoon, while spreading the light in Bethnal Green, on being unexpectedly kicked in the stomach by a costermonger. It gave him, he told me, a strange, dreamy feeling, together with an odd illusion of having walked into a thick fog. And the reason I mention it is that my own emotions at this moment were extraordinarily similar.

When I had last seen this butler, if you recollect, on the occasion when he had come to tell me that Madeline Bassett would be glad if I could spare her a moment, I mentioned that he had flickered. It was not so much at a flickering butler that I was gazing now as at a sort of heaving mist with a vague suggestion of something butlerine vibrating inside it. Then the scales fell from my eyes, and I was enabled to note the reactions of the rest of the company.

They were all taking it extremely big. Pop Bassett, like the chap in the poem which I had to write out fifty times at school for introducing a white mouse into the English Literature hour, was plainly feeling like some watcher of the skies when a new planet swims into his ken, while Aunt Dahlia and Constable Oates resembled respectively stout Cortez staring at the Pacific and all his men looking at each other with a wild surmise, silent upon a peak in Darien.

It was a goodish while before anybody stirred. Then, with a choking cry like that of a mother spotting her long-lost child in the offing, Constable Oates swooped forward and grabbed the lid, clasping it to his bosom with visible ecstasy.

The movement seemed to break the spell. Old Bassett came to life as if someone had pressed a button.

'Where — where did you get that, Butterfield?'

'I found it in a flower bed, Sir Watkyn.'

'In a flower bed?'

'Odd,' I said. 'Very strange.'

'Yes, sir. I was airing Miss Byng's dog, and happening to be passing the side of the house I observed Mr Wooster drop something from his window. It fell into the flower bed beneath, and upon inspection proved to be this helmet.'

Old Bassett drew a deep breath.

'Thank you, Butterfield.'

The butler breezed off, and old B., revolving on his axis, faced me with gleaming pince-nez.

'So!' he said.

There is never very much you can do in the way of a telling come-back when a fellow says 'So!' to you. I preserved a judicious silence.

'Some mistake,' said Aunt Dahlia, taking the floor with an intrepidity which became her well. 'Probably came from one of the other windows. Easy to get confused on a dark night.'

'Tchah!'

'Or it may be that the man was lying. Yes, that seems a plausible explanation. I think I see it all. This Butterfield of yours is the guilty man. He stole the helmet, and knowing that the hunt was up and detection imminent, decided to play a bold game and try to shove it off on Bertie. Eh, Bertie?'

'I shouldn't wonder, Aunt Dahlia. I shouldn't wonder at all.'

'Yes, that is what must have happened. It becomes clearer every moment. You can't trust these saintly looking butlers an inch.'

'Not an inch.'

'I remember thinking the fellow had a furtive eye.'

'Me, too.'

'You noticed it yourself, did you?'

'Right away.'

'He reminds me of Murgatroyd. Do you remember Murgatroyd at Brinkley, Bertie?'

'The fellow before Pomeroy? Stoutish cove?'

'That's right. With a face like a more than usually respectable archbishop. Took us all in, that face. We trusted him implicitly. And what was the result? Fellow pinched a fish slice, put it up the spout and squandered the proceeds at the dog races. This Butterfield is another Murgatroyd.'

'Some relation, perhaps.'

'I shouldn't be surprised. Well, now that that's all satisfactorily settled and Bertie dismissed without a stain on his character, how about all going to bed? It's getting late, and if I don't have my eight hours, I'm a rag.'

She had injected into the proceedings such a pleasant atmosphere of all-pals-together and hearty let's-say-no-more-about-it that it came quite as a shock to find that old Bassett was failing to see eye to eye. He proceeded immediately to strike the jarring note.

'With your theory that somebody is lying, Mrs Travers, I am in complete agreement But when you assert that it is my butler, I must join issue with you. Mr Wooster has been exceedingly clever — most ingenious — '

'Oh, thanks.'

' — but I am afraid that I find myself unable to dismiss him, as you suggest, without a stain on his character. In fact, to be frank with you, I do not propose to dismiss him at all.'

He gave me the pince-nez in a cold and menacing manner. I can't remember when I've seen a man I liked the look of less.

'You may possibly recall, Mr Wooster, that in the course of our conversation in the library I informed you that I took the very gravest view of this affair. Your suggestion that I might be content with inflicting a fine of five pounds, as was the case when you appeared before me at Bosher Street convicted of a similar outrage, I declared myself unable to accept. I assured you that the perpetrator of this wanton assault on the person of Constable Oates would, when apprehended, serve a prison sentence. I see no reason to revise that decision.'

This statement had a mixed press. Eustace Oates obviously approved. He looked up from the helmet with a quick, encouraging smile and but for the iron restraint of discipline would, I think, have said 'Hear, hear!' Aunt Dahlia and I, on the other hand, didn't like it.

'Here, come, I say now, Sir Watkyn, really, dash it,' she expostulated, always on her toes when the interests of the clan were threatened. 'You can't do that sort of thing.'

'Madam, I both can and will.' He twiddled a hand in the direction of Eustace Oates. 'Constable!'

He didn't add 'Arrest this man!' or 'Do your duty!' but the officer got the gist. He clumped forward zealously. I was rather expecting him to lay a hand on my shoulder or to produce the gyves and apply them to my wrists, but he didn't. He merely lined up beside me as if we were going to do a duet and stood there looking puff-faced.

Aunt Dahlia continued to plead and reason.

'But you can't invite a man to your house and the moment he steps inside the door calmly bung him into the coop. If that is Gloucestershire hospitality, then heaven help Gloucestershire.'

'Mr Wooster is not here on my invitation, but on my daughter's.'

'That makes no difference. You can't wriggle out of it like that. He is your guest. He has eaten your salt. And let me tell you, while we are on the subject, that there was a lot too much of it in the soup tonight.'

'Oh, would you say that?' I said. 'Just about right, it seemed to me.'

'No. Too salty.'

Pop Bassett intervened.

'I must apologize for the shortcomings of my cook. I may be making a change before long. Meanwhile, to return to the subject with which we were dealing, Mr Wooster is under arrest, and tomorrow I shall take the necessary steps to — '

'And what's going to happen to him tonight?'

'We maintain a small but serviceable police station in the village, presided over by Constable Oates. Oates will doubtless be able to find him accommodation.'

'You aren't proposing to lug the poor chap off to a police station at this time of night? You could at least let him doss in a decent bed.'

'Yes, I see no objection to that. One does not wish to be unduly harsh. You may remain in this room until tomorrow, Mr Wooster.'

'Oh, thanks.'

'I shall lock the door — '

'Oh, quite.'

'And take charge of the key — '

'Oh, rather.'

'And Constable Oates will patrol beneath the window for the remainder of the night.'

'Sir?'

'This will check Mr Wooster's known propensity for dropping things from windows. You had better take up your station at once, Oates.'

'Very good, sir.'

There was a note of quiet anguish in the officer's voice, and it was plain that the smug satisfaction with which he had been watching the progress of events had waned. His views on getting his eight hours were apparently the same as Aunt Dahlia's. Saluting sadly, he left the room

293

in a depressed sort of way. He had his helmet again, but you could see that he was beginning to ask himself if helmets were everything.

'And now, Mrs Travers, I should like, if I may, to have a word with you in private.'

They oiled off, and I was alone.

I don't mind confessing that my emotions, as the key turned in the lock, were a bit poignant. On the one hand, it was nice to feel that I had got my bedroom to myself for a few minutes, but against that you had to put the fact that I was in what is known as durance vile and not likely to get out of it.

Of course, this was not new stuff to me, for I had heard the bars clang outside my cell door that time at Bosher Street. But on that occasion I had been able to buoy myself up with the reflection that the worst the aftermath was likely to provide was a rebuke from the bench or, as subsequently proved to be the case, a punch in the pocket-book. I was not faced, as I was faced now, by the prospect of waking on the morrow to begin serving a sentence of thirty days' duration in a prison where it was most improbable that I would be able to get my morning cup of tea.

Nor did the consciousness that I was innocent seem to help much. I drew no consolation from the fact that Stiffy Byng thought me like Sidney Carton. I had never met the chap, but I gathered that he was somebody who had taken it on the chin to oblige a girl, and to my mind this was enough to stamp him as a priceless ass. Sidney Carton and Bertram Wooster, I felt — nothing to choose between them. Sidney, one of the mugs

— Bertram, the same.

I went to the window and looked out. Recalling the moody distaste which Constable Oates had exhibited at the suggestion that he should stand guard during the night hours, I had a faint hope that, once the eye of authority was removed, he might have ducked the assignment and gone off to get his beauty sleep. But no. There he was, padding up and down on the lawn, the picture of vigilance. And I had just gone to the washhand-stand to get a cake of soap to bung at him, feeling that this might soothe the bruised spirit a little, when I heard the door handle rattle.

I stepped across and put my lips to the woodwork.

'Hallo.'

'It is I, sir. Jeeves.'

'Oh, hallo, Jeeves.'

'The door appears to be locked, sir.'

'And you can take it from me, Jeeves, that appearances do not deceive. Pop Bassett locked it, and has trousered the key.'

'Sir?'

'I've been pinched.'

'Indeed, sir?'

'What was that?'

'I said 'Indeed, sir?''

'Oh, did you? Yes. Yes, indeed. And I'll tell you why.'

I gave him a *précis* of what had happened. It was not easy to hear, with a door between us, but I think the narrative elicited a spot of respectful tut-tutting.

'Unfortunate, sir.'

'Most. Well, Jeeves, what is your news?'

'I endeavoured to locate Mr Spode, sir, but he had gone for a walk in the grounds. No doubt he will be returning shortly.'

'Well, we shan't require him now. The rapid march of events has taken us far past the point where Spode could have been of service. Anything else been happening at your end?'

'I have had a word with Miss Byng, sir.'

'I should like a word with her myself. What had she to say?'

'The young lady was in considerable distress of mind, sir, her union with the Reverend Mr Pinker having been forbidden by Sir Watkyn.'

'Good Lord, Jeeves! Why?'

'Sir Watkyn appears to have taken umbrage at the part played by Mr Pinker in allowing the purloiner of the cow-creamer to effect his escape.'

'Why do you say 'his'?'

'From motives of prudence, sir. Walls have ears.'

'I see what you mean. That's rather neat, Jeeves.'

'Thank you, sir.'

I mused a while on this latest development. There were certainly aching hearts in Gloucestershire all right this PM. I was conscious of a pang of pity. Despite the fact that it was entirely owing to Stiffy that I found myself in my present predic., I wished the young loony well and mourned for her in her hour of disaster.

'So he has bunged a spanner into Stiffy's

romance as well as Gussie's, has he? That old bird has certainly been throwing his weight about tonight, Jeeves.'

'Yes, sir.'

'And not a thing to be done about it, as far as I can see. Can you see anything to be done about it?'

'No, sir.'

'And switching to another aspect of the affair, you haven't any immediate plans for getting me out of this, I suppose?'

'Not adequately formulated, sir. I am turning over an idea in my mind.'

'Turn well, Jeeves. Spare no effort.'

'But it is at present merely nebulous.'

'It involves finesse, I presume?'

'Yes, sir.'

I shook my head. Waste of time really, of course, because he couldn't see me. Still, I shook it.

'It's no good trying to be subtle and snaky now, Jeeves. What is required is rapid action. And a thought has occurred to me. We were speaking not long since of the time when Sir Roderick Glossop was immured in the potting-shed, with Constable Dobson guarding every exit. Do you remember what old Pop Stoker's idea was for coping with the situation?'

'If I recollect rightly, sir, Mr Stoker advocated a physical assault upon the officer. 'Bat him over the head with a shovel!' was, as I recall, his expression.'

'Correct, Jeeves. Those were his exact words. And though we scouted the idea at the time, it seems to me now that he displayed a

297

considerable amount of rugged good sense. These practical, self-made men have a long way of going straight to the point and avoiding side issues. Constable Oates is on sentry go beneath my window. I still have the knotted sheets and they can readily be attached to the leg of the bed or something. So if you would just borrow a shovel somewhere and step down — '

'I fear, sir — '

'Come on, Jeeves. This is no time for *nolle prosequis*. I know you like finesse, but you must see that it won't help us now. The moment has arrived when only shovels can serve. You could go and engage him in conversation, keeping the instrument concealed behind your back, and waiting for the psychological — '

'Excuse me, sir. I think I hear somebody coming.'

'Well, ponder over what I have said. Who is coming?'

'It is Sir Watkyn and Mrs Travers, sir. I fancy they are about to call upon you.'

'I thought I shouldn't get this room to myself for long. Still, let them come. We Woosters keep open house.'

When the door was unlocked a few moments later, however, only the relative entered. She made for the old familiar armchair, and dumped herself heavily in it. Her demeanour was sombre, encouraging no hope that she had come to announce that Pop Bassett, wiser counsels having prevailed, had decided to set me free. And yet I'm dashed if that wasn't precisely what she had come to announce.

'Well, Bertie,' she said, having brooded in silence for a space, 'you can get on with your packing.'

'Eh?'

'He's called it off.'

'Called it off?'

'Yes. He isn't going to press the charge.'

'You mean I'm not headed for chokey?'

'No.'

'I'm as free as the air, as the expression is?'

'Yes.'

I was so busy rejoicing in spirit that it was some moments before I had leisure to observe that the buck-and-wing dance which I was performing was not being abetted by the old flesh and blood. She was still carrying on with her sombre sitting, and I looked at her with a touch of reproach.

'You don't seem very pleased.'

'Oh, I'm delighted.'

'I fail to detect the symptoms,' I said, rather coldly. 'I should have thought that a nephew's reprieve at the foot of the scaffold, as you might say, would have produced a bit of leaping and springing about.'

A deep sigh escaped her.

'Well, the trouble is, Bertie, there is a catch in it. The old buzzard has made a condition.'

'What is it?'

'He wants Anatole.'

I stared at her.

'Wants Anatole?'

'Yes. That is the price of your freedom. He says he will agree not to press the charge if I let him have Anatole. The darned old blackmailer!'

A spasm of anguish twisted her features. It was not so very long since she had been speaking in high terms of blackmail and giving it her hearty approval, but if you want to derive real satisfaction from blackmail, you have to be at the right end of it. Catching it coming, as it were, instead of going, this woman was suffering.

I wasn't feeling any too good myself. From time to time in the course of this narrative I have had occasion to indicate my sentiments regarding Anatole, that peerless artist, and you will remember that the relative's account of how Sir Watkyn Bassett had basely tried to snitch him from her employment during his visit to Brinkley Court had shocked me to my foundations.

It is difficult, of course, to convey to those who have not tasted this wizard's products the extraordinary importance which his roasts and boileds assume in the scheme of things to those who have. I can only say that once having bitten into one of his dishes you are left with the feeling that life will be deprived of all its poetry and meaning unless you are in a position to go on digging in. The thought that Aunt Dahlia was prepared to sacrifice this wonder man merely to save a nephew from the cooler was one that struck home and stirred.

I don't know when I have been so profoundly moved. It was with a melting eye that I gazed at her. She reminded me of Sidney Carton.

'You were actually contemplating giving up Anatole for my sake?' I gasped.

'Of course.'

300

'Of course jolly well not! I wouldn't hear of such a thing.'

'But you can't go to prison.'

'I certainly can, if my going means that that supreme maestro will continue working at the old stand. Don't dream of meeting old Bassett's demands.'

'Bertie! Do you mean this?'

'I should say so. What's a mere thirty days in the second division? A bagatelle. I can do it on my head. Let Bassett do his worst. And,' I added in a softer voice, 'when my time is up and I come out into the world once more a free man, let Anatole do his best. A month of bread and water or skilly or whatever they feed you on in these establishments will give me a rare appetite. On the night when I emerge, I shall expect a dinner that will live in legend and song.'

'You shall have it.'

'We might be sketching out the details now.'

'No time like the present. Start with caviar? Or cantaloup?'

'And cantaloup. Followed by a strengthening soup.'

'Thick or clear?'

'Clear.'

'You aren't forgetting Anatole's Velouté aux fleurs de courgette?'

'Not for a moment. But how about his Consommé aux Pommes d'Amour?'

'Perhaps you're right.'

'I think I am. I feel I am.'

'I'd better leave the ordering to you.'

'It might be wisest.'

I took pencil and paper, and some ten minutes later I was in a position to announce the result.

'This, then,' I said, 'subject to such additions as I may think out in my cell, is the menu as I see it.' And I read as follows:

Le Diner

Caviar Frais
Cantaloup
Consommé aux Pommes d'Amour
Sylphides à la crème d'Écrevisses
Mignonette de poulet petit Duc
Points d'ásperges à la Mistinguette
Suprême de fois gras au champagne
Neige aux Perles des Alpes
Timbale de ris de veau Toulousaine
Salade d'endive et de céleri
Le Plum Pudding
L'Etoile au Berger
Bénédictins Blancs
Bombe Néro
Friandises
Diablotins
Fruits

'That about covers it, Aunt Dahlia?'

'Yes, you don't seem to have missed out much.'

'Then let's have the man in and defy him. Bassett!' I cried.

'Bassett!' shouted Aunt Dahlia.

'Bassett!' I bawled, making the welkin ring.

It was still ringing when he popped in, looking annoyed.

'What the devil are you shouting at me like that for?'

'Oh, there you are, Bassett.' I wasted no time in getting down to the agenda. 'Bassett, we defy you.'

The man was plainly taken aback. He threw a questioning look at Aunt Dahlia. He seemed to be feeling that Bertram was speaking in riddles.

'He is alluding,' explained the relative, 'to that idiotic offer of yours to call the thing off if I let you have Anatole. Silliest idea I ever heard. We've been having a good laugh about it. Haven't we, Bertie?'

'Roaring our heads off,' I assented.

He seemed stunned.

'Do you mean that you refuse?'

'Of course we refuse. I might have known my nephew better than to suppose for an instant that he would consider bringing sorrow and bereavement to an aunt's home in order to save himself unpleasantness. The Woosters are not like that, are they, Bertie?'

'I should say not.'

'They don't put self first.'

'You bet they don't.'

'I ought never to have insulted him by mentioning the offer to him. I apologize, Bertie.'

'Quite all right, old flesh and blood.'

She wrung my hand.

'Good night, Bertie, and goodbye — or, rather *au revoir*. We shall meet again.'

'Absolutely. When the fields are white with daisies, if not sooner.'

'By the way, didn't you forget *Nonais de la*

Méditerranée au Fenouil?'

'So I did. And *Selle d'Agneau aux laitues à la Grecque.* Shove them on the charge sheet, will you?'

Her departure, which was accompanied by a melting glance of admiration and esteem over her shoulder as she navigated across the threshold, was followed by a brief and, on my part, haughty silence. After a while, Pop Bassett spoke in a strained and nasty voice.

'Well, Mr Wooster, it seems that after all you will have to pay the penalty of your folly.'

'Quite.'

'I may say that I have changed my mind about allowing you to spend the night under my roof. You will go to the police station.'

'Vindictive, Bassett.'

'Not at all. I see no reason why Constable Oates should be deprived on his well-earned sleep merely to suit your convenience. I will send for him.' He opened the door. 'Here, you!'

It was a most improper way of addressing Jeeves, but the faithful fellow did not appear to resent it.

'Sir?'

'On the lawn outside the house you will find Constable Oates. Bring him here.'

'Very good, sir. I think Mr Spode wishes to speak to you, sir.'

'Eh?'

'Mr Spode, sir. He is coming along the passage now.'

Old Bassett came back into the room, seeming displeased.

'I wish Roderick would not interrupt me at a time like this,' he said querulously. 'I cannot imagine what reason he can have for wanting to see me.'

I laughed lightly. The irony of the thing amused me.

'He is coming — a bit late — to tell you that he was with me when the cow-creamer was pinched, thus clearing me of the guilt.'

'I see. Yes, as you say, he is somewhat late. I shall have to explain to him . . . Ah, Roderick.'

The massive frame of R. Spode had appeared in the doorway.

'Come in, Roderick, come in. But you need not have troubled, my dear fellow. Mr Wooster has made it quite evident that he had nothing to do with the theft of my cow-creamer. It was that that you wished to see me about, was it not?'

'Well — er — no,' said Roderick Spode.

There was an odd, strained look on the man's face. His eyes were glassy and, as far as a thing of that size was capable of being fingered, he was fingering his moustache. He seemed to be bracing himself for some unpleasant task.

'Well — er — no,' he said. 'The fact is, I hear there's been some trouble about that helmet I stole from Constable Oates.'

There was a stunned silence. Old Bassett goggled. I goggled. Roderick Spode continued to finger his moustache.

'It was a silly thing to do,' he said. 'I see that now. I — er — yielded to an uncontrollable impulse. One does sometimes, doesn't one? You remember I told you I once stole a policeman's

305

helmet at Oxford. I was hoping I could keep quiet about it, but Wooster's man tells me that you have got the idea that Wooster did it, so of course, I had to come and tell you. That's all. I think I'll go to bed,' said Roderick Spode. 'Good night.'

He edged off, and the stunned silence started functioning again.

I suppose there have been men who looked bigger asses than Sir Watkyn Bassett at this moment, but I have never seen one myself. The tip of his nose had gone bright scarlet, and his pince-nez were hanging limply to the parent nose at an angle of forty-five. Consistently though he had snootered me from the very inception of our relations, I felt almost sorry for the poor old blighter.

'H'rrmph!' he said at length.

He struggled with the vocal cords for a space. They seemed to have gone twisted on him.

'It appears that I owe you an apology, Mr Wooster.'

'Say no more about it, Bassett.'

'I am sorry that all this has occurred.'

'Don't mention it. My innocence is established. That is all that matters. I presume that I am now at liberty to depart?'

'Oh, certainly, certainly. Good night, Mr Wooster.'

'Good night, Bassett. I need scarcely say, I think, that I hope this will be a lesson to you.'

I dismissed him with a distant nod, and stood there wrapped in thought. I could make nothing of what had occurred. Following the old and tried Oates method of searching for the motive, I had to confess myself baffled. I could only suppose that this was the Sidney Carton spirit bobbing up again.

And then a sudden blinding light seemed to flash upon me.

'Jeeves!'

'Sir?'

'Were you behind this thing?'

'Sir?'

'Don't keep saying 'Sir?' You know what I'm talking about. Was it you who egged Spode on to take the rap?'

I wouldn't say he smiled — he practically never does — but a muscle abaft the mouth did seem to quiver slightly for an instant.

'I did venture to suggest to Mr Spode that it would be a graceful act on his part to assume the blame, sir. My line of argument was that he would be saving you a great deal of unpleasantness, while running no risk himself. I pointed out to him that Sir Watkyn, being engaged to marry his aunt, would hardly be likely to inflict upon him the sentence which he had contemplated inflicting upon you. One does not send gentlemen to prison if one is betrothed to their aunts.'

'Profoundly true, Jeeves. But I still don't get it. Do you mean he just right-hoed? Without a murmur?'

'Not precisely without a murmur, sir. At first, I must confess, he betrayed a certain reluctance. I think I may have influenced his decision by informing him that I knew all about — '

I uttered a cry.

'Eulalie?'

'Yes, sir.'

A passionate desire to get to the bottom of this Eulalie thing swept over me.

'Jeeves, tell me. What did Spode actually do to the girl? Murder her?'

'I fear I am not at liberty to say, sir.'

'Come on, Jeeves.'

'I fear not, sir.'

I gave it up.

'Oh, well!'

I started shedding the garments. I climbed into the pyjamas. I slid into bed. The sheets being inextricably knotted, it would be necessary, I saw, to nestle between the blankets, but I was prepared to rough it for one night.

The rapid surge of events had left me pensive. I sat with my arms round my knees, meditating on Fortune's swift changes.

'An odd thing, life, Jeeves.'

'Very odd, sir.'

'You never know where you are with it, do you? To take a simple instance, I little thought half an hour ago that I would be sitting here in carefree pyjamas, watching you pack for the getaway. A very different future seemed to confront me.'

'Yes, sir.'

'One would have said that a curse had come upon me.'

'One would, indeed, sir.'

'But now my troubles, as you might say, have vanished like the dew on the what-is-it. Thanks to you.'

'I am delighted to have been able to be of service, sir.'

'You have delivered the goods as seldom before. And yet, Jeeves, there is always a snag.'

'Sir?'

'I wish you wouldn't keep saying 'Sir?' What I mean is, Jeeves, loving hearts have been sundered in this vicinity and are still sundered. I may be all right — I am — but Gussie isn't all right. Nor is Stiffy all right. That is the fly in the ointment.'

'Yes, sir.'

'Though, pursuant on that, I never could see why flies shouldn't be in ointment. What harm do they do?'

'I wonder, sir — '

'Yes, Jeeves?'

'I was merely about to inquire if it is your intention to bring an action against Sir Watkyn for wrongful arrest and defamation of character before witnesses.'

'I hadn't thought of that. You think an action would lie?'

'There can be no question about it, sir. Both Mrs Travers and I could offer overwhelming testimony. You are undoubtedly in a position to mulct Sir Watkyn in heavy damages.'

'Yes, I suppose you're right. No doubt that was why he went up in the air to such an extent when Spode did his act.'

'Yes, sir. His trained legal mind would have envisaged the peril.'

'I don't think I ever saw a man go so red in the nose. Did you?'

'No, sir.'

'Still, it seems a shame to harry him further. I don't know that I want actually to grind the old bird into the dust.'

'I was merely thinking, sir, that were you to threaten such an action, Sir Watkyn, in order to avoid unpleasantness, might see his way to ratifying the betrothals of Miss Bassett and Mr Fink-Nottle and Miss Byng and the Reverend Mr Pinker.'

'Golly, Jeeves! Put the bite on him, what?'

'Precisely, sir.'

'The thing shall be put in train immediately.'

I sprang from the bed and nipped to the door.

'Bassett!' I yelled.

There was no immediate response. The man had presumably gone to earth. But after I had persevered for some minutes, shouting 'Bassett!' at regular intervals with increasing volume, I heard the distant sound of pattering feet, and along he came, in a very different spirit from that which he had exhibited on the previous occasion. This time it was more like some eager waiter answering the bell.

'Yes, Mr Wooster?'

I led the way back into the room, and hopped into bed again.

'There is something you wish to say to me, Mr Wooster?'

'There are about a dozen things I wish to say to you, Bassett, but the one we will touch on at the moment is this. Are you aware that your headstrong conduct in sticking police officers on to pinch me and locking me in my room has laid you open to an action for — what was it, Jeeves?'

'Wrongful arrest and defamation of character before witnesses, sir.'

'That's the baby. I could soak you for millions. What are you going to do about it?'

He writhed like an electric fan.

'I'll tell you what you are going to do about it,' I proceeded. 'You are going to issue your OK on the union of your daughter Madeline and Augustus Fink-Nottle and also on that of your niece Stephanie and the Rev. H. P. Pinker. And you will do it now.'

A short struggle seemed to take place in him. It might have lasted longer, if he hadn't caught my eye.

'Very well, Mr Wooster.'

'And touching on that cow-creamer. It is highly probable that the international gang that got away with it will sell it to my Uncle Tom. Their system of underground information will have told them that he is in the market. Not a yip out of you, Bassett, if at some future date you see that cow-creamer in his collection.'

'Very well, Mr Wooster.'

'And one other thing. You owe me a fiver.'

'I beg your pardon?'

'In repayment of the one you took off me at Bosher Street. I shall want that before I leave.'

'I will write you a cheque in the morning.'

'I shall expect it on the breakfast tray. Good night, Bassett.'

'Good night, Mr Wooster. Is that brandy I see over there? I think I should like a glass, if I may.'

'Jeeves, a snootful for Sir Watkyn Bassett.'

'Very good, sir.'

He drained the beaker gratefully, and tottered out. Probably quite a nice chap, if you knew him.

Jeeves broke the silence.

'I have finished the packing, sir.'

'Good. Then I think I'll curl up. Open the window, will you?'

'Very good, sir.'

'What sort of night is it?'

'Unsettled, sir. It has begun to rain with some violence.'

The sound of a sneeze came to my ears.

'Hallo, who's that, Jeeves? Somebody out there?'

'Constable Oates, sir.'

'You don't mean he hasn't gone off duty?'

'No, sir. I imagine that in his preoccupation with other matters it escaped Sir Watkyn's mind to send word to him that there was no longer any necessity to keep his vigil.'

I sighed contentedly. It needed but this to complete my day. The thought of Constable Oates prowling in the rain like the troops of Midian, when he could have been snug in bed toasting his pink toes on the hot-water bottle, gave me a curiously mellowing sense of happiness.

'This is the end of a perfect day, Jeeves. What's that thing of yours about larks?'

'Sir?'

'And, I rather think, snails.'

'Oh, yes, sir. 'The year's at the Spring, the day's at the morn, morning's at seven, the hill side's dew-pearled — ''

'But the larks, Jeeves? The snails? I'm pretty

sure larks and snails entered into it.'

'I am coming to the larks and snails, sir. 'The lark's on the wing, the snail's on the thorn — ''

'Now you're talking. And the tab line?'

''God's in His heaven, all's right with the world.''

'That's it in a nutshell. I couldn't have put it better myself. And yet, Jeeves, there is just one thing. I do wish you would give me the inside facts about Eulalie.'

'I fear, sir — '

'I would keep it dark. You know me — the silent tomb.'

'The rules of the Junior Ganymede are extremely strict, sir.'

'I know. But you might stretch a point.'

'I am sorry sir — '

I made the great decision.

'Jeeves,' I said, 'give me the low-down, and I'll come on that World Cruise of yours.'

He wavered.

'Well, in the strictest confidence, sir — '

'Of course.'

'Mr Spode designs ladies' underclothing, sir. He has a considerable talent in that direction, and has indulged it secretly for some years. He is the founder and proprietor of the emporium in Bond Street known as Eulalie *Sœurs*.'

'You don't mean that?'

'Yes, sir.'

'Good Lord, Jeeves! No wonder he didn't want a thing like that to come out.'

'No, sir. It would unquestionably jeopardize his authority over his followers.'

'You can't be a successful Dictator and design women's underclothing.'

'No, sir.'

'One or the other. Not both.'

'Precisely, sir.'

I mused.

'Well, it was worth it, Jeeves. I couldn't have slept wondering about it. Perhaps that cruise won't be so very foul, after all?'

'Most gentlemen find them enjoyable, sir.'

'Do they?'

'Yes, sir. Seeing new faces.'

'That's true. I hadn't thought of that. The faces will be new, won't they? Thousands and thousands of people, but no Stiffy.'

'Exactly, sir.'

'You had better get the tickets tomorrow.'

'I have already procured them, sir. Good night, sir.'

The door closed. I switched off the light. For some moments I lay there listening to the measured tramp of Constable Oates's feet and thinking of Gussie and Madeline Bassett and of Stiffy and old Stinker Pinker, and of the hotsy-totsiness which now prevailed in their love lives. I also thought of Uncle Tom being handed the cow-creamer and of Aunt Dahlia seizing the psychological moment and nicking him for a fat cheque for *Milady's Boudoir*. Jeeves was right, I felt. The snail was on the wing and the lark was on the thorn — or, rather, the other way round — and God was in His heaven and all right with the world.

And presently the eyes closed, the muscles

relaxed, the breathing became soft and regular, and sleep which does something which has slipped my mind to the something sleave of care poured over me in a healing wave.

We do hope that you have enjoyed reading this large print book.

Did you know that all of our titles are available for purchase?

We publish a wide range of high quality large print books including:
Romances, Mysteries, Classics
General Fiction
Non Fiction and Westerns

Special interest titles available in large print are:
The Little Oxford Dictionary
Music Book
Song Book
Hymn Book
Service Book

Also available from us courtesy of Oxford University Press:
Young Readers' Dictionary
(large print edition)
Young Readers' Thesaurus
(large print edition)

For further information or a free brochure, please contact us at:
Ulverscroft Large Print Books Ltd.,
The Green, Bradgate Road, Anstey,
Leicester, LE7 7FU, England.
Tel: (00 44) 0116 236 4325
Fax: (00 44) 0116 234 0205

Other titles published by Ulverscroft:

RIGHT HO, JEEVES

P. G. Wodehouse

Gussie Fink-Nottle — a shy man, obsessively devoted to the study and care of newts — has done the unthinkable and fallen in love. With Madeline Bassett, the soppiest of specimens, who thinks that stars are God's daisy chain, and that bunny-rabbits are gnomes attendant upon the the fairy queen. Hopelessly incapable of expressing his feelings, Gussie enlists Jeeves to advise him how to woo Madeline. Then Bertie, fed up with being constantly overlooked in favour of his valet, puts his foot down and insists upon helping out his chum himself. But playing Cupid will land Bertie in a terrible tangle . . .

THANK YOU, JEEVES

P. G. Wodehouse

Bertie Wooster's incessant strumming on the banjolele has provoked complaints from the occupants of the neighbouring flats, and the building manager has issued an ultimatum: chuck in the playing, or clear out. So the young master intends to withdraw — along with his faithful valet, of course — to a country cottage where he can twang the strings day and night. But Jeeves refuses to resign himself to such a cacophonous existence, and hands in his notice. In high dudgeon, Bertie prepares to travel to the rural paradise of Chuffnell Regis — only to find that Jeeves is bound for the same destination . . .